MAGI

T. D. Cooper

Happy Readi'
TD Coop

Dedication

My joy has been discovered in writing for a younger audience as well as everyone else. Thank you Meena, Mick, Konnor, and Cooper for inspiring me. May you find my love and entertainment between these pages. As before if not for the support group around me, Frank H. Weeden, W. Delre' Designs, Allie Kat, Bruce, and Jessica, these pages wouldn't be as fanciful.

Contents

The Magical Ringed Land

Chapter One

The Family

Regina Edwards' dark amber eyes flickered open. The familiar sound of the shower was absent. "Did that kid oversleep, again? I can't afford to be late for school and I have to take a bath," she groaned. Even at the tender age of twelve, Regina had the maturity of an adult. She headed for the bathroom off the hall, stopping to glance at her reflection in the mirror that hung on the wall outside the door. She had a sore spot on her chin. "Great, a zit!" she groaned, pinching it between her two index fingers. All she succeeded in doing was making a swollen red spot on her light honey skin.

Regina knocked on the bathroom door, "Matthew, are you in there?" No answer. So she opened the door, stuck her head in, "Matthew!" she called. No Matthew, no leftover steam, and as far as she could tell, he hadn't been there. "Thanks, Matt!" she growled, storming out of the bathroom to hunt him down. "He is messing up the routine. Why can't he take a shower at night? Because his precious hair will be curly instead of straight, not to mention the hot water runs out after the other three take their baths!" she muttered snidely.

1

Living in a house with five other siblings, only one of which was actually her brother, was, in itself, a challenge, but she was grateful for Mrs. Hillsdale, a tiny woman with graying hair and dark eyes. Last spring, Mr. Hillsdale had succumbed to cancer. The whole house had felt the loss, especially Matthew.

She swept the raven hair out of her face and dropped it in a bunch, to cascade down her back. This would make the third day in a row she'd been cheated out of a real shower. She wasn't looking forward to another spit bath. Washing her hair in the bathroom sink, or her body with a cold washcloth, wasn't her idea of the way to start the day. It lacked something. Somehow, it never felt like the soap was truly rinsed off.

Mrs. Hillsdale had a schedule that she insisted the entire household strictly adhere to. Regina rolled her eyes and stuck her head in his bedroom door. "Matthew! Matthew Rogan, are you out of bed?" she spoke softly. She didn't want to wake up her brother Dyson. He was still in bed, but Matthew wasn't. "Fantastic!" Regina swore sarcastically.

"I'll just take his spot," she smirked, returning to her room. She saw that the bed next to hers was empty. She shared this room with a tall, blonde, blue eyed, fifteen-year-old girl named Pam Smith. "She's already up doing her chores." Mrs. Hillsdale's house was nothing if not organized. "Schedules… strict schedules!"

Regina collected her toiletries and headed out the door. If she was to get her hair dry and chores finished before school, she'd have to take her shower now. She set her things on the counter. "That zit really needs to go," she muttered, staring at it and trying to pop it again. This time, she was successful. "Well, it looks worse, but it feels better," she talked to herself in the mirror. "Stop dallying. Pam will be here soon," she scolded, turning on the water.

Regina understood that with this many people in the house, rules were essential. Her chores kept things tidy and Mrs. Hillsdale happy, so she made it a habit to make the beds and throw the dirty clothes into the hamper each morning before school. On the weekends, she was in charge of the laundry. When she stayed on top of her chores she was allowed to participate on the school volleyball team.

Pam, her roommate, was required to be up before the sun and off to the stables. Her chores were to gather eggs, feed the cow and horse, and clean the stalls. If Regina hoped for a pleasant morning without a sibling showdown, she'd better be finished in the bathroom before Pam finished her chores.

Her third roommate was a sixteen-year-old, somewhat chubby girl, named Veronica Porter. She had the personality of a doormat and her hair was so many colors that Regina didn't even know how to describe her, except to say that she liked to cook, so she had kitchen detail. Now that Regina thought about it, she didn't smell the customary bacon and eggs wafting up the stairs.

"What's going on this morning?" Regina mumbled, crinkling her brow, and stepping out of the shower. She wrapped a towel around her wet hair, dried herself with another, and slipped her arms through the sleeves of her robe.

Just then, she heard the baby crying. "Good grief! Where is everyone this morning?" Regina fumed, running into the nursery, which was actually a large walk-in closet, in the Hillsdale's bedroom.

"Hey, Sally! Where's Mrs. H?" she said cheerfully. Sally Mortimer smiled a big toothy grin, fluttering her big azure eyes, and swiping her hand over the top of her blonde curly head of hair. Regina picked up Sally, her three-year-old foster sister, from the crib. Her pants hadn't been changed since last night. "Yuck!" she frowned, removing Sally's night clothes, and changing the soiled diaper. "You smell delightful," she giggled. Sally cooed. "Here, we might as well get you dressed," Regina slid her arms into a sweatshirt with the words, *Queen of the House*, written on the front, and a pair of stretch pants. She slipped clean socks on her feet and her new tennis shoes. Regina swung her onto her hip and headed down the hall.

"Let's go get Dyson up," Regina said. Sally grinned. Regina opened the door and walked into the room. "He's gone! He was just here!" She started to close the door when she heard sniffing coming from the closet. Dyson sat in the back of the closet, behind all the clothes and shoes. He shook and spluttered.

"Dyson, little man, what are you doing in here?" Regina bent down and cuddled her true brother, who had turned eight last week. His straight, brown hair, stood up in several different directions, tear-stained, freckled cheeks, and glistening blue-green eyes always stole her heart. He instantly jumped into her free arm, hugging her neck tightly. "Tell me…" she implored.

4

"A man hit Mrs. Hillsdale," Dyson choked and stuttered, wiping snot across his face. Regina plucked a couple of tissues from the box and wiped away his tears. "Where are your glasses?" she asked. Dyson pointed to the lampshade by his bed. Regina slid the brightly colored green earpieces over his ears.

"Better?" He nodded.

"Now, start again... Mrs. Hillsdale was hit, by who?" Regina asked, shaking her head, positive she'd misunderstood, but Dyson's head bobbed up and down as he repeated himself. "Okay, come on! Where's Matthew?" Dyson pointed toward the hall. "Great!" Regina took hold of Dyson's hand, and with Sally on her hip, she led him into the hall, and the top of the stairs. Hearing nothing, she slowly and silently stepped down onto the first step.

The house was unusually quiet this morning, and either they were all having cereal, which Mrs. Hillsdale didn't tolerate, or Veronica was on strike. But still, Mrs. Hillsdale would be picking up the slack for Veronica. She always made sure all the children in her care were fed and clothed appropriately. They wore hand-me-downs, and each got a new outfit with shoes for birthdays and Christmas, so it was an acceptable situation if you were a kid who needed a place to live. Besides, Mrs. Hillsdale was kind and loving. She hugged and kissed each of them and tucked them in at bedtime, even if you were almost a teenager. Regina smiled. She felt fortunate to live under the Hillsdale's roof and maybe she even loved Mrs. Hillsdale. She wasn't sure what love was, exactly, but perhaps the Hillsdales were as close as she would ever be to the love of a family. She certainly knew of other foster kids that didn't have it as good as she did.

Dyson's sobs grew more pronounced and louder with each step down. "Shhh!" Regina hissed, squeezing his little hand tighter in her own, not from anger, but from apprehension. Her skin began to prickle on her arms and the hair stood up on the back of her neck. Something was definitely off this morning, and her intuition was screaming for her to run. But she had to find the others and make sure they were alright.

The stairs creaked with each step down, making it harder to listen for trouble. She had no choice, as there was one way out of the house and that was down the stairs. "Perhaps I ought to leave you and Sally on the porch and investigate on my own," Regina whispered to Dyson.

"No! I don't want to be alone," Dyson sobbed. By this time, Sally had begun to whimper and press closer into Regina's side.

"Alright, I won't leave you alone, but you can't say I didn't warn you. I don't like the feeling I'm having…" she spoke softly, rubbing the goosebumps from her arms. Dyson sniffed.

When she finally found the bottom step she called out softly. "Mrs. Hillsdale?! Matthew?! Pam?! Veronica?!" (Although she knew Veronica would never answer her.) No one answered back. She heard a choking sob coming from the kitchen.

Regina looked down at Dyson and saw that he'd heard it too. He had stopped his blubbering, but was now holding his breath. Regina poked him. Dyson looked at her with wide eyes. "Breathe!" she whispered, returning his look with a calmer one of her own. She tugged him along, forcing his feet to shuffle forward.

Regina glanced at Sally. She looked scared with her wide eyes, darting here and there. Regina hugged her close. "It's okay!" Sally nodded. They inched their way into the kitchen where they found Matthew seated at the table. Regina first noticed his jet black hair hadn't been combed and it was especially messy. He usually didn't leave his room without every hair in place. She saw his rigid posture and tight shoulders. His palms were flat against the wooden tabletop.

Matthew stared up into Regina's face with wide, dark brown eyes full of fear. Regina watched as he forced his eyes to move from the pantry then to something behind her over and over again. She followed the path with her own gaze, but didn't catch on until he'd done it a few more times. Regina realized he was trying to tell her to get out of the kitchen, and she started to back out with the smaller children.

Regina took a couple of steps backwards, but Dyson had melded into her leg, making her movement awkward and cumbersome. Sally had hidden her face in Regina's shoulder. When Regina looked up again, a man with a stocking cap covering his face emerged from the food closet with Mrs. Hillsdale. He had one arm wrapped around her chest and the other held a knife to her throat.

Regina felt the blood drain from her head as she made eye contact with Mrs. Hillsdale. She felt dizzy and her legs were so heavy she couldn't move. Regina didn't know if she was more frightened of the knife at Mrs. Hillsdale's throat, the fear in Mrs. Hillsdale's eyes, or the fact that Mrs. Hillsdale was as white as a ghost. Regina's skin began to crawl with panic and it became harder for her to breathe. She untangled Dyson from her thigh and freed herself to take a couple of steps backward, but she was shaking so hard she almost dropped Sally. She hesitated. As soon as she stopped, Dyson reattached himself to her leg, making it impossible for her to move. A second later, another movement caught Regina's eye. It came from behind the masked man and forced Regina to look beyond the knife blade.

Veronica sidled out with a smirk on her face. She grabbed a hunk of Matthew's hair at the crown, dragging him up and out of the chair. Regina now understood why his hair was standing up in the back. He screeched in pain, reaching for her hand.

"Shut-up," Veronica growled, forcing him to stay on his feet. They moved toward Regina. "Get upstairs, all of you!" she bellowed.

Terrified, Regina obeyed. She'd never heard Veronica say that many words all at once, and she'd never seen this side of her.

"Don't hurt Mrs. H. We won't get in the way," Regina pleaded, shuddering with each step up the stairs. She stole a glance back at her foster mother, who was trembling to the point of having to be held up by the masked man.

"Shut-up!" Veronica snarled. "I've had it with this house, with all of you kids, and doing all the work around here! Do you know where Hillsdale keeps her cash?" Regina shook her head. "I know she trusts you and sends you to the store all the time. Rumor has it she has piles of cash stashed someplace around here."

"No! I don't know," Regina whispered.

"Me… All I ever get to do is cook and clean for you bunch of leeches. I have dreams and I want a life!" Veronica ranted. They reached the top of the stairs. "Get in there! There's no window in this room with access to a roof, and I can hear if you open this door! I should know. After all, she's caught *me* trying to sneak out enough times. Believe me, this house is like a jail for teenagers!"

Veronica flung Matthew through the bedroom opening. He skidded across the floor and rolled to a stop. Regina stepped past her and received a solid shove in the middle of her back. She stumbled forward and sprawled across the bed, thankfully protecting Sally from falling to the floor. Dyson bumped into the edge of the mattress and ricocheted onto the carpet. His cries became full blown hysterics. "Shut-up!" Veronica shouted, cocking her arm with every intention of backhanding him across the face. Regina flew off the bed, stepping between them. This caused Sally to scream.

"Just stop!" Regina snapped. "You're scaring them!"

Veronica turned her eyes on Regina, who stared her down. "We won't cause you any trouble. Please don't hurt Mrs. H!" Regina said calmly. Veronica spun on her toes, marching from the room, and slamming the door. Regina heard something solid fall to the floor and shatter. The large antique mirror was the only thing out there that Regina could think of that was made of glass.

"Is everyone alright?" she bent down to check the condition of the three children. Matthew had a rug burn on his elbow that he was poking. "Don't touch it. It should scab up soon. Thanks for being the big, brave man," Regina said, rubbing his full head of hair and forcing it to lie back down. "You'd put any full grown man to shame and you're only ten," she said with a grin.

Matthew shrugged, moving her hand off his head. He scooped up Sally. She nuzzled against his chest, quieting down. Dyson had a strangle hold on Regina's neck and she had to physically pry his arms off of her. "Were going to be alright. They'll get what they're after and leave. We'll be alright, I promise," Regina said confidently, but she wasn't so sure she believed her own words.

She'd never seen Veronica speak or behave like that. Regina didn't think she had a mean bone in her body. This was so unlike her. Normally, she was too shy to look anyone in the eye, much less take this kind of stand against her own family; well, the only family she'd ever known. Her parents had been jailed for not taking care of her when she was a baby. She'd been with Mrs. Hillsdale since she was six months old. Regina didn't understand why she would turn on all of them.

And who was that guy in the kitchen? Regina thought he looked strong. He was tall, but she noticed his dirty appearance and tattoos more than anything else. She quivered, thinking about his black eyes staring at them through the eye holes of the mask. Veronica had never talked to a boy that Regina ever knew about, so where did she find him?

Oh, but poor Mrs. Hillsdale! She was so scared. Regina just knew she was more afraid for her wards than the fear of being hurt, and she was certain Mrs. Hillsdale didn't care about the money Veronica was talking about. She'd never heard that there was a stash of cash in the house. Regina blew off the thought and decided to concentrate on getting everyone out of the house. She could help Mrs. H if she could get to a phone.

"Come on, we need to stick together and not panic. Matt, come sit here on the bed with Sal and Dy. I need to put some clothes on." The three siblings moved into a huddle on the bed. Regina slipped out of her bathrobe and pulled on some jeans and a sweatshirt from the floor. She put on a pair of athletic shoes, then hurriedly combed out her hair and French braided it.

"Okay, Matt, you're dressed and have shoes; good! Dyson, I don't know who dressed you this morning, (he wore a striped t-shirt with a plaid over-shirt), but I guess it will have to do, and Sal, you're good and warm for this fall morning." She smiled, trying to be reassuring. "Matt, dump out my backpack and pack sweatshirts and socks along with anything else you think we might need."

"What do you mean? Are we going someplace?" Matthew said with a frown.

"If I can figure a way to get you guys out of here, yes." She didn't wait for a retort from Matthew. "Dyson, are you doing okay?" She waited for him to respond. He nodded. "Okay, go stand by the door and tell me if you hear anyone coming." He sprinted over to the door and placed his ear squarely in the middle. "Sally, sit still, please!" Regina couldn't believe it, but she didn't move a muscle.

"We need to get to a phone and then hide from Veronica," Regina whispered, explaining what she had planned. Regina went to the window, forced the lock open, and pushed with all her might. "Ouch! This dumb thing is painted shut! Matt there are a pair of scissors in the desk," she said, pointing.

"Here!" said Matthew, handing them to her. "But that man said for us to sit still and he wouldn't hurt Mrs. H," he said.

"You're going to trust a masked robber over my instincts?" Regina replied. She pried at the paint with the scissors and pounded on the window frame, eventually forcing it to break loose. The screen was easy to dislodge and she dropped it to the ground. "Matthew, do you know where Pam is?" He shook his head. Regina sighed. "Okay how are we going to get down?"

"Let's make a rope out of sheets. I've seen it done in the movies," Matthew offered with a smile.

"Okay, we got nothing else," she giggled, feeling like a rebel using poor English. They were stripping beds and tying knots in the ends of the sheets when they heard something bang against the outside of the house beneath the window. Regina ran and looked out to see Pam. She'd brought a ladder from the barn and laid it up against the stucco under the window. She was at the bottom motioning them to climb out. Regina clapped and returned a huge smile back down to Pam.

"We're saved," Regina nodded. "Okay, Matthew, go first. I'm going to send Dyson right after you. I want you to climb down slowly and stay together." She looked both boys in the eyes and waited until they each nodded that they understood.

Regina helped Matthew onto the ledge and then onto the ladder. He climbed down three rungs and then she lifted Dyson out. The boys were well on their way to safety. Regina took a sheet and made a sling to put Sally in and tied it across her chest and over her shoulders. She climbed out the window and made her way slowly down the rungs.

"Come on! Come on! I hope Veronica didn't hear me bang this against the house," Pam urged impatiently. Regina's foot hit bottom and sunk into the soft dirt in the flowerbed. She exhaled, feeling like she hadn't taken a breath in the last ten minutes. The palms of her hands were wet with sweat and tears threatened to spill from under her thick lashes. "Everyone alright?" Pam asked. They all nodded.

It felt good to have an older person taking over the leadership role. Regina hadn't had time to fall apart and be the little girl, until this minute. She searched Pam's crystal blue eyes for the next step in their escape plan. "Regina, you've done well so far, but we're not out of this, yet. I need you to take the kids and head in that direction. I'm going to go help Mrs. H," Pam said, as if saving Mrs. Hillsdale were as easy as picking up milk at the corner deli. Regina shook her head adamantly at the sound of her having to leave without Pam and be in charge again.

"It will be okay, if you go that way. They won't follow you. I called 911 with the phone in the barn. I will wait for the police to get here and show them where Mrs. H is. Don't worry. We'll come get you in a little bit. Just get the kids out of here," Pam said emphatically. Regina hesitated. She really didn't like this plan. "Go! Now!" Pam screamed.

They all heard the bedroom door open. "What are you guys banging around in here?" Veronica yelled, rushing to the window and poking her head out.

"Pam what are you doing!?" Veronica screamed.

"Go! For the last time, get out of here!" Pam shouted.

"What about you?" Regina hesitated.

"I'll be fine! Just go!" Pam insisted.

Veronica turned with a groan and left the window.

Regina with Sally strapped to her chest, and the two boys, fled as fast as they could through the pasture and into the forest. She could hear Pam screaming at them to run and Veronica screaming at Pam for letting them go.

Chapter Two

The Escape

"Matthew, stop! I can't… Stop! I can't go anymore!" Regina spluttered, heaving and struggling with the added weight of Sally. She dropped to her knees.

"Okay, come this way. Let's go to my fort. It's over here, in the middle of these trees. We can wait it out there," Matthew said.

Dyson ran to Regina's side and helped her up. The small group slowed their pace and wove their way through the tightly knit grove of trees, brush, and rocks of the hillside. Matthew seemed to know this part of the woods like the back of his hand. Boy, was Regina thankful! She glanced around, recognizing nothing.

Regina didn't know much about Matthew. He hadn't been with the family long, but he was smart and good with his hands. She knew he liked to design and build things. Mr. Hillsdale taught him many things, and before he got sick, they spent hours in the barn designing chicken coops, flower boxes, and cabinets. They also liked to go on campouts in the woods. They packed all their gear in packs and spent many weekends fishing and hunting.

The day Matthew and his friends came to Mr. Hillsdale to ask him to help them build a fort, he was thrilled. He donated old scraps of wood and tin to the boys. He helped with the layout and construction. Mr. Hillsdale also taught Matthew how to design pulleys to open cupboard doors and trapdoors. They hid cabinets inside walls, the furniture, and the floor. The last thing they built and installed was a periscope.

Shortly after the completion of the clubhouse, the boys invited Regina to have a look. Matthew wound her around and around through the trees. "Matt quit walking me in circles," she complained. He frowned and delivered her directly to the hidden front door. She was wined and dined with a variety of tasty treats including a glass of champagne in a plastic cup, although the fizzle was gone, making it kind of flat.

"Here we are!" Matthew gloated. Dyson and Regina looked startled.

"But, where's the fort?" Dyson exclaimed.

"Right here! In front of you!"

"I don't remember it being so… Stealthy," Regina said admiringly.

"Exactly! Come this way," Matthew chortled. He lifted a bush, a pulley spun, and a door opened, leading the way into a large open room.

The kids walked in, awed by the cleanliness and cozy layout. A large, worn, woolen area carpet covered most of the dirt floor. In the middle of the rug was a ratty sofa, and

16

on either side of it sat two tattered chairs, repaired with duct tape. A big, square, wooden coffee table filled the space in the middle. Old magazines, like the ones you'd see in a doctor's office sat neatly arranged in the middle of the table. Lanterns sat on end tables, made out of old crates and cabinets lined the walls. Three cots with sleeping bags, pillows, and blankets were piled in the corner.

"Make yourselves at home!" Matthew said grandly, knowing they were impressed.

"Wow, you guys have really done a lot since I was here, last time," Regina marveled, looking up at the ceiling and noticing a trapdoor. She assumed it would open and let the stars be visible at night. Regina chose a section of the couch and made herself comfortable. She untied Sally and let her stretch her legs.

"Matt, you built this?! It's really cool!" Dyson liked what he saw.

"Me and my boys did… Well, Mr. H helped a little," he grinned. "Here, I have bottles of water." He lifted the top of the coffee table. Out popped another box lined with insulation and filled with water bottles and ice. He pulled out four crystal clear containers, handing each of them a bottle. Regina opened Sally's and she guzzled it.

"Humery…" Sally complained.

"I know Sal. We're all hungry. You wouldn't, by any chance, have some scrambled eggs in here someplace, would you?" Regina teased.

"No, but I have some Pop Tarts," he grinned, reaching into his pocket, he removed a key and unlocked a padlocked cupboard. The cupboard had a lined and sealed storage space, making it as protected from animals as it could be. "Oh, man… There are only two packages," Matthew frowned.

"It will be fine! We each get one, Sal," Regina explained. Sally grinned, standing at Matthew's toes waiting for him to unwrap the pastry. She took hers and returned to the couch to sit by Regina.

"I'm sorry there isn't more, but we kinda had a feast the other day," Matthew sighed. "Parker and Sam were supposed to go shopping after school and restock the place. I guess they haven't had time."

"This is perfect! For a while," Regina nodded and smiled.

"I have some Saltines, but other than that we're pretty much… foodless," Matthew showed them the package of crackers. He went to another cabinet and pulled out some napkins. They sat comfortably, drinking water, and eating Pop Tarts.

"Why didn't Pam come with us?" Dyson asked, unexpectedly.

"I don't know, Dy. It didn't make any sense to me either," Regina shrugged.

"Do you think Mrs. H is okay?" Dyson asked.

"I sure hope so. I think we should stay right here until we feel it's safe to go home," Regina said. They all nodded in agreement.

"Yeah, at least we can have a roof over our heads if it rains or gets dark," Matthew added, "and we're pretty safe from animals and such."

"Good plan," Regina said, nodding.

"So make yourselves comfortable. I have blankets over there, magazines right here, and a first aid kit on the wall. Oh, and matches for the lanterns in that drawer," Matthew pointed out everything.

"Wow, you really are set up," Regina laughed. Dyson frowned.

"What's up, little man," Regina asked, recognizing Dyson's pained face.

"Where's the bathroom?" he whispered in Regina's ear.

"Oh, no problem! Here is a roll of toilet paper and see that big grove of trees downwind? Pick yourself a spot," Matthew chuckled.

"Outside?" Dyson complained.

"When ya gotta go…" Matthew snickered. Dyson marched off without the paper, into the grove. He was in no position to argue. He returned a few minutes later, much relieved and a little embarrassed.

"Feel better, buddy?" Regina asked, teasing him. Dyson grinned. "You don't happen to have any diapers in here?" she said, poking fun at Matthew.

He thought for a minute, "No, but I do have an idea. How about this," Matthew rummaged around in his boxes and cabinets. He came back with a roll of paper towels, a plastic storage bag, and a roll of duct tape.

"Hey, I think you're onto something," Regina said. Between Matthew and herself, they came up with a workable diaper for Sally, and even a couple of spares. They relaxed and began to forget their plight for the next few minutes. It wasn't long before they were giggling and teasing each other. "We're getting a little loud," Regina was saying, when a bell chimed in the distance.

Matthew came to attention quickly, causing the rest of them to freeze and hold their breaths. "What is it?" Regina mouthed.

"One of my booby-traps has been triggered," Matthew whispered, heading for the periscope.

"Booby-traps?" Regina said too loudly. Matthew quickly put his finger to his lips and hushed her, nodding his head. He unfolded the periscope and began to scan the perimeter. He focused on a party of three trampling through the forest.

"Dy, hand me the crackers and water," Regina urged him, pointing to each item. She stuffed them into her backpack along with the homemade diapers. "Sal, come here; it's time to get in the sling," Sally toddled toward her and let Regina stuff her back inside the twisted sheet.

Matthew folded the scope up and moved it out of the way, "Let's go," he motioned.

"Why… Who is it?" Regina whispered.

"Pam."

"Well that's good! She's come after us," Regina said, smiling. Matthew made his eyes wide and shook his head.

"She's not alone," Matthew whispered. "I think we ought to go now! They're almost here!"

"That can't be, Matt! You have to be confused," she argued. Pam had always been a good sister and loyal to the family. She complained about her designated chores, just like everyone else did, but they all did work according to their abilities. "I don't understand." Regina stammered.

"Me either…" Matthew said, interrupting Regina's revere. "Can we have this conversation away from here?" Matthew insisted.

Regina stood with Sally strapped firmly into her sling. "You knew something wasn't right… Look, you're ready to go," Matthew noticed all the items and cupboards packed up and closed.

"Yeah, well no point in taking chances. How are we going to get ahead of them?" Regina asked Matthew. He was removing an old beat up rug he had lying across another section of the dirt floor. Beneath it was a wooden trapdoor. He lifted it and motioned for Dyson and Regina to enter.

"It's dark!" Dyson shuddered.

"Here take this flashlight," Matthew said, offering him the light out of the same drawer with the matches. Dyson took it eagerly, turning it on as he entered the dark hole in the ground. He flashed the light around inspecting the dirt-walled tunnel that was about three feet tall. Matthew arranged the rug to fall back in place when the trapdoor closed.

They heard a raspy-voiced man scream at Pam, "Where is this fort you've been talking about?"

"It's right around here… Someplace," Pam whimpered. About that time the raspy-voiced man found the door behind the bush and was trying to open it.

"Let's go!" Matthew whispered, taking the light and the backpack. "Come on! They're here!" he gently nudged Regina, moving her forward. They crawled through the tunnel bent at the waist and made their way underground.

"Wow, the dirt smells damp, kinda like rain just before it hits," Regina whispered loudly. Dyson and Matthew looked back over their shoulders at the same time, giving her a look of surprise.

"Are you nuts?" Dyson said irritably.

Regina snorted, "Well, it does! Besides it's the little things that keep me calm."

The tunnel wasn't very long. They emerged behind a rock formation that gave them plenty of cover from their trackers. The best part was they hadn't left any footprints to give themselves away. "Safe for now. They can't follow unless they find the tunnel. Where to, now?" Matthew sighed.

"Let's head out of the woods, in that direction," Regina said, pointing toward the morning sun. "Seems to me, there is a farm on the other side of the hill."

"I think you're right. One of my friends was talking about some rich dude with a bunch of cattle, living over there somewhere," Matthew waved a hand.

They set out through the woods, traveling over a creek where they refilled their water bottles. After an hour or so they reached the edge of the tree line. "Okay, here we are. You know once we head that way, we're going to be out in the open. They will be able to see us," Matthew said.

"I know. What do you suggest?" Regina waited.

"I don't know. I'm just saying," Matthew sighed.

"If we can make it over that mound and down the other side we will be hidden, I think," Regina said. Matthew considered her assumption.

"Let's just go home," Dyson whimpered. Regina hugged him closely.

"We can't, buddy. Who knows what's happening there?" she whispered into his ear.

"That's an awful lot of grass to run across, and we're going to have to push it. Dyson, you up for a jog? And Reg, you're carrying about a third of your weight in that pack. We can't help…" Matthew said.

"You're the inventor. What should we do?" Regina snapped. Matthew looked put out. "I'm sorry. I know you're right, but what are our choices?"

"Isn't this the way Pam told us to come?" Matthew asked. Dyson shook his head.

"She told us to go toward Old Man Holman's farm," Dyson shrugged.

"That's the opposite direction. Why did we come this way?" Matthew grumbled. Regina glared at him.

"I can make that run," Dyson said, seeking to calm the tension.

"He's right! She told us to go south and we went through the woods instead," Regina said.

"Well, how did she find us in the woods?" Matthew murmured, more to himself than to the others.

"I don't know," Regina shrugged. "Maybe she went to the Holman's and we weren't there!"

"Yeah, and I made the mistake of showing her the fort last week," Matthew grumbled.

"You took me in circles so I'd never find it, and you took her straight to it," Regina frowned.

"No, not exactly, but she left and went straight home," Matthew wouldn't look at her.

"Okay, we have to get out of here, if we go back to the house we don't know what we'll find and…" Regina sighed.

"We don't know what they will do with us!" Dyson said. "So let's go, already!"

"I'm game!" Regina exhaled, looking at Matthew.

"Let me double back and see if they're on our trail. You guys wait here. I'll be right back," Matthew slithered back through the trees before Regina could object.

"That kid can sneak away faster than…"

"Stop arguing Reg," Dyson interrupted.

"That's what we do, but you're right, I'm sorry." The small group sat quietly each lost in their own thoughts, waiting. Regina was tightening the sheet around Sally when Matthew returned.

"All clear… It's now or never."

"Did you see anyone?"

"No!"

"Matt you go first, Dyson, stick close to Matt, and Sal and I will bring up the rear. Let's go!" Regina said. The children headed out in a fast pace through the tall green grass that stretched as far as the eye could see. The small hill was getting closer. Dyson tripped over a stick and slid in the mud. Regina scooped him up and set him back on his feet in one motion. Matthew turned in time to watch her in amazement, but didn't stop. "It's okay, just a little mud. I'll clean you up when we get behind the mound," she assured Dyson.

"I'm okay, Reg. Stop treating me like a baby," Dyson complained, stuffing his glasses back onto his nose. Muddy fingerprints streaked across them. Regina rolled her eyes, but kept running.

When they reached the top of the hill, Matthew made a quick survey of the landscape before following the others down the other side. Regina collapsed in the ravine at the bottom. Short fast pants were causing a pain in her side and her back was killing her. She lay flat on a bed of grass. Sally was still tied to her hip. She'd flopped across Regina's chest. Regina stared up into the rich blue sky, consciously forcing herself to breathe in through her nose and out through her mouth.

Sally rolled over pointing up at the white fluffy clouds. "Look! Pretty," she gurgled. Out in the open, Regina felt the cool breeze puff across her sweaty form, cooling her, and settling her labored breathing.

Sally wiggled free of her confines, running back up the hill toward Matthew. He grabbed her around the waist and brought her back down out of sight. "Sally, stay down here," Matthew scolded. She giggled.

"I'm hungry," said Dyson, no longer able to ignore the rumble deep in his stomach. Matthew opened the pack and pulled out the crackers and water. Dyson snorted with disappointment and Sally was not interested in the crackers at all. She started to fuss.

"Me too," Matthew sighed, "and these are not going to fill me up!"

"I hear ya! But I don't see anything that resembles a farm or a place to get a burger," Regina groaned.

"What are we going to do? I think we went the wrong way. I don't see any ranch mansion or whatever you called it," Matthew said. He'd been a good sport, but all of them were rapidly losing what bravery they'd had.

"Who was Pam with, exactly?" Regina muttered.

"Some tall, muscular man. He had tattoos all over his face and those big holes in his earlobes. He sounded just like the guy in the kitchen," Matthew said.

"You didn't recognize him? Maybe he was a police officer," Regina argued.

"With tattoos on his face? Why didn't he have on a uniform? And I saw a knit cap stuck in his back pocket," Matthew retorted.

"I think Pam's trying to kill us, too," Dyson cried.

"No one is trying to kill us. We just need to think," Regina tried to change her tone from curt to reassuring. The last thing she needed, was for the little ones to start freaking out. Sally had been so good thus far, and she didn't want that to change.

"Yucky," Sally screamed, throwing her cracker onto the ground. "Bo'le…" she cried.

"I don't have a bottle, Sal, just a drink of water," Regina took a deep swallow to let Sally know she was drinking it too. Sally sipped and quieted down to a low whimper.

"Matt, we have to get these kids some shelter and food. Look, we only have a few hours of daylight left," she

27

said, pointing to the sun that had moved past its zenith. "Help me think!"

Dyson withered into the long grass, forgetting the mud that was caked on his knees. "I'm not moving another foot. I want food!" he demanded, cleaning off his glasses on his shirttail. Regina tried to hand him a cracker. "NO! No more crackers!" he shrieked.

Regina had begun to lose all hope, when something made her look up. In the distance was the outline of a huge structure. "There, look! The mansion! That must be the one the cattle rancher owns. Come on! Let's go," she cheered.

"Where did that come from? It wasn't there, five minutes ago," Matthew shaded his eyes and gulped a couple of swigs of water, before he sealed the backpack and threw it over his shoulder. They all took off with renewed hope.

Chapter Three

The House

"I hope they will feed us. Do you think they will feed us, Reg?" Dyson huffed and puffed, working hard to keep up with Matthew.

"Yes, I think they will feed us, little man," Regina said. "Look, Sally, we're going to have help soon," Regina pointed to the faded image of the mansion in the distance. Sally sniffled, holding on tightly to Regina and her sling.

The four children had been running through the grass and mud for a while now. Regina slowed. The others slowed to a skip, with their spirits brightened. It was only a matter of time before they'd be rescued, and in Dyson's case, eating. The hill behind them seemed to have flattened into the green, grassy terrain. "Oh, you guys, I need to rest," Regina complained, falling to her knees, clutching her side. Sally reached up and patted her on the cheek. "Does that house look any closer to you?"

"Not really," Dyson grumbled. Their enthusiasm started to wane.

"It reminds me of a mirage, all wiggly and out of focus." Matthew puffed, out of breath. He too, fell to his knees.

"You're right! That's exactly what it looks like a mirage," Regina exclaimed.

"So, what does that mean?" Dyson whined.

"I'm not sure… It's strange!" Regina rubbed her eyes.

A flash caught her eye, causing her to jerk her head. "Check out that car." She pointed off to the right of them. "It looks like the Hillsdale's SUV," Regina coughed, clearing her throat. All eyes turned toward the car traveling at a high rate of speed on the highway.

"That's gotta be Mrs. Hillsdale's car! She's looking for us," Dyson cheered, bounding toward the road. Matthew jumped to his feet and joined Dyson. They waved their hands, screaming, "Mrs. H! Over here!" Regina walked quickly. She couldn't force her legs to run one more step after carrying Sally all day.

The truck whizzed past, the driver not seeing the children. Matthew and Dyson dropped their arms and slumped with disappointment, giving Regina a chance to catch up. "At least we know there is a road this direction," Regina grinned. "She won't stop looking, until she finds us."

"I'm glad Mrs. H is alright!" Dyson choked. He was crying again. This day had been hard on him. Regina understood.

Their parents had been ripped from their lives in a similar fashion, when they were eight and three, respectively. Regina rubbed her temples with her knuckles, trying to force the unwanted images from invading her mind, but it was no use. She could still see the two men in long robes barge through the front door and into their home. She heard her dad's voice, "Hide!" he'd shouted, pushing her brother into her arms.

By the time he'd secured his children's safety the intruders were firing at him. Regina remembered hearing the invaders shout, "Die Atlanteans!" Followed by a loud pop and a whizzing sound. She pictured the Roman candles they'd lit on Independence Day, her curiosity causing her to peak over the kitchen island. She saw sparks flying out of the man's hands directly at her father. Her mother appeared at the top of the stairs, but she was too late to save her father. He collapsed face down on the floor. Regina smelled singed hair and burned flesh.

The next fireball flew at her mother. But she caught it and threw it back at the intruders, hitting one of them. He crumpled, taking out a large vase in the entry and vanished into a hole in the floor. Regina gasped as her mother raised her hands, firing lightning bolts at the second man. "Run Regina! Get Dyson out of here!" she'd screamed, dodging volleys of fireballs. But the last one hit its mark. Her mother fell, tumbling down the staircase.

"No!" Regina shrieked, jumping up, and bolting around the island toward her mother. Regina felt a jolt strike her in the chest. She froze. Energy sizzled through her, giving her a burst of vitality.

"Momma!" Regina screamed.

"Save Dyson!" her mother cried with her last breath before collapsing at the bottom of the stairs. Regina took one look at the man with his long dreads and red eyes. She screamed, spun around, and scooped up Dyson. The back door slammed open and the two children escaped out the door.

Regina crashed into the arms of a woman she knew who lived down the street, shivering and shaking. Tears began to flow. She sobbed uncontrollably, holding Dyson tightly in her arms.

"They're gone! You're safe," the woman spoke softly, consoling the two children.

"What shall we do? There's a scorch mark in the entry by a broken vase," a man dressed as a policeman asked the neighbor lady.

"Are the police on their way?" the neighbor whispered.

"Yes! They should be here in about five minutes."

"Let them figure it out. Another one of those unexplained murders," she mouthed. "We have to get the children out of here. No one must know they are alive."

"Okay, I've got a car waiting!"

"I'm thankful the boy is too young to remember anything," the neighbor whispered. "It's going to be interesting to see if she remembers any of it." Regina looked up into the man's eyes and watched his head move up and down. She remembered being frightened and confused.

"They're coming," the fake police officer warned.

"Take her... I've got him!"

Regina heard the car door slam, the engine start, and the car ease away from the curb. "Sparks, fire, hands," Regina repeated over and over again.

"Yes dear?" the neighbor muttered, sharing a look with the officer.

"Sparks! Mommy! Fire!" Regina sobbed.

"It's going to be okay," the neighbor said soothingly.

"We're going to fix this... I promise!" the fake policeman said as they drove away.

Sparks, really? What did I see that night? More importantly how did I get outside? The professional therapists had alleged that she must have seen something so horrible, she invented the flying sparks. "*When she is ready she will remember exactly what happened that night, and she won't be that frightened little girl hiding in the kitchen,*" they'd said.

Regina shrugged. *What did the therapist know? They weren't in the house that night.* Regina knew what she'd seen. The man shot fire out of his hands. She'd explained it countless times, but no one would listen.

The next thing she remembered was being taken directly to Mrs. Hillsdale's house. She and Dyson were not allowed to attend their parents' funerals. They were given the new sir name of Edwards and ordered to never speak of the episode again.

Regina understood that this was strange, but she was too young to do anything about it, so she never spoke about any of the details of her parents' death; not even to Dyson.

Regina missed her mom, missed her herb scent, and being kissed goodnight. Mrs. Hillsdale was great, but not the same as loving her mother. She felt tears well in her eyes and fought hard to keep them from spilling down her cheeks. These were not memories she enjoyed reliving, and until today, she'd managed to control the thoughts.

She was sure Dyson remembered some of it, too, even though he wasn't much older than Sally at the time. She had run to his room just the other night, to comfort him from the night terrors that haunted him.

Regina wiped a wayward tear. *I still see the sparks.* She rolled her eyes.

"House go," Sally said, pointing in the direction of the mansion. Regina glanced over her shoulder. Sally was right. The great house had disappeared.

"Look! The car is coming back!" shouted Dyson, redirecting Regina's attention. He took off, running, hoping to intercept the suburban this time. Matthew chased after him, passing him as the SUV raced up the road. Just then, the brakes squealed and the car slid sideways. The smell of burning rubber waft through the air as the car slid to a stop. Regina watched as the back wheels spun and the backend flipped around. It headed back in the direction of the children.

Relief washed through her. *This day was almost over.* She took three quick steps in the direction of the car. *Wait... I've never seen Mrs. H drive like...* And suddenly it dawned on Regina that it couldn't have been Mrs. Hillsdale behind the wheel. "Dyson, stop!" she screamed.

Matthew slowed. He looked at the oncoming SUV and saw a male behind the wheel. Dyson was running at full speed. He hadn't heard a word from Regina's lips. All he cared about was Mrs. Hillsdale and being in her arms again. Matthew caught him around the chest. The force of the collision took both boys to the ground. The tires squealed again as the SUV came to a full stop. Veronica bailed out of the passenger side door, nearly falling to the ground. Regina had reached the boys who lay sprawled in the thick grass.

"Get up! Get up!" she yelled at Dyson. Matthew was already getting up from the ground. Veronica was a mere twenty-five yards away, huffing and puffing from the exertion. "We have to go!" Regina urged. The male figure was out of the driver's side door, racing around the front of the car and gaining on Veronica. Regina knew they would never outrun him. Panic consumed her. She yanked Dyson to his feet. Matthew grabbed Dyson's hand and they ran back the way they'd come.

"Where are we going?" Matthew called from behind Regina and Sally.

"That way!" Regina pointed back toward their hill and the woods. Before she finished her sentence, the mansion appeared before them. Regina inhaled sharply, skidding to a stop. Matthew and Dyson almost ran over her. She couldn't begin to imagine where the mansion had come from, but she didn't care. "Get inside!" she screamed.

"It's nothing more than a dilapidated, broken down, pile of rubble," Matthew complained. "Besides, where did it come from?"

"Who cares? It's a place to hide," Dyson altered his course, danced over the fallen bricks and mortar that lay all around the grounds outside the mansion, and began searching for a way inside.

"I'm not going in there! That place looks haunted," Matthew screeched.

"I'm open to suggestions. Dyson has a point; maybe we can hide in a room. There looks to be lots of them," Regina said with a groan. Sally was heavy and she wasn't sure she could make it into the woods. Her legs were so rubbery she could barely hold herself up and her lungs burned like she was breathing fire. "If I don't make it, take care of Dyson," Regina half whispered as the boys sprinted past her.

"Reg, don't say that!" Dyson yelled over his shoulder. "Keep going!"

"Get back here," Veronica shouted in-between her labored breaths. The sound of her voice brought Regina back to life. She continued to put one foot in front of the next as fast as she could. "Your precious Mrs. Hillsdale is waiting for you…" Veronica cackled.

"Out of the way, woman!" Regina heard the raspy voice of the man from the fort. The sound of him caused Regina to gasp and try harder. She was afraid to look back. If she fell, Sally would be hurt, and she wouldn't allow herself to fail. She concentrated on each footstep, making sure she didn't trip. Her exhaustion had vanished for the moment and she felt a surge of energy.

Sally clung to the sheet, staring wide eyed behind Regina, crying, "Go! Go! Go! Comin'!" Sally wailed.

"Hang on, Sal! I'm doing the best I can," Regina puffed.

"Hurmpf," the raspy voiced man belched as he hit the ground.

"Get up, Marcus!" Veronica squealed. "They're getting away!"

Regina exhaled a sigh of relief. She paused, weighing her options on how to enter the mansion. At first glance, the steps leading to the front door were part of the rubble she had been carefully stepping around. It was a good two feet over her head and she saw no way of reaching the landing. Matthew had found a broken window on a lower level that he'd climbed through and then dragged Dyson along with him. "Come on, Regina!" he shouted, but she knew it would take too long for her to untie Sally so they could fit through the opening.

"I can't fit through there! I have to find another way," she shouted to Matthew. "Get in there and hide! I'll catch up with you later!"

Dyson stood behind Matthew, sticking his head out under Matthew's arm. They both watched Regina from inside the mansion, "Reg, he is on his feet again coming at you," Dyson screamed. "Run! Faster!"

She moved to her left along the front of the mansion. All the windows large enough for her to go through were either not broken, or too high for her to reach from the ground. She was almost to the far end of the structure. Marcus was upon her.

Sally screamed.

Regina ducked. Marcus missed, swiping at her arm. "You go after the boys! I've got these two," he yelled to Veronica.

"Get what boys?! Where did they go?!" Veronica hissed.

Regina heard Marcus stumble. Out of nowhere, a hole in the ground appeared with a staircase leading down. An explosion landed beside her. She flinched, but didn't stop to think about where she was going. She scuttled down the steps and into the storm cellar. At the bottom, she listened for Marcus, but didn't hear him behind her. A door overhead slammed shut. All light was extinguished and she and Sally were left standing in pitch black.

"Daak!" Sally cried. Regina couldn't see her hand in front of her face. She tried to move, but everywhere she stepped, her toes kicked pieces of the crumbling house.

"Oh man, its dark," Regina whispered, scooting her feet along the floor. "Ouch!" she cried, stumbling forward.

Cobwebs wrapped around her eyelashes. Her hands flew out in front of her to brace for a fall, but instead she hit a wall. Sally's head smacked against it. "I'm so sorry! Are you alright?" Regina rubbed Sally's head and kissed it tenderly.

"Ooooh!" Sally yelped.

After making sure Sally wasn't hurt badly, Regina inched along the wall until she found another opening. The further into the cellar she wandered, the darker it became, and the more Sally blubbered. "Shh, shh! We're all right," Regina soothed her with a calming voice. *I think...* But with the smell of damp mold invading her nose, her heart pounding through her chest, and her flesh crawling with fear, Regina wasn't sure she was convincing anyone.

"If I only had a flashlight," she mumbled to herself.

Regina felt something cold and hard settle into the palm of her hand. She jumped, startled, trying to throw the object away, but it was stuck to her hand. Suddenly a light popped on, and her breath abandoned her. In her hand was a flashlight! Blinking hard, "I'll figure it out later. There's nothing strange, here. It's just your imagination," she told herself, over and over again.

The light made her navigation much easier. She stepped around the trash cluttering the floor, all the while, listening for Marcus. Cobwebs dangled from the ceiling and reflected in the round circle of light. Regina avoided the ones she could, and shuddered when one stuck to her face. She envisioned a man-eating spider crawling up her back, but quickly forced the thought away.

A rat squeaked as it ran along the baseboard. Regina squealed, panting, and making sure she watched it disappear out of the circle of light. They came to the foot of a staircase. "Shall we go up?" Regina asked Sally. Sally nodded. Regina took hold of the rail and climbed hesitantly. Sally held her breath.

At the top of the stairs, Regina pushed a door open. It creaked, and the rat she'd seen earlier raced through the opening. "That's right, little rat, you go first," she muttered. "Scare away the ghosts!" Sally stared at her wide-eyed.

They entered what looked to be a pantry, which lead to the kitchen. The ceramic tiles were cracked and chipped, leaving great gaping holes that gave way to rotting wooden floorboards. The spot where the refrigerator should have been, dribbled with water from a copper tube. The sink had black scum caked on it and the stove was missing its burners. There was a big plate glass window in the breakfast nook smeared with mud, but clear enough to allow the afternoon sun to lighten the room.

"This place is disgusting, but at least we have some light," she nudged Sally.

Regina saw an image pass by the window out of the corner of her eye. She quickly ducked into the empty refrigerator space and peeked out the picture window. Regina could see the woods in the background and the green knoll in front of them. Veronica was looking up and through the mansion as if she didn't see it. Regina edged along the wall to the window to get a closer look and maybe hear what was being said. She saw that Marcus also looked bewildered.

"Where did they go?" he growled.

"How should I know? They were here one second and gone the next," Veronica snapped.

"Let's get back to the house. Pam has lived in the area the longest. Maybe she knows something we don't. Or maybe we can torture something out of the old lady." Regina's heart sank with fear, but just as fast, it lightened. Mrs. Hillsdale was still alive and maybe Pam was really on their side. She did, after all, bring them a ladder and help them out the window. *I'm so confused! What am I supposed to believe?* Regina decided she would think about that later. She watched Marcus and Veronica walk out of view and head toward the car. Now she had to find the boys and get out of this creepy place.

"Umery," Sally cried.

"Oh Sal, how can you think about food, now? But you know what… So am I! Let's find the boys and get out of here." Regina hugged Sally, turning to leave the kitchen. Sitting on the counter in plain sight, was a picnic basket; a brown wicker basket, complete with a checkered lining, handles, and flip-up lids on the sides. Regina stood still, scanning the room. "That wasn't here a minute ago," she looked all over the kitchen and saw no one. She inched her way up to the basket, reaching her hand out, running her fingers over the top and onto the handles.

"O'en it!" Sally urged.

"What do you think is in here and where did it come from?" Regina quipped, cautious but curious. Sally giggled, clapping her hands. "Do you think it's safe," she asked

Sally, not waiting for an answer. Regina's stomach was growling so loud that she thought it would give away their hiding place. Her hunger pangs won out over caution. She slid her finger under the lip of the lid and lifted it slowly. The scent of fried chicken, deviled eggs, and potato salad filled the air.

Regina's mouth watered uncontrollably. *Just what I was wishing for...* Sally leaned toward the basket, falling out of her sling. She was not going to be denied something to eat again today, or have to eat another cracker. Regina dug into the basket, pulling out plates, napkins, and flatware. She opened the tops of Tupperware exposing the delectable treats. Regina handed Sally a chicken leg and an egg. Sally sat on the counter that now had been completely repaired -- no more missing tiles, and it was clean! The sink glistened, the stove was complete and shiny, and a double-door refrigerator stood in the empty spot. Regina blinked, rubbing her eyes. "Later..." she muttered, shaking her head.

Regina scooped a giant helping of potato salad onto a plate and helped herself to a chicken leg. She turned to see behind her a table and chairs, neatly covered in a gingham tablecloth, with a small bouquet of yellow daisies sitting in the center. Regina carried Sally over and sat her in a chair. Both girls ate, looking out the now crystal clean window until they could eat no more. Regina gulped down a large glass of milk.

"Bo'le?" Sally whimpered.

"Well, let's see," Regina grinned. She reached back in the basket and a fresh bottle of ice cold milk waited for her. "Look what else I found," Regina came up with fresh baked chocolate chip cookies, and they were still warm as if they'd just come from the oven.

"I don't know who left the food, but thank you very much," Regina whispered into the air.

Sally squealed with delight, "Yeah, than ou!" she nodded happily.

"We need to find the boys. I think we saved them some lunch," Regina giggled. Sally nodded. Regina slipped Sally back into the sling, picked up the basket, and pushed the door open that led into the next room. "Oh, wait I left the flashlight on the counter," Regina said, hurrying back through the door. The kitchen had returned to the same dilapidated state it was when they first walked in, and the flashlight had fallen through the broken tiles on the countertop and rolled across the floor. It took Regina a few minutes to find it, and when she did, she dropped it into the basket and left, afraid to look back into the kitchen.

"Sally, I don't know what's going on around here and it's freaking me out, but now is not the time to question... I'll take what I can get, even if it's from ghosts. I think," she said with a shudder. Sally grinned. Her eyes were following something to the left of Regina. Sally cooed and giggled, waving at it. Regina was afraid to ask and just let it be.

The next room had wallpaper peeling and chunks of plaster missing from the walls, exposing the raw wood beneath. A chandelier hung from the ceiling, dripping with cobwebs. And the floor crunched with every step from the disintegrating room. "I guess this was the dining room," Regina muttered, looking around.

She and Sally stumbled through two or three other large, empty rooms, one with a cement floor and tattered pieces of carpet, one with a hardwood floor and a vaulted ceiling, and one with large black and white marble squares on the floor and walls. Everything about these rooms was a ramshackle mess.

"Dyson, Matthew, where are you?" she whispered, poking her head in room after room with no answer. Regina's voice became more strained with each failure to locate the boys.

"Where are they, Sally?" Regina sighed. "This place is so big, we could be walking in circles around each other," she paused. "We should have never separated… Do you think they went back outside?" Regina gulped. Sally patted her on the back and grinned.

"You aren't worried. Why aren't you worried?" Regina whispered. "No, I guess I don't think they went back outside, either. They were more afraid of Veronica than the ghosts in here," Regina muttered to Sally, not really expecting her to answer, but hoping her own horror would calm. *Oh, I need a place to sit down and rest. My back hurts and I'm tired of carrying Sally, but I don't dare put her down… what if she gets away from me and I lose her too?*

Regina felt hot tears welling up in her eyes, and this time, she didn't have the strength to stop them. A steady stream of salty water ran over her cheeks and dripped off her chin. Sally hugged her and patted her back, which made Regina sob that much more. Sally took Regina's cheeks in her tiny little hands, pointing Regina's face directly in front of her own. She smiled her big toothy grin. Regina inhaled and exhaled. A calm washed through her, making her feel better.

Regina pushed through another door and into a room that smelled musty and of decay. The ceiling, made of frosted glass, was broken. *The sun is still up! Good!* The floor was gray cement and in the center was an enormous hole. "It's an empty pool." Regina recognized the black tiled lines along the bottom. "Look, Sal! A lap pool," Regina wiped the tears from her chin.

Her fingers trickled over a metal ladder's handles that stood meaningless on the edge of the pool with carved steps cut into the wall. They stopped halfway to the bottom. A diving board lay toppled over next to its stand, and to Regina's surprise, a concrete picnic table stood all alone at the farthest end of the pool.

Regina edged her way over to it, brushing off the dirt and broken glass. She sat down and cuddled with Sally. Sally wanted down, pushing herself away from Regina. She fidgeted until Regina gave in and let her stretch her legs. "Now you stay close to me. I don't feel like chasing you down. Phew! You need a diaper!" Regina held her nose. Sally stared blankly at her. "Oh, all right. Whatever," Regina groaned. "Stay away from the edge of the pool! I don't have the diapers, anyway."

Regina watched as Sally wandered around the pool, looking over the edge, and picking up broken pieces of pool tiles. Regina rubbed the small of her back, stretched the back of her legs, and yawned. She looked around the room, feeling safe and yet, terrified. How could she have two such different emotions at the same time?

Sally found a spot at the edge of the pool and sat down, letting her feet dangle over the edge. She chattered quietly. Regina wasn't sure, but Sally seemed to be visiting with someone or something. *Can this day be any freakier?* Regina sighed, perusing her surroundings. *I should be horrified. This mansion appears when I need it most, it presents a basement for me to hide in, a flashlight to see in the dark, and food when I'm starving. It also shuts out the very people who are trying to get me. What is this place?* She sighed and whisked her hair out of her eyes.

Chapter Four

Ghosts?

Regina wiped a leftover tear from her thick lashes and took several deep breaths, letting them out slowly. Should she be afraid or should she be thankful? *I'll think about it later!* Right now she had to find the strength to search for the boys.

And where is Dyson? I hope he's okay. She exhaled. A loud noise echoed through the room, making Regina jump. She ran to Sally's side. She'd heard it too, but wasn't afraid. "Sally, what do you see?" Regina whispered. Sally pointed toward the door.

"Momma!" Regina looked up, following Sally's finger, pointing at nothing.

"What?" Regina squinted and blinked hard. The figure of a woman began to materialize. She glided toward them. Regina picked Sally up and began to retreat slowly, one small step at a time.

"That isn't Mrs. Hillsdale." She glared, watching a tall woman in a long, black full skirt, white blouse, and a tweed cape that wrapped around her shoulders. She had a welcoming smile and soft, comforting blue-green eyes. Her auburn hair was neatly coiffed in a French braid and rolled up the back of her head. A hint of recognition began to fill Regina. She felt a warm glow push through her fear. Regina stopped. "Could that be…? Naw!" she whispered, shaking her head.

The door banged open and Matthew barreled up the side of the pool with Dyson directly behind him. Regina glanced at the boys. A surge of relief ran through her as she ran to Dyson, taking him in her arms and squeezing him tightly. She bumped fists with Matthew. Sally, feeling squished, squirmed and freed herself.

"Really Reg, you act like you haven't seen me for months," Dyson teased.

"I feel like I haven't! Where have you two been? I've been looking all over for you! We need to get out of this house. I don't know how to explain this, but to say some strange things have been happening, is an understatement," Regina couldn't stop talking. Her eyes brimmed with tears again.

"I know! This place is a trip!" Matthew exclaimed. Dyson nodded.

"You guys aren't afraid?" Regina asked incredulously.

"Afraid of what?" Matthew asked.

"Who *are* you two? I can't believe you're not afraid of all the quirky things going on around here! Haven't you seen anything strange?" The boys glanced at each other. Matthew shook his head 'no'.

"Who's Sally talking to?" Dyson flicked his head, directing their attention to the pool's edge. She'd wandered back to the far end of the pool and resumed her conversation with her imaginary friend.

Regina didn't bother to look over her shoulder at Sally, "At first I thought it was Mrs. H, but now I'm not sure who it is," Regina shrugged. When she glanced back at Sally no one was with her. After what she'd been through today, she wasn't surprised. "She's been talking and giggling to her fictional friend, ever since we found our way into this nightmare."

"Right… You saw someone, Reg?" Matthew laughed. "Carrying Sally all day must have affected your brain. Sally is just being three," Matthew chided.

"Yeah, I did or thought I did. Maybe you're right," Regina sighed.

"Hey, I'm still starving. Where are we going to find something to eat? I'm pretty sure this dump isn't going to feed us."

"Yeah, me too. My stomach hurts and I feel like I'm going to barf," Dyson whined.

Regina continued to watch Sally chatter away with a make-believe someone… "Hmm, I can fix that. Hold on boys! I have just the thing," Regina said boastfully. They looked at her, puzzled. She strolled back to the concrete bench.

Matthew and Dyson made eye contact, each wrinkling their brows. "I'm really beginning to worry about you

Reg... Have you truly lost your mind?" Matthew said. She didn't answer him and kept walking.

"Where are you going, Reg?" Dyson screamed, falling to his knees.

He was at the end of his patience. His foster mother had been ripped from his life, he'd been chased all day, and he hadn't eaten much since last night. No wonder he was nauseous. Regina decided he'd be fine, and kept walking instead of answering him.

"Come on!" she urged. Matthew shrugged and followed, and Dyson crawled partway on his hands and knees, until he discovered the sharp broken tiles on the ground were painfully poking into his hands. Regina reached behind the bench and lifted up the wicker picnic basket. She set it on the cement table.

"Where did you get that?! Is there food in it?!" Matthew's eyes popped open wide, racing to where Regina stood.

"Reg, does that really got food in it?" Dyson swooped in and stuck his head under the flap before anyone could respond. "Look Matt! Chicken nuggets, hot French fries, and root beer!" he chortled.

"What? No, there were chicken legs, deviled eggs, and potato salad," Regina said, pulling the basket away from the boys and rooting through it. "I don't understand..." she mumbled.

"Hey, give it back, Reg!" Matthew yelled, grabbing the basket out of her hand and pulling out a handful of fries.

The boys were stuffing food in their mouths so fast they didn't bother to chew, and their jeans made for a better napkin than the actual thing. Regina stepped away from their feast. Sally was happily sitting on the edge of the pool. Regina joined her.

"Hey Sal, who are you talking too?" Regina spoke softly. Sally giggled and pointed to an empty space beside her. Regina followed her hand. She saw nothing. "Does this person have a name?" Regina picked up Sally and held her in her lap.

Sally clapped her hands together and put her fist up to her mouth. "Momma," Sally cooed. Regina stared at Sally, up at the boys, and back at Sally.

Momma, who?

"Oh yeah, throw me a diaper, Matt," Regina sighed, remembering Sally needed a change. She purposefully held her breath. Dyson trotted over and dropped a homemade diaper on Regina's head before he ran back to the basket. Regina started to remove Sally's pants, but she wasn't wet or smelly. In fact, she was clean and dry and had on a store-bought diaper, rather than one of their homemade ones. *What is going on here?* "Hey, guys, tell me where you've been," Regina asked hesitantly.

"Around," Matthew responded with his mouth full of chicken.

"Yeah, we were lost on the second floor. We kept running into torn up room after torn up room, and broken down stairs. We couldn't find the stairs we went up, so it took a while to come back down. But we found a place where we think an elevator could have been," Dyson said, proud of his discovery. Regina didn't look impressed. "Anyway, this ball of light…"

"Dyson!" Matthew exhaled and stared him down.

"Appeared before us. It danced all through the air, so we followed it. It finally led us here," Dyson mumbled, slurping root beer from a straw.

"Dyson, we weren't going to tell anyone we saw that light," Matthew complained.

"Oh yeah, well, it's just Reg. She doesn't care. Besides, she thinks she saw Mrs. H," Dyson shrugged. He could tell Matthew was put-off with the confession.

"Why don't you tell her you were bawling like a baby, too," Matthew grumbled.

"It wasn't only me!" Dyson fired back.

"It's okay! I had my moment too," Regina admitted solemnly. "Hey, who do you…? I mean, what do you think that ball of light could have been?" She blushed.

The boys snickered at her. "I mean, I would swear I saw someone come in that door, just before you guys showed up." she said softly. Matthew thought for a minute and then shrugged. Dyson didn't bother to react; he just kept stuffing food in his mouth.

"Hey Dy, I think you'd eat Brussels sprouts if they were in that basket," Regina laughed. Dyson only smirked.

"So, where did you get a picnic basket?" Matthew asked.

"It was in the kitchen. I just turned around, and there it was!" She decided not to elaborate.

"Where do you think it came from?" Matthew asked, between fries.

"I don't know," Regina said curtly. She was too tired and scared to answer Matthew's tedious questions. Besides, if she had, it meant she had to think about her day and that was the last thing she had in mind.

"Sorry... I just don't understand where a picnic basket, flashlight, and Mrs. H came from," Matthew said thoughtfully.

"I'm tired. I didn't mean to snap. I don't get it either, and I never said it was Mrs. H." Regina said.

"It's the house. It's taking care of us," Dyson chirped. Regina shivered at the thought, followed by deafening silence.

"You could be right. Just before Veronica reached us, I was wishing the mansion wasn't so far away and there it was in front of us. And by the way, Veronica and Marcus couldn't see it," Regina said as if a lightbulb flashed.

"How do you know?" Dyson asked, looking up from his food.

"I watched them from a window in the kitchen. They thought we vanished into thin air."

"Huh?"

"Yeah, weird, huh!"

"So, they aren't in here looking for us?" Dyson said relief flooding his face. Regina shook her head and smiled.

"So, now what?" Matthew exhaled. He'd turned around and leaned back against the tabletop, rubbing his full belly. "I don't think I've ever eaten that much, all at once. Boy, was it good," he chuckled.

"Well, it looks like it is starting to get dark. Maybe we ought to find a room, upstairs. One that is clean and rat free, hopefully. And… we stay the night… here!" Regina suggested, having second thoughts as she looked at her surroundings.

"Stay here… in this ghost-fest; this crumpled down old building? What if it collapses on our heads in the middle of the night?" Matthew said.

"It's better than wandering around the woods in the dark, and I'll bet they will have your fort staked out. Besides, I'm more afraid of those creeps back at home, than a couple of ghosts," Regina snapped. Everyone looked up, looking surprised at her suggestion. "I'm sorry! I don't think I can carry Sal another foot!" They all nodded.

"But we stay together, right?" Matthew exhaled. Regina bobbed her head up and down and smirked.

Matthew packed up the leftovers and arranged them in the basket. He found the flashlight and brought it out. "We might need this upstairs."

"Don't you have one from the fort?" Dyson asked.

"Yes, but let's use one at a time and save batteries."

"Okay, everyone hold hands. Matt you go first with the backpack, then Dyson. Sally, you take Dyson's hand, and I'll take the basket and Sal's other hand. We'll turn left out the door and go up the first staircase we come to. Hopefully, there's a bedroom upstairs we can feel safe in until morning," Regina said, bringing up the rear of the small group. She had second thoughts that this was the best plan or that it would be the safest place for the night, but she didn't feel like there was any other choice.

They exited the natatorium and turned left. After walking down a long hall they ended up in the foyer. The floor was covered in broken marble tiles and chunks of plaster from the walls. A huge chandelier hung over their heads, and a mammoth curved stairway led up. "Look at that light! I'll bet we could all fit up there!" Matthew exclaimed.

"I bet we could too, but how would we reach it? It's as tall as the house," Dyson added.

"Dy, I don't think he meant it literally," Regina chided.

"Maybe I did!" Matthew snickered. "It might be fun!"

He led the group over to the gaping hole that would have been the entry doors. He stood back and peered over the edge. It was at least an eight foot drop to the ground, littered with piles and piles of concrete rubble and bricks spread about, leaving the imagination free to design the steps and landing.

"Careful!" Regina barked. Matthew looked over his shoulder and glared. "Okay, I think we're all tired. Let's go," Regina tugged them back toward the stairs. Matthew resumed his place at the head of the line. A few steps later, they stood at the bottom of the staircase, looking up at its gentle curve. The handrail was broken and gone in spots, and some of the steps were broken or missing entirely.

"Do you see that?" Matthew frowned.

"Umm, I do," Regina groaned.

"Okay, just checking," Matthew said. He placed his foot on the first step, tested its stability, and added his full weight. The four followed him step for step, stair for stair, holding hands, passing Sally, the basket, and backpack back and forth as they climbed.

At one point, Matthew leaped over a missing step, letting go of Dyson's hand. "Don't let go of him," Regina huffed.

"Well, if I missed, I didn't want to take him down with me, and now you can hand him over," Matthew snapped.

"Exactly! I can't do this if you get hurt," she inhaled strongly. "Now, take his hand and I'll hold the other and hand him to you." They moved Sally the same way, and then Regina stepped over the hole. The higher they got the more dilapidated the staircase became.

"Halfway there, Reg! Look up!" Matthew groaned. There were three steps missing, impassable with no way to inch around and too wide to leap. Just then the stair that Matthew was standing on broke away. Dyson screamed. Regina grabbed Sally securely around the chest. Matthew had disappeared in the hole. Dyson fell to his knees, peeking over the ledge into what looked like oblivion to Regina. To Dyson's relief, Matthew had caught himself on a support beam that braced the staircase. He was dangling about nine feet off the ground, but had a firm grasp on the joist.

"He's here!" Dyson yelled to Regina. "But I can't reach him!" "Okay, hold Sally over here. Don't let her go!" Regina closed her eyes and took in a deep breath. "Hold on, Matt! I'm coming!"

"Could you speed it up?" he squirmed desperately. Regina lay down on the step and reached into the hole. Matthew had his fingers interlaced and wrapped around the six-inch beam. He was swinging freely.

"Give me your hand," she urged.

"Uh, can't let go. You take my arm," he grunted.

"No, no, I got it. Swing your leg up to me and I'll catch that," she suggested. Matthew swung his lower body back and forth until he could fling his leg up to Regina. She missed. He groaned.

"Sorry! Again! Come on! You can do it! I almost had it!" Matthew inhaled, repositioned his hands until he had a firm grasp, and began swinging his legs again. This time Regina caught his ankle. She lifted it over the rotted wood of the stair step and hooked his heel on solid ground. Matthew strained and pulled to get his body up. Regina guided his other foot into place, then hooked her fingers into his belt loops, pulling him with all her strength. After considerable work, Matthew was able to let go of the beam and climb the rest of the way onto the step.

Regina hugged his neck and patted his back. Matthew sat on the step and breathed. "Don't do that again," Regina growled, catching her breath.

"Are you wonky? I didn't plan that!" Matthew stared at her unbelievingly. She grinned and they all had a good laugh for a moment.

"What is with this house?" Regina grumbled into the air. "I wish this staircase was as good as new!" she called out forcefully.

"Like *that* is going to work! Everybody knows you need a magic word," Dyson teased.

"A magic word?"

"Yeah, like, 'Abracadabra!'"

"You know, whenever I get scared, I say, 'Harriett! Get me out of this!'" Before their eyes, the staircase and entry morphed into a beautiful room, grand enough for royalty. The white marble floor glistened, double mahogany doors with leaded pane glass inserts closed the opening to the outside, and crystal clear windows appeared beside each door. The monstrous chandelier turned shiny gold, with imitation candles and tiny shades that lit the entire room. Dyson jumped when broken pieces of marble flew through the air and started repairing the staircase, filling in the holes, and last, but not least, the rusted wrought iron rail turned white and the mahogany banister returned to perfection. White plaster flitted through the air onto the walls and ceiling, completing the transformation.

"Wow!" the children watched with wide eyes and gaping mouths until the last chip of paint found its place.

"Why didn't you do that before I fell and almost killed myself?" Matthew yelled.

"Stop gawking and get up to the top before it changes again," Regina bellowed, grabbing Sally, and pushing Dyson forward.

Sally shrieked with happy laughter. She pointed to the top of the stairs, dropping Regina's hand and climbing on her hands and knees, trying to reach the landing at the top. Matthew froze in his tracks causing Dyson to run squarely into his behind. "Move it, Buster," Dyson grumbled.

Standing above them on the landing was a woman, young enough to be Regina's older sister. She had the same auburn hair and Dyson's blue-green eyes. Her smile was warm and comforting. A warm glow began to fill Regina; the same one she'd experienced downstairs in the indoor pool.

"That's the same woman I saw earlier," Regina gulped.

She motioned the small group to join her.

"Whoooo is she," Matthew stuttered, leery of moving another inch.

"Do you see her?" Regina whispered. Dyson peeked around Matthew and said nothing. Regina bent forward and held Sally at bay. She wiggled and tugged to free herself. "Hold still!" Regina scowled.

"Yeah!" Matthew said. "I see her!"

"She's the same person I saw down at the pool..."

"Yeah, you said that already," Matthew said with his mouth gaping.

"I think she's my mom, Harriett Worthington," Regina muttered, not knowing whether to scream or run to her.

"But your mother is dead!" Matthew spluttered.

"I know," Regina whispered, stepping forward, not taking her eyes off of the woman she wanted to call Mom. Harriett continued to motion for them to advance toward her. Regina, bravely or desperately, climbed the steps. She wasn't sure. Her heart pounded in her chest, her hands trembled, but she couldn't stop herself from wanting to be closer to the woman before her.

"Stop! What are you doing?" Matthew's voice cracked. Regina ignored his command.

Sally giggled and clapped, pushing on Regina, and trying to get around her. Regina kept her firmly behind her. She reached the last step at the top. "Momma, is it you?" she whispered. The woman reached out her arms and pulled Regina into her chest with a hug of love and sorrow that only a mother could give. Regina melted, never wanting to leave. She inhaled deeply, breathing in the same herbs she remembered so well and had dreamed about for the last four years.

Sally cried at Harriett's knees, stomping her feet, and tugging on her long skirt. When the embrace came to its conclusion, Regina stepped back. Dyson hid behind Matthew, who hadn't moved an inch. "Dyson, it is okay, baby, I am your mother," Harriett spoke softly. Her voice a soothing song that sang to each of them as she stooped to pick up Sally. Sally quieted and settled her head against Harriett's shoulder.

"Dy, come here. She really is our mom," Regina said to him, returning her gaze to her mother's eyes, fearing she'd disappear again. Dyson shook his head and stayed behind Matthew. Regina smiled coyly. "Oh, sorry Matthew, this is my mom, Harriett Worthington."

"It's very nice to meet you… Mrs. Worthington?" Matthew questioned, looking apprehensively at Regina.

Harriett smiled and nodded. "Yes, why is that…?" Regina whispered.

"Dyson is not ready. It will be fine," Harriett said, smiling and ignoring Regina's sarcasm. Regina motion for both boys to climb the stairs. Matthew inched his way up. Dyson had his arms wrapped tightly around his waist making it difficult for Matthew to walk.

"Follow me," Harriett said.

Regina waited for the boys to step in front of her. She took Dyson by the hand and let Matthew lead. Dyson hadn't said a word, but Regina noticed he wasn't quivering or holding his breath. Good sign, she supposed.

As they entered the hall at the top of the stairs the paint, plaster, and boards were all in disarray. Matthew looked over his shoulder at Regina and Dyson to see if they were seeing what he was seeing. The two sibling's eyes danced along, watching tiny pieces of mansion float through the air and land in their proper places, repairing the walls, windows, and floor a few feet ahead of them and then after they'd passed, returning to chaos.

"What is happening?" Matthew mouthed. Regina had a silly, contented grin on her face and didn't hear his question. Matthew shrugged and continued to scrutinize their surroundings and escort.

Somewhere about halfway down the long hall Harriett stepped up to a door and knocked three times. She turned the perfectly polished brass door handle and pushed the door wide open. Inside, a beautiful room awaited. Harriett swept her hand slowly, inviting them inside. Regina stepped over the threshold first, and beheld a room so large, Mrs. Hillsdale's whole house could have fit inside. The walls were a soft pale blue with white wood accents. Big picture windows were draped with sheer, wispy curtains, and a fireplace filled the space between them. A roaring fire blazed in the hearth, warming the room. An assortment of pictures of happy children at play hung on the walls.

A ladder stretched from the floor to a loft halfway across the room, and under the loft was a full-sized bed so puffy, it looked like it could float away. The quilted bedspread had squares of flowers across the top with row after row of eyelet ruffles to the floor. A small night stand sat between the window and bed. A lamp lit the small corner with the same ruffles on its shade. A bookcase, desk, and large walk-in closet filled with clothes was to the left of the bed. Sitting on the bed was Regina's favorite teddy bear from when she was eight years old; the very one she'd slept with every night as a small child. She hadn't seen it since that dreadful night.

Regina broke loose from the group when she recognized it, scooping it up and burying her face in the fur. She cried softly. Dyson realized she was upset and ran after her. He tried to console her, but didn't quite understand. Regina hugged his neck, "It's alright… I'm alright! It's just…" she cried.

Matthew had climbed the ladder up into the loft. "Dyson! Dyson get up here," he yelled. Regina pushed him away and nodded her head for him to go. Dyson sprinted to the ladder and climbed as fast as his small frame would allow. His mouth dropped open at the sight of the room above Regina.

Beds fashioned in the shape of log cabins sat apart on each wall, giving each boy privacy and a place to call their own. Attached to each cabin was a desk and small bookcase. Each boy had a small walk-in closet, toy box, and directly in the center of the room was a slot-car racetrack complete with their favorite Nascar racecars, operated by handheld remote controllers. Regina heard the engines fire and the boys' excited laughter.

Regina scanned the room and found Harriett sitting in a rocking chair, Sally snuggled up on her lap, gently sleeping. To the left of Harriett was a twin bed with safety rails and piles of stuffed toys of all sizes. A closet, changing table, and toy box were also close by.

The center of the large room was a common area with couches, comfy chairs, and an entertainment center complete with a massive flat screen TV, video recorder, and all the games and movies they could want. The last thing Regina noticed was a closed door. She hoped it led to a bathroom.

Chapter Five

Are You My Mother?

Regina stepped out of the lukewarm water onto a fluffy mat. She'd been soaking in a large, oblong porcelain tub, with hot steamy water, scented lavender soap, and thick frothy bubbles. Languishing in the coveted bath eased the tired muscles of her legs and back. She'd almost fallen asleep but the water had turned cool. Several plush terry towels sat on a shelf over the toilet, and hanging on the back of the door was a long flannel nightgown. "Where did *that* come from?" she pondered, donning the gown. The door creaked open, but no one startled as she tiptoed across the floor toward her special room. Her eye caught a dark figure sitting next to Sally's bed. She jerked her head sideways, seeing a woman wearing a black dress with a crisp white apron and a funny looking stiff white hat. She was transparent. "Whoa, who's that?" Regina whispered, careful not to wake Sally. She'd had a big day and needed her sleep. Regina wasn't sure what would frighten Sally more; being surrounded by four or five giant stuffed animals, or having a ghost sitting next to her.

"A nanny. She will stay by her side all night. So you do not have to worry," Harriett answered, bringing her finger to her lips to quiet Regina. Next to Harriett, in the comfy chair, was Dyson. He'd fallen asleep curled up on Harriett's lap, while she twirled a lock of his auburn hair.

Regina squeezed her eyes tight, hoping the vision of that awful night wouldn't seep into her mind, but it did. She felt herself transported back in time. The family was watching a movie together. Regina snuggled up to her father and Dyson slept on her mother's lap while she twirled his hair. The fire had gone cold and instead of adding a log, Harriett had gone upstairs to get a lap blanket. That's when the men busted down the front door and Regina's life was changed forever. She blinked hard, erasing the images.

"Looks like he's warming up to you," Regina sniffed. Harriett nodded and smiled.

Regina shivered, scurrying across the room, partly because she was cold, but mostly to outrun the memories. She was done with the emotion of this day and was eager to put it all behind her, somehow. She didn't think it was going to be so easy, but she would try anything to think about it all later! She couldn't resist one last glance behind her, checking for Matthew. He lay stretched out on the couch, watching the latest Minion movie.

Regina reached her quiet section of the room, and lying at the foot of her bed was a pink pair of fuzzy slippers. She slipped them over her feet and began gently rubbing the water out of her hair with the towel.

"How was your bath?" Harriett asked softly, standing directly behind Regina. She twitched, startled.

"It was heaven!" Regina said, flopping onto the edge of her bed with her comb. She began ripping through the snarls of her wavy locks. *Where did she come from?* Regina thought silently, glancing back at Dyson. He was undisturbed with a blanket covering him. Regina stared back at her mother, who had helped herself to the comb. Reaching for the bear that she'd left on her pillow, Regina snuggled it and let her mother comb out her tangles.

"I used to do this when you were little, but it was not quite this long," she said.

"Yeah, I've never had it cut, except for a trim here and there, in Mrs. Hillsdale's kitchen," Regina said. She felt angry, somehow. Maybe it was because she missed all the little things or she could just be exhausted.

"How are you doing with all of this?" Harriett cleared her throat, changing the subject.

"To be honest, I'm afraid to think," Regina confessed, more controlled. She closed her eyes and let the warmth of a mother's love filter through her. Mrs. Hillsdale did the very best she could and Regina loved her for it, but she'd missed her mother. They'd been a close family before Harriett died and it had been hard for her and Dyson since then. "I'm afraid I'm going to wake up and this is going to be a miserable dream," Regina whispered.

"It might be better for everyone if that were so," Harriett said with a frown.

"Maybe, but a lot of good has come out of today too. I don't want you to be gone again. But I don't want Mrs. Hillsdale to be dead, either," she paused to consider. "I don't want you to be another nightmare! I've lived that once," Regina sighed, trembling.

Harriett wrapped her in her arms and held her there. Regina cried softly, "Are you really my mother?"

"I am," Harriett hesitated, letting the thought sink in. "I am truly sorry I was taken from you and Dyson when you were so young. It was not my choice... If that helps."

"Mommy?" Regina murmured. Tears streamed out of her amber eyes and down her face.

"It is all going to be all right... You will see," Harriett whispered, rocking her back and forth.

Regina yawned, "My hair will be a frizzy mess if I don't..." she gulped. Her hand caught the dried braid hanging down her back. "What?" Regina said, surprised.

"Not to worry, my sweet! You get some sleep and we will talk in the morning," Harriett spoke softly, pulling down the bed covers. Regina climbed into the cool clean sheets as Harriett pulled the blankets up to her chin and tucked her in. Harriett handed her Mr. Wuzzles, the bear, and Regina tucked him under the covers, holding him close. Harriett kissed her on the forehead and Regina breathed in her fragrance of lavender.

"Oh, the boys!" Regina exclaimed, sitting up suddenly.

"I will take care of them," Harriett said, guiding her back down onto the pillows and returning the blankets. Regina snuggled down and yawned. She was asleep within moments.

Regina awoke to the bright sunlight streaming in through the window next to her bed. Birds sang outside. She stretched and sat up, her hair was still in its braid and she was still in the puffy warm bed. *It hadn't been a dream*, she smiled, bounding onto the floor, sliding her feet into the slippers, and pulling the sheer curtain away from the window. Her eyes beheld green lawns, large leafy shade trees, and flower gardens full of vibrant colors. Birds sang in the trees and a large yellow butterfly flittered across the yard. Regina grinned with anticipation.

"Dyson!" she called. She waited for an answer, nothing came. Regina sprinted over to the ladder and looked up toward the loft. "Matthew!" she heard no response. "Sally, are you here?" She spun and looked into her bed. She was gone, too. Regina's heart sank to her stomach. "Harriett! Mom! Where is everyone?" Panic started to fill her.

Regina reached for the doorknob to the hall and before she touched it, it swung open. In popped Dyson and Matthew. Regina exhaled.

"What's wrong with you? You look like you've seen a ghost!" Matthew laughed. "Oh, I guess you have," he roared.

"Not funny! Where have you been?" Regina snapped.

"Reg, wait until you see this place! It has everything. We brought you a cinnamon roll. Here!" Dyson pushed a gooey, sugary pastry into her hand. "Get dressed so we can go explore!"

Matthew plopped onto the couch and turned on the television. He flipped through the channels and paused on the news. The headline that the reporters were all talking about, said, "Foster children missing and caretaker unable to speak. This is the third case of foster children missing from their homes. Authorities don't believe the foster parents are to blame."

"You'd better believe Mrs. Hillsdale isn't to blame! That creep, Marcus, is to blame and so is Veronica," Matthew spewed. He had no more than finished his sentence when Harriett walked through the door.

"I do not want you kids to worry about Mrs. Hillsdale..." Harriett started to say.

"We have to tell the police what happened to Mrs. H so she doesn't get in trouble," Regina argued.

"I know you think you will be helping her, but trust me, she does not need your help," Harriett said.

"What do you mean? We can't just leave her there with Marcus and Veronica," Regina insisted, and Dyson stood next to her nodding his head.

"Maybe she's right, Reg... I mean, what can we do? We're just kids," Matthew muttered.

"Well, we can call the police and report what happened!" Regina was beside herself with disbelief. Why were these people leaving Mrs. Hillsdale out there to fend for herself?

"Get dressed and let us meet in my office," Harriett said.

"Office... You have an office?" Regina gasped.

"Yeah, Reg, you aren't going to believe how cool everything is," Dyson said.

"Go now! Get dressed. I think you will be interested to hear what I have to tell you." Harriett turned on her heels and strode out the door.

"So, how do we find her?" Regina muttered under her breath.

"Just call out my name and I will be here," Harriett's voice echoed throughout the room. The children stopped their fidgeting and stared into the empty room waiting for the voice to finish its message.

"See now that's what I'm talking about! What is this place, and who just left us?" Regina snorted. "I say we get out of here, ASAP!"

"She says she's our mom. I don't want to leave," Dyson said sadly. Regina hugged him close.

"Okay, okay. Let's go talk to her. I'm curious too," Regina whispered to the top of his head. "Where's Sal?"

"Oh, she's with that nanny from last night," Matthew said, and burped loudly. He'd been drinking a soda. Dyson began to snicker. Matthew laughed.

"That was a good one!" Dyson pounced Matthew on the couch and a wrestling match ensued.

"You two are disgusting!" Regina groaned, spinning on her heel and returning to her room to change. She could hear the boys tussling and laughing. She rolled her eyes, taking a big bite out of her pastry. "Yum, this is good," she grinned.

"Harriett!" Regina called out into the empty room.

Harriett strolled through the door. "Oh, I see you found the clothes in the closet. I thought that color of blue would look good on you. The dark blue-green really makes your eyes sparkle," she said. Regina felt Harriett's maternal love being showered upon her, but she wasn't in the mood to accept all of… Whatever all this was. And now that she had rested and had a clear head… Well, maybe she would reserve judgment until she'd listened to what Harriett had to say.

"Follow me," Harriett said, after waiting for Regina to comment about the clothes, which she didn't.

They left the room and entered the hallway. A group of girls Regina's age meandered down the corridor. They were dressed in matching navy blue skirts, white blouses, and tweed capes. They each wore white knee-high socks and black saddle shoes. They carried school books in their arms and stared at Regina as they passed by.

Regina rubbed the back of her neck uncomfortably. "Who are they?" Regina whispered to Harriett, but before she could answer, three boys, Dyson's age, raced up the hall almost running over them.

"Slow down, boys," Harriett called. They didn't seem to heed her warning and Harriett groaned. "I will deal with them later." Further down the hall, Regina noticed a small group of boys a little older than herself. They were huddled together telling some kind of secret.

"Dickson Remington, what do you have there?" Harriett redirected her attention to the small group of young men. Regina felt her heart skip a beat when her eye caught the young man that answered the call. He was tall and lanky, with blondish-brown hair, and a mischievous lopsided grin. Regina quickly looked away, afraid someone would read her mind.

"Oh, good morning, Ms. Worthington!" Dickson said. Harriett stood before him snapping her fingers. "But, I… I don't know what you mean!" Dickson was turning bright red. He pulled at the red tie around his neck. Harriett didn't say another word. She just waited patiently with her hand held out. Dickson finally placed a small leather pouch on her palm. "We weren't going to use it on any of the teachers. I promise," he swore.

"Uh-huh!" Harriett exhaled. "Now get to class before I send you all to detention," Harriett ordered.

"Yes, Ma'am!" Dickson said, catching Regina's stare before she looked away. He hesitated, watching her, then trotted in the direction of his friends.

"Class?" Regina cleared her throat, stuttering, and blushing. She couldn't help but think his dark turquoise eye color was different than anyone she'd ever seen before. She glanced over her shoulder. He was watching her. She hesitated.

"This way, please." Harriett said, ushering them through a door at the end of the hall. Regina stumbled into the room.

This room was large with a window behind a crystal clear desk and a white leather chair. There was a tall crystal glass lamp with a light beige shade sitting on the corner of the desk and a grouping of picture frames. Regina couldn't see who was in the pictures. To the left of the desk was a floral print couch and two tall, wingback chairs all sitting in a group. A glass top coffee table was in front of the couch and a bushy light-colored rug lay on the hardwood floor. Several large leafed plants decorated the corners of the room. She had a fire blazing in the hearth and hanging above it was a large golden snake eating its tail. It formed a perfect circle with an olive branch twining through the middle. Below it read, *Never Ending Peaceful Life*." Regina stared, thinking it was a strange emblem and wondered what it meant.

"Make yourselves comfortable. Would you like some tea? I believe I have some glazed donut holes." Dyson nodded with a big grin. Regina sat in one of the chairs and the boys bounced on the sofa. Harriett joined the children after a brief stop to open a window.

"I know you have a lot of questions, but let me see if I can explain before we get to those," Harriett smiled. The three sat quietly, waiting. "We are a school," she began, "and a refuge for some," she added.

Regina's brows scrunched together. "Yes, questions!" Harriett smiled and stood. "I might as well just lay it out. Regina, you have always been one for cutting to the core of things." Harriett smiled. "So, here it is… We come from a magical world that met its end from a fiery volcano many, many years ago. You have probably heard of it… Atlantis." She paused. Recognition flashed in each of their eyes, but they continued to sit quietly. "Yes, we are descendants from the lost island of Atlantis. Centuries ago, our country was thriving, happy, and peaceful. We were a shipping port in the middle of the Mediterranean Sea. Travelers from all over came to us to trade their wares, but that is not all; our civilization was far more advanced than most of the others, partly because we were innovative, and partly because of our magic!" she continued.

"When the end came, we gathered every living creature, artifact, and piece of wealth we had, and left. At first, we spread throughout the lands and seas, looking for another place like Atlantis, but could not settle on the right place. And then the unthinkable happened…" Dyson and Matthew were quiet as mice and hadn't taken their eyes off of Harriett. Regina started to say something, but Harriett spoke again before she could ask her a question.

"Instead of uniting as one, our people split into two. Atlantis emerged with two philosophies. The King believed in harmony and peace, that all should strive to help and care for all life. His half-brother believed in an all for one attitude. Take what you need for your own power, regardless of consequences. This led to the King's people being hunted!"

The children were too mesmerized by the story to say anything.

"Let us talk about magic. Our magic comes in many forms. Some of us were born with magic, and others of us have the ability to use what is around and *make* magic," Harriett explained. "So, with that said… We are a school for lost Atlanteans. We are here to teach you how to use your power safely. We teach you control, to use nature, and we protect you from the evil that would steal your power for their own benefit."

"B-B- But," Regina stuttered, mouthing words that wouldn't come out.

"I have powers?" Matthew sputtered, staring at his hands. Dyson's eyes were wide with astonishment.

"Not yet, Matthew. You have not come of age. Regina will soon come into her power. She will be thirteen in five months. I know this because her father and I were both magical. Matthew, your mother was a top notch sorceress, but your father possessed no magic. You may or may not have your own magic, but you will be able to manipulate the elements to create magic -- after we teach you, of course."

"Are you a teacher?" Dyson whispered.

"I am the head mistress," Harriett said, and took Dyson in her arms.

"This is all very hard on all of you, I know. You see, the first thing we all do, as parents, is make special arrangements for our child's care in case we are not able to provide it any longer, so we have safeguards in place. Mrs. Hillsdale knows about our society. She is non-magical, but her family originated from Atlantis. Her ancestors married humans until they had bred the magic out of their lines. Sadly, they were afraid of the demon hunters and wanted off their radars and to live normal lives. Mrs. Hillsdale has been one of our rescue houses for many years. She and her husband, George, provided a normal, safe environment for you. We are not sure how your identities were discovered," Harriett waited a moment for this information to sink in.

"It was Marcus and Veronica. They held a knife at Mrs. Hillsdale's throat and then locked us in our room upstairs. Pam helped us escape," Regina almost screamed.

"We have to go get Mrs. Hillsdale!" Dyson cried.

"You cannot leave here, sweetheart. The mansion is not even in Glenville anymore," Harriett said.

"Where are we?" Matthew gasped.

"We move around a lot. We can hear the call of sorcerers when they are in trouble. That is how we knew to come for you."

"I wished it," Regina whispered, deep in thought.

"Yes!"

A beautiful white dove flew in through the window and landed on a perch next to Harriett's desk.

"Excuse me for a minute," she said politely, getting up and walking silently over to the bird. Regina watched every step she took. The bird began to sing a beautiful melody and after a moment or two, Harriett whispered something to the bird. It then flew out the window and into the distance.

Harriett returned to the couch and placed Dyson back on her lap. "I have been informed that Mrs. Hillsdale is in the hospital. Marcus tortured her, trying to force her to reveal your whereabouts," Harriett said sadly, looking at the floor.

"I want to see Mrs. Hillsdale," Dyson said. She hugged him close.

"Is she going to be alright? What about Pam?" Regina asked.

Harriett looked up, making eye contact with Regina, "I am sending one of our healers to the hospital. The

Unicorn Horn ought to do the trick and heal her," Harriett assured Regina. "We have not located Pam."

"I don't understand any of this… Unicorn Horn?" Regina fired back. She didn't take her eyes off of Harriett.

"Unicorns are magical creatures…" Regina nodded that she knew that part. "At the end of their lives their horns are donated and ground into dust that has magical healing powers."

"That's good, right? It can heal Mrs. H?" Matthew surmised. Harriett smiled.

"Let us go for a walk," Harriett said, standing and taking Dyson's hand. "Maybe get some lunch."

Regina stood slowly, exhaling loudly, and rolling her eyes. "Whatever," she moaned.

The group walked toward the door, following Harriett. "What does the emblem over the fireplace mean?" Regina asked, pointing to the snake.

"Oh, that is our crest. It is an Ouroboros. It symbolizes the eternity of life and energy unending. A snake eating its tail encircles the Earth and protects it from the chaos beyond. The olive branch running through it brings peace to the Earth and eternal life." Harriett smiled and continued to the door.

Regina thought for a moment and smiled. She finally found a reason to hope and believe in what was happening. *Perhaps I haven't given Harriett and this place a chance.* "Hey, wait a minute; why are we going to tour this dump? I saw enough of it, yesterday," Regina groaned.

"Oh, Reg, you don't know… This is no dump," Matthew chuckled as the door opened. They walked into the brightly lit hallway and turned left heading back to the marble staircase. Regina's eyes opened wide in surprise. She couldn't get over the fact that it was clean, carpeted, and complete, as if it had been built yesterday.

"What happened to the rats?" Regina whispered, punching Matthew.

"I told you, you were in for a shock," he chuckled. "Come on!"

Regina continued to follow Harriett quietly. They made their way down the curved, marble staircase and ended up in the foyer. Harriett opened the front door and stepped onto the massive slate stoop. She led them down the steps onto a driveway that circled around a lush green lawn. Growing in the grass were huge bay leaf, olive, and willow trees. Bushes and flowers that Regina didn't recognize, filled the flower beds. The curved drive seemed endless and looked to never have been driven on. Bees buzzed and butterflies fluttered from flower to flower.

In the distance, Regina caught sight of a beautiful snow white horse. His mane flowed down the length of his neck and all way to the ground. His tail did the same. Regina watched, waiting for him to hear them and run, but instead, he turned in their direction and bowed. Regina's mouth fell open. A long thin, twisted horn grew from his forehead. She nudged Matthew in the ribs and pointed. He looked up with much the same expression. They watched silently as Harriett prattled on about something, until another beast with the same frosty white coat that almost looked blue, walked up alongside the first unicorn and then the two meandered off together. Matthew and Regina shared a look and a giggle before they tuned back and reengaged with what Harriett was explaining.

"Ah, yes; our magical pair of unicorns have allowed you to see them this morning. They only let the most trustworthy gaze upon them," Harriett smiled.

"Unicorns?" Dyson asked. "Is that what they were?"

"Indeed," Harriett smiled, leading them onto the grass. She turned them around to look back at the mansion. Regina couldn't believe her eyes. Not a single window was cracked, not a brick or stone out of place, and not a single chip in the paint could be seen. Regina gasped at the sheer size of the mansion. It reached the clouds in height and the edges seemed to fade out of view.

"Impressive, do you not agree?" Harriett said, looking at Regina who was gaping in astonishment. "We are fully equipped with anything and everything you would ever need. Notice that the girls' dormitories are to my left, each floor representing a compatible age group, and the boys' dormitories are to my right. Until, of course, you are in high school. Then, your floors will be comprised of all high school aged students."

"I thought you said only thirteen-year-olds were admitted." Matthew interrupted.

"I also said we do rescues. For instance, you four." she paused and let him consider her words before she continued. "The middle is comprised of classrooms, dining halls, kitchens, offices… well, you get the idea. The upper floors are out of bounds and the hospital is in the basement."

She clapped her hands together and sighed. It was clear to Regina that Harriett was proud.

"But I don't… Why was this place a spooky wreck yesterday, and who does the cleaning?" Regina stammered.

"Well, we cannot have just anybody walking through our doors now, can we?" Harriett said blithely, obviously not expecting an answer. Regina stared. "Actually, it is a test of sorts, to see if you are ready to become a member of our society," Harriett explained, attempting to quell the expression of incredulity on Regina's face.

"A test?! We almost died!" Regina barked. Her emotions were so rattled she didn't know if she was happy, amused, or angry. "What's the next exam, scrubbing the floors?" Regina flushed a rosy pink while yelling, causing her to end her tirade in a whisper. She was embarrassed by her own outburst.

"Oh no, dear, we have Brownies who live to serve our society."

"Brownies?" Matthew mouthed, wrinkling his brow.

"You will learn about our magical helpers in time and what they require from us. But let me tell you, most of our teachers are from the hereafter," Harriett said, smiling. All three of the children gasped at once. "And you will notice when we speak we do not use contractions. Most of us were assassinated by demon hunters and when they stole our magic… Well, it was kind of a side effect to our grammar." She folded her hands and walked forward.

"Come along, come along," Harriett motioned them back up the steps. "Lots to see!"

As they walked back into the mansion, Harriett quietly said to Regina, "I would imagine you are curious to know about Sally." Regina nodded, realizing she'd forgotten about Sally. Harriett opened a double door and they entered the nursery. Sally jumped up and ran straight into Regina's arms.

"Reg, I li it ere," she said in her baby talk.

"That's nice, Sal… What have you been doing?" Regina asked, setting Sally down on her feet, and letting her lead them across the room.

Regina saw that there were a number of children in the nursery, ranging in age from newborn, who each had their own nanny, to four years. "There are never more than three to a nanny after they reach the age of two."

"Are all these kids orphans?" Regina asked over her shoulder.

"Pretty much," Harriett acknowledged.

"Wow! Why? What happened to their parents?" Matthew blurted out.

"Well, it is simple really. All the normal reasons you would lose your parents, plus, we are hunted," Harriett said under her breath.

"Really? Hunted?" Dyson grimaced.

Harriett sighed, "So, Sally, did you tell Regina about the picture you painted?"

Sally giggled and pointed to the easel. "Oh, Sal! It's beautiful!" Regina exclaimed, angling her head, trying to place the image. "You know; from this angle it looks like a butterfly. One with lots of colors!" Regina winked.

Sally grinned widely with her finger in her mouth, swaying, "Butfly!" Everyone giggled.

"Excuse me," Harriett said, walking toward the window. Regina watched her carefully, while listening to Sally, Dyson, and Matthew analyze the painting. Harriett stopped in front of the window, opening it to let an oversized dove fly to a perch. They had a conversation much like the one she witnessed earlier.

"We need to talk," Harriett spoke softly. "Sally, may I borrow your brothers and sister for a moment, please?" she asked, bowing slightly. Sally ran off to her new playmate who was playing with the plastic dishes in a child-sized kitchen.

Harriett led them out of the nursery and into a garden room. This room was filled with green succulent plants and a large, sprawling chaste tree. Its lavender, fingerlike flowers filled the room with a pleasant aroma. Harriett offered them a seat at a round, wrought-iron table with a glass top.

"Would you like anything?" she asked. "I know! How about lunch?" And before they could answer, the table was filled with a variety of chips, sandwiches, and lemonade. Dyson helped himself to a peanut-butter and jelly. He placed it on a china plate and chose a bag of bar-b-que chips. Matthew chose ham and cheese, and Regina helped herself to tuna. "Very good," Harriett said, smiling, and when they were finished, she waved her hand and a plate of homemade chocolate chip cookies, still hot, appeared.

Regina was becoming used to the magic and it didn't seem to ruffle her as much. "So, what did you want to say away from Sally?" Regina inquired, swallowing a gulp of milk with her cookie.

Harriett cleared her throat and looked each of them in the eye, "I am very sorry to report that my healer could not heal Mrs. Hillsdale. She is beyond repair and is not expected to survive much longer," Harriett said solemnly. Dyson screeched in despair and jumped into Regina's arms. He sobbed inconsolably.

"What do you mean?! Why can't you do some magic and fix her?! Bring her here and put her in the mansion's hospital! You have to do more!" Regina shouted, burying her face in Dyson's tousled hair. They cried together. Matthew sat stone-faced and didn't utter a sound.

"I understand this is devastating and I am terribly sorry. Marcus used dark magic on her that repelled our good magic. She is resting comfortably and she sent you all a message," Harriett handed it to Regina.

Kids,

Please don't be sad. I've known all along that this could be my destiny. Know that I love you. You are where you should be. I have always believed that everything happens for a reason and I taught that to all of you.

Be happy for me… I get to see Mr. Hillsdale soon!

Love to all and take care of each other,

Mrs. Hillsdale

Regina read the note out loud to everyone. Harriett left the room to let them grieve.

"Is this our fault?" Matthew mumbled.

"I don't think so. How could we know any of this?" Regina sniffed. Matthew shrugged. Dyson wiped his eyes and snuggled deeper into Regina's lap. She stroked his hair and kissed the top of his head. Regina motioned for Matthew to come closer and made room for him to join the embrace.

They stayed together quietly for a time, and when they were ready, Regina called, "Harriett!"

They huddled together on the couch upstairs in their room. "Can I get you anything?" Harriett asked.

Regina looked into Dyson's eyes and then Matthew's, "No, we're good… Unless you want to take us to see her one last time," Regina said hopefully.

"Yeah, take us to see her," Matthew demanded, while Dyson pushed his glasses up and nodded his head.

"No, I do not think it is a good idea for you to go out in the open. It is not safe!" Harriett replied.

"No, really. We want to see her. We insist…" Regina spoke up.

"It is out of the question. You cannot protect yourselves out in the world. Marcus will be looking for you. He is after your magic."

"Steal something we don't even have yet?" Regina retorted.

Harriett glared. "Stealing innocent magic is the best possible rush. It is pure, untamed magic. No one has put controls on it. Do you understand?" she explained.

"Then send someone with us. We need to say goodbye," Regina argued and Dyson folded his hands as if he were praying.

"I don't want to stay here unless I can go see Mrs. Hillsdale. You can't keep me here! It's kidnapping, or something!" Matthew argued. Harriett looked each of them in the eye, reading their souls.

"You owe us," Regina paused. Harriett tilted her head considering the statement. "We were never allowed to say goodbye to you and dad, and it was traumatic. It left scars…" Regina fired back.

"Let me see what I can arrange. This is against my better judgment, but I will try," Harriett sighed and disappeared out the door. Regina, Matthew, and Dyson cheered quietly, thrilled that they'd won this argument.

Chapter Six

Never Ending Peaceful Life

Saying Goodbye

Regina paced around their room, twisting and popping her knuckles. Matthew flipped through TV channels nervously, and Dyson kept running to the bathroom. "It's almost dark outside. When are they going to send us home?" Regina fussed.

"Relax! They'll be here when they're ready," Matthew fired back.

"When did *you* become so snotty?" Regina fumed.

"Don't fight!" Dyson whined.

"Harriett!" Regina screamed, followed by a groan and a loud pop of her middle finger. Harriett materialized almost immediately in the middle of the room. Regina jumped at the sight of her. "It's about time," her snarky comment drew an intense stare from Harriett.

"Follow me!" Harriett said with a frown. Matthew flew off the couch, startled at the sound of her voice.

"Where did you come from?" Dyson spluttered, charging out the bathroom door.

"Ghost!" Harriett said sarcastically. "You three are as white as sheets… If you cannot handle a little materializing, then you are not going to fare well out there," Harriett scolded. "Maybe this is not a good idea."

"No, no, we're ready. You just startled us," Regina assured her. Harriett paused to consider her decision to let them go. Regina fidgeted from foot to foot, trying to look confident.

"Okay, follow me," Harriett whispered.

She walked them down the hall and into her office. She turned, giving them a final look before she approached the blank wall beside her desk. With a sweeping motion she said, "Revealelecto!" A door with a glass window appeared before them. Harriett opened it. Inside was a gate that she unlatched and ushered everyone inside. She pushed a button that read, *Cloud* and said, "Ascendelecto!" The small room began to climb, up through the mansion.

"Now listen to me carefully!" Harriett said sternly.

Regina, Matthew, and Dyson yawned, popping their ears, but gave her their full attention. "I am sending Puddlefoot with you. He is a Brownie." Harriett raised her index finger to silence Matthew. "He will be invisible unless he is needed. Now, it is very important that you do not embarrass or anger him."

"Embarrass? How do you embarrass a… Puddlefoot?" Regina giggled.

"Like that!" Harriett barked.

"Sorry," Regina frowned.

"Oh, and when you can, feed him bread and cream -- real cream, not milk!" Harriett said just before the elevator rumbled to a stop.

Regina turned to Matthew, wiggling her finger in her ear, and crossing her eyes, "Bread and real cream," she mouthed. Harriett glared. "My ear won't open," Regina complained, looking away.

The door opened to a hallway. As they exited the lift, Harriett swept her arms in the same circular motion, "Concealelecto." The elevator and door vanished.

"Come on! Do not lag, Dyson!" Harriett commanded, floating along at a quick pace. Regina took his hand. The three raced up the hallway behind Harriett.

"Where are we?" Regina puffed from the exertion. She couldn't see anything! It was as if they were running through a cloud or thick fog. Harriett led them around a corner and through a door into a... forest. Regina skidded to a stop on fresh dirt. Giant redwood trees stood before her. Some so large Regina couldn't put her arms around them. The scent of fresh mountain air and fir trees tickled her nose. A full moon hung in the star-filled sky and the sound of falling water could be heard in the distance.

"Puddlefoot!" Harriett whispered.

Regina looked up and from behind a tree she saw a three-foot-tall figure, as perfectly proportioned as a man, strolling toward them. She held her breath, keeping a close eye on their visitor. "Puddlefoot, so glad you could join us," Harriett smiled.

Puddlefoot looked like a man in every aspect, except for his button nose between his big, oval, slate gray eyes, and thick lipped mouth. His brown hair stuck straight out, creating points above his ears, but also framed his face perfectly. He wore a skin tight muscle shirt with leather bands wrapped up and down his arms, and a neckerchief around his neck.

"Puddlefoot, this is Regina, Matthew, and Dyson, the ones I was telling you about. Will you please take care of them?" Harriett asked.

Puddlefoot tipped his head, hid his eyes, and bowed low. "Pfffft!" The odor that followed almost made Regina gag. Matthew and Dyson started giggling and before they knew it, they were all in full blown hysterics.

"I am sorry. Brownies are known for their… Expulsions. Puddlefoot, we have discussed this," Harriett sighed.

"Yes, Madam Harriett. I'm sorry, but honored to protect your family. We need to be leaving if we hope to catch the wind to Glenville," Puddlefoot said shyly in a deep, gravelly voice.

"Yes, you are right," Harriett replied. She turned to Regina, "Remember what I said. You say your good-byes and get right back here. Do not engage Marcus or Veronica," she ordered, pulling each one of them into her arms. She then snapped her fingers three times. Within a few seconds, a dwarf led a large lizard with mammoth red wings attached to its back, four short legs, reddish-brown scales the size of a man's hands, for skin, and twisted horns on either side of his head, through the trees. They stopped beside Puddlefoot.

"It's a dragon!" Dyson gawked. "Cool!"

Regina stepped back, letting the creature have more space. "This place just gets stranger by the minute," she muttered.

Puddlefoot patted the beast on the red blaze that filled his chest. "Hey, Henry, you ready to go?" Henry stretched his long neck toward the sky and shook his long narrow snout up and down.

"Henry? It's a boy?" Dyson marveled.

"Yes, girl dragons are too ferocious and can't be tamed," Puddlefoot explained.

"Can I touch him?"

"We really need to go. All aboard!" Puddlefoot growled and picked up Dyson. He tossed him easily onto Henry's back in between his wings. He sat on a rawhide pad fashioned into a saddle. Straps were woven into the saddle for its riders to hold on to. "There… Stroke his scales right between his shoulder blades and watch what he does," Puddlefoot chuckled as he tossed Matthew up behind Dyson.

Dyson did as he was instructed and rubbed Henry's back. Fire shot from his nose and mouth in a long stream catching a bush ablaze. "Oh, wow! Awesome!" Dyson exclaimed. Puddlefoot laughed hysterically, watching Regina leap out of the way and screech.

"Not funny! Puddlefoot!" she scolded. He laced his fingers together and offered a step up. She climbed in behind Matthew. Puddlefoot picked up what looked to be an empty backpack and hung it over his shoulder along with a leather pouch. He had a sword hanging from his hip and a tool belt strapped around his waist. Next he leaped onto Henry's back and gently nudged him in the flank.

"Pfffft!"

"Oh, Puddlefoot!" Regina moaned. The boys burst into laughter.

"Safe journey!" Harriett said softly. "And good luck!" she mouthed as they flew up over the trees and into the dark sky. The wind whistled through their hair as they caught the updraft and rode it in the direction of Glenville.

"Wheeee!" Dyson screamed. Matthew stretched his arms out from his sides as if he were flying. Regina slowly began to relax, loosening her strangle hold on the leather strap, and breathed in the fresh crisp air.

"We're almost to our destination. I'm going to land, Henry, on top of the hospital. He will be safe up there and we can use the stairs down to the fifth floor. Mrs. Hillsdale is in room 524," Puddlefoot instructed.

"Isn't... Can't someone see us coming?" Regina groaned.

"Oh, right! I forgot to throw the magic dust," Puddlefoot fiddled with the pouch on his belt. Regina watched him reach in and bring out a pinch of dust. He sprinkled it over all of them.

"Magic dust? What's it made of?" Matthew perked up, interested.

"Plants we grow around Magic House. They make it in the lab, so, I'm not sure what's exactly in it."

"Are we invisible? I don't feel any different!" Regina babbled. Puddlefoot smirked, but Regina ignored him.

Henry descended through the clouds until the city lights appeared, and before they knew it, they had landed on the roof of the hospital. "I have to remember to get him a steak. Raw, preferably," Puddlefoot smiled.

"Raw? Ick... Gross!" Regina pretended to retch.

"I'll get it for him," Dyson cheered, rubbing him between the shoulders. He shot out another stream of red, yellow, and blue flames.

"Dyson! Stop it! We are in town. Someone will see," Matthew cautioned.

"Nobody can see us," Puddlefoot laughed.

Matthew slid off the side of Henry, landing loudly. He stepped away from Henry. "Wait for me!" Dyson screeched.

"Someone is going to hear *you*!" Matthew whispered, stepping back into the shadow of Henry.

"Oh, yeah!" Dyson muttered. Regina secured Dyson under the arms and slid him into Matthews's hands, and then slipped to the ground. "Are you coming, Puddlefoot?"

"I'm right beside you!" he said, poking her in the shoulder. "Pffffft!"

Dyson and Matthew snickered.

"Why can I see Matthew and I can't see you?" Regina stumbled over the words, fanning her face.

"I'm invisible..." Puddlefoot said sarcastically.

"I can see that, but you don't smell invisible," she snapped. "But, why? How?"

"I can't make you invisible without Henry and the magic powder. I'm a magical creature," he coughed. Regina considered his explanation for a moment and then nodded. "Shall we..." Puddlefoot nudged Regina into the lead. "Quiet as mice!" he added, as they opened the outside door.

"Hold hands, you two. Dyson get in the middle of us," Regina ordered. They crept down metal stairs and through another door. They entered another stairwell made of concrete walls and more metal stairs. As they passed each floor Regina peeked through the window to the floor they had reached and saw a number on the wall. "That was seven," she whispered.

They silently continued down until they reached the fifth floor. "Let me go first. You three wait here," Puddlefoot said. They nodded. Puddlefoot opened the heavy door a fraction of an inch and easily slid through. Matthew and Dyson held Regina's gaze for a moment. She ruffled their hair and smiled. Puddlefoot was back faster than a clock could tick ten times.

"Veronica is sitting in the room with Mrs. Hillsdale. I didn't see Marcus, but he can't be far away. She looks to be getting restless, so maybe she will go for a walk soon. I might be able to implant the thought," Puddlefoot suggested. Regina nodded her approval. "Okay, take my hand, Regina. The rest of you, stay close and be quiet. We need a close place to hide until I get her out of the room. Remember, you'll be in the open for a few seconds, so be mindful."

Puddlefoot led them down the stark white, shiny corridor. They hugged close to the wall, tiptoeing and scurrying like mice. Puddlefoot opened a door and pushed them into a linen closet. Dyson collapsed on top of a pile of clean folded, white sheets that were sitting on the bottom shelf of a cabinet. Regina reached up and pulled a string that lit a single light bulb overhead. Matthew stepped on her toe, "Ouch!"

"Sorry!"

"Quiet!" Puddlefoot said hoarsely.

"Nice closet!" Regina quipped. She began fumbling through the shelves. "Hey, I have an idea," she puffed, pulling out a white uniform and a candy striper's apron.

"That won't work. You're too young. Besides, what about your shoes? They aren't white," Matthew shook his head and looked in Puddlefoot's direction for support.

"Matthew, you're so negative! Everything doesn't have to be in perfect alignment like all your inventions," Regina said, rolling her eyes and exhaling soundly.

"It might work. Good thinking, Regina. At least it will give you a little cover," Puddlefoot backed her up. Matthew rolled his eyes as Regina was sticking out her tongue.

"Can you two be a little nicer to each other?" Dyson sighed.

"Look, here's a cart. If I take this middle shelf out, Dyson and Matthew can sit here. We cover it in a sheet and you push it up the hall. No one is going to be looking at your feet," Puddlefoot muttered as he ripped the shelf out, stuffed Dyson and Matthew on the bottom rack, and snapped his fingers. A white sheet hovered over the cart and dropped over it covering the boys.

"Turn around while I change," Regina insisted.

"The boys are covered and you can't see me." Puddlefoot snickered.

"Turn around!"

"Oh, all right," he groaned.

"Okay, I'm decent," Regina giggled. "What about Veronica?"

Puddlefoot opened the closet door and peered out the crack. "Oh, there she goes, up the hall. Let's go!" Puddlefoot grabbed the cart and wheeled it out into the corridor. Veronica turned into the public restroom. Regina pushed the four-wheeled table down the hall. Puddlefoot slowed and pulled some magazines and a flower arrangement off a table in the waiting room, setting them on top of the cart.

"Like no one is going to notice magazines floating through the air," Regina whispered snidely, looking around to see if anyone did notice.

"Dyson get your head back under the sheet," Matthew fumed. "You're going to give us away."

Dyson groaned.

"Shh!"

After a dozen or so steps, Puddlefoot pushed the door to room 524 open and Regina pushed the boys through into the room. "I'm going to wait in the hall. Now remember, don't lollygag," Puddlefoot warned. "Pfffft!"

"Quick! Close the door," Regina spat.

Regina turned, pausing to stare at the tiny figure under the white sheet. Her gray hair seemed lifeless against the stark white pillowcase and her normally vibrant tanned skin looked pale and almost chalky. Her eyes twitched under her closed lids and her thick lashes crisscrossed while lying against her cheeks. Mrs. Hillsdale had tubes and wires coming out of her all over the place, and her breathing was unusually shallow. Regina had to force herself to breathe.

Dyson bailed out from under the drape and stood before the bed. Regina saw the tears well up in his eyes. She took his hand and walked him to the side of the bed, where he laid his head beside her on the sheet. Regina caressed Mrs. Hillsdale's hand. Matthew made his way out from under the cart. He stood, took one look at her, and went to sit in the corner chair.

"I'm sorry, Mrs. Hillsdale, that this has happened to you. We wanted to come and tell you how much we love you and to thank you for taking us in for all those years. We found the Magic House and mother is doing her best to make us feel welcome," Regina paused to sniff. The tears streamed down her cheeks. Dyson was blubbering now and Matthew cried quietly across the room.

"Reg, what are you doing here?" Mrs. Hillsdale mumbled. "Not safe!" she could barely be heard. Dyson leaped onto the bed and laid his head on her chest. She stroked his hair. "Matthew, come." she said softly. "You're a good boy. You'll do good things, one day. Dyson, son, this is hardest on you, but don't worry about me. I'll tell Mr. H hello from you," she coughed and sputtered. "Regina, find Pam! She's in trouble. They made her do some horrible things. Promise me you'll find her and forgive her!" Regina nodded. "I love you all. Now don't worry about me and don't be sad. Everything is going to be better now," she whispered.

Regina bent down and kissed her on the cheek. Matthew snorted and sniffed as he took her hand and brought the back of it to his cheek, sneaking a kiss on the top of it. Dyson hugged her neck, until she almost couldn't breathe.

The door opened a crack, "Veronica's coming back," Puddlefoot said softly. "We have to go now!"

"Go, all of you, and take care of each other. You all are going to do great in your new school." Mrs. Hillsdale closed her eyes and fell back to sleep.

Dyson had to be forcefully pulled off her chest and Matthew slowly climbed back under the cart. Regina pushed Dyson under and rearranged the sheet. "Come now!" Puddlefoot was getting anxious.

Regina's heart wasn't in the task before her. All she wanted to do was sit by Mrs. Hillsdale and sing to her. She used to do that for them when anyone was sick. She felt the tears race down her cheeks and drip off her chin. Dyson gulped loudly under the cart. Matthew sniffled.

"Regina, snap out of it. We've got to get out of here," Puddlefoot whacked her on the back. Regina startled. She saw Puddlefoot standing before her waving his hands for them to exit the room. "Regina, are you with me? Snap out of it girl! We're going to get caught," he almost screamed at her.

Regina shook her head and became completely aware of her surroundings. "Oh, I'm sorry… What?" she whispered.

"Let's go, now!" Puddlefoot growled. "Kids!" he muttered silently, turning invisible, and opening the door. "Are you ready?" he barked. Regina nodded.

"Shh, under there," she whispered sternly and wheeled the cart out the door.

"Hey! Hey! You there! Stop!" Veronica yelled. Regina looked over her shoulder and saw Veronica trudging down the hall after them. Regina picked up her pace and Puddlefoot pulled the cart faster. The elevator bell chimed and Marcus strolled off the lift.

"Marcus, get them! There they are!" screamed Veronica. He turned and looked in the direction of the cart. Regina was now running and pushing the cart as fast as she could. Matthew poked his head out from behind the sheet and Dyson held on for dear life. Marcus leaped in their direction.

"Puddlefoot, do something!" Regina squealed. Just then the sheet flew off the cart and enveloped Marcus. Matthew rolled off the cart and came up running. This lightened the load and allowed Regina to run faster. They passed the linen closet and were headed for the stairwell.

Marcus struggled with the sheet, trying to remove it from around his head and shoulders. Regina took a quick peek over her shoulder to see Veronica catch up to him. She grabbed a corner of the sheet just as a nurse came out from behind the nurse's station, "Hey, you kids can't be running in here!" she shouted. Marcus barged right into her in his attempt to rid himself of the last corner of the sheet. The nurse sprawled on the floor and Veronica leaped over her in an effort to keep up with Marcus.

Puddlefoot made it to the stairwell door, throwing it open, and letting it bang into the wall. Matthew bound through. The cart tipped over. Dyson skidded on the floor. Regina pulled him up by the collar and forced him up the stairs. Puddlefoot kicked the cart, sliding it into Marcus and Veronica. They hit the floor. Puddlefoot squeezed through the closing door, stopping to fill the lock with magic dust.

Matthew had reached the seventh floor when he tripped, skinning his shin. He rolled over clutching at his leg and moaning. "Come on, Matt! Brush it off!" Regina growled, reaching for his arm and pulling him up. They hesitated and gasped when Marcus began banging on the stairwell door.

"Regina, you can't hide from us forever! We'll get you eventually," Veronica screeched. Regina felt a shiver climb up her spine. Somehow, Regina knew she'd have to deal with Veronica, but not tonight.

Puddlefoot sprinkled Unicorn Horn on Matthew's leg when they reached Henry. It was healed before they all mounted the dragon and lifted off the roof toward the stars. Regina breathed a huge sigh of relief. Matthew and Dyson couldn't catch their breath.

Puddlefoot snickered, "That was close!"

"Okay, Henry, head for Magic House," Puddlefoot commanded.

"No, we can't! I promised to go get Pam," Regina shrieked at Puddlefoot.

"Oh no, missy, I have been instructed to take you back to Magic House."

"Pfffft!"

Chapter Seven

Oh… Puddlefoot

"I have to get permission, before we can alter the plan," Puddlefoot interrupted.

Regina groaned, fanning away the foul air, "Then get permis…"

Thunder rumbled overhead and lightning flashed. "All this arguing and I didn't notice this storm building," Puddlefoot growled.

"Yeah, it sure came up fast," Matthew remarked, staring up into the heavens.

Lightning flashed. They felt the hair on the backs of their necks prickle. "That was close," Matthew squealed. The thunder and lightning clashed again. Henry jerked, causing the kids to scream.

"Something is wrong. Thunderstorms don't come up that fast or have strikes on top of each other, unless they are…" Puddlefoot shouted. "We have to get undercover, now!" Lightning flashed again. Henry roared. Fire shot from his mouth and nose. His wings folded and he fell into a spiraling dive.

"Ahhh!!!" Dyson shrieked, somersaulting and sliding down Henry's neck. He grasped at the scales along his neck, wedging his fingers between them and holding on for dear life.

"Dyson!" Regina shouted.

"Hold on! I'm coming!" Matthew yelled, hooking his arm through the strap and reaching for Dyson. Puddlefoot worked frantically to gain control of Henry.

The ground was coming up fast. Matthew grunted and groaned, stretching and reaching over Henry's neck with the inky blackness of the night sky all around them. Matthew and Dyson's fingertips touched. Regina took hold of Matthew's feet, allowing him the extra inch to scoot forward. Matthew locked hands with Dyson.

"We're gonna crash!" Regina hollered, squeezing her eyes shut.

Puddlefoot saw the smoldering wing. He reached into his pouch, pulled out the Unicorn Horn, and sprinkled it over Henry's wing. He began to heal. Henry extended his wings and at the last moment, hit the forest floor at a run. He threw his riders to the ground and then rolled head over tail through the black dirt.

Dyson skidded to a stop on his belly, coming up with a mouthful of dirt. Matthew jumped, tumbled, and landed on his feet, while Regina was thrown free. She sat upright on the ground, legs sprawled out in front of her, as she struggled to breathe. Her breath had been knocked from her. Puddlefoot materialized. "Is everyone alright?" he shouted.

Regina patted herself down, "I'm all here," she puffed. "I think!"

"We're all good," Matthew assured everyone. Dyson was busy spitting dirt and forest loam from his mouth and nose. He couldn't speak.

"I think we need to get out of the open! That wasn't a natural storm," Puddlefoot insisted. Henry nudged Dyson with his nose. Dyson stroked him between his nostrils. High overhead, the clouds raged like nothing any of them had ever seen. "Let's go!" Puddlefoot took a hold of Henry's bridle. "Stay close to Henry so we can stay invisible. If I had to guess, I'd say we're being hunted," he instructed.

Lightning continued to strike and the thunder rolled, muffling the natural sounds of the woods, and making it an eerie and frightening place in the dark. Rain began to fall in sheets so thick, they were all drenched in seconds. And to make it worse, sparks rained down on top of their heads, as the lightning scorched a tree.

Dyson had been lifted onto Henry's back. He sat on the saddle with his mouth open, letting the water rinse the last particles of dirt off his tongue. Matthew ran alongside Henry, trying to keep up, and Regina just tried to hold it together. "Can't we just wish for the Magic House?" she yelled at Puddlefoot.

"I've already put in a call, but they're off on another mission and won't be in the area for three days. They were expecting us to fly to them," Puddlefoot explained.

"Matthew, what about your fort?" Dyson suggested. His voice was broken up by the bouncing from Henry's gate.

"Um, where are we?" Matthew stopped to get his bearings. "I think it's just over that rise," he smiled, pointing in the direction of a large rock.

"That's the rock that hides the entrance to the tunnel," Regina cheered.

"Okay, let's try that," Puddlefoot agreed.

"What are we going to do with Henry? We can't leave him out in the rain and lightning. He's hurt!" Dyson said, when they arrived at the entrance to the fort.

Puddlefoot exhaled, searching for the perfect spot. He brought out his pouch and stood before a large rock embedded in the side of a small hill. He muttered some sort of chant. Regina stared at him disbelievingly. Then Puddlefoot threw the dust at the rock. An opening appeared. The three children gasped.

Puddlefoot sprinkled more Unicorn Horn on Henry's side. He snorted and walked into the cave, disappearing out of sight.

"He'll be alright until morning and then we'll have to find him some food," Puddlefoot said. "Let's get inside where it's dry."

Matthew went through his secret pulleys and latches, working them in sequence, until the door opened and they could enter. Puddlefoot brought several logs into the fort and lay them on the floor. He carefully rolled up the carpet, putting it aside, dug a hole in the dirt, and lit the logs. They turned instantly into coals.

"Interesting… No flames and no smoke! I didn't think it was safe to have an inside fire without ventilation." Matthew looked questioningly at Puddlefoot.

"It isn't. This is a magic fire and now we have instant warmth," Puddlefoot quipped.

Regina warmed her hands over the red coals. Dyson pulled a chair up and removed his shoes. They were full of water. "Puddlefoot, do you have my other clothes? This dress and apron are sopped." Regina shivered. Puddlefoot reached into the backpack and tossed her the clothes she'd worn that morning. Matthew checked his food storage bins and to his surprise, they had been restocked by his friends. The first thing he did was hand Puddlefoot a loaf of bread.

"Thank you," Puddlefoot said with a sweeping bow. "I believe we can share."

"Hey, Matthew, look here! You have a bunch of those little creamers from restaurants," Regina said surprised. Matthew looked over his shoulder as he was pulling out the peanut butter and jelly from a secret cupboard.

"Cool! Puddlefoot will probably like those," he grinned.

"Do you have a steak in there?" Dyson joked.

"No, but if he doesn't care what kind of meat it is, I'll set a rabbit snare," Matthew suggested, looking at Puddlefoot.

He nodded, "Henry would like that!"

With their clothes dry and their hunger pangs tamed, "Where are those snares? Puddlefoot asked.

"Right here!" Matthew pulled them out of an underground storage cupboard and helped Puddlefoot set them.

"What was that storm all about?" Regina asked, as soon as they returned.

"It was magic! If I had to guess, either Marcus or Veronica has the ability to manipulate the weather."

"Weather?" Matthew questioned and yawned.

"Yes! All magic is tied to the elements, Earth, wind, fire, metals, and water, or combinations of each. Anyway, I think Marcus took an existing mild squall and turned it into a storm to knock us out of the sky. He couldn't see us, so hopefully they don't know where we are... Or if they got us!" Puddlefoot sighed. Regina looked about and could see they were all deep in thought.

"Let's get some sleep. You have any blankets in here?" Puddlefoot lightened the mood.

"Yes, in this cabinet, and I have cots over there," Matthew pointed to the corner.

"Good! Good! Do you mind if I move them over by our fire?" Puddlefoot asked. Matthew gave his okay and the cots instantly filled the space around the coals. Regina tucked Dyson in and Matthew lay down on his cot. Both boys were asleep before Regina could get comfortable.

"I'll keep watch!" was the last thing Regina heard from Puddlefoot, before her eyes fluttered closed.

Regina's eyes were the first to open the next morning. The rain had stopped and the sun was shining. She lay under the blanket, stretching, and yawning. Dyson and Matthew still slept soundly, but Puddlefoot was missing. She popped out of her makeshift bed in search of him. "Puddlefoot, are you here?" she called softly. No answer.

She turned. A table full of hot cereal and hot chocolate with little marshmallows appeared. "Wow!" Regina cheered, startled. She sat down and stirred cream into her bowl.

"Do I smell oatmeal?" Dyson's head emerged from under his blanket. He ran to the table, hitting it, knocking the paper cups over.

"Careful!" Regina snipped.

"Sorry!"

"Matt… You better come and eat, or I'm going to eat yours," Dyson chuckled.

"Pfffft!"

"Oh, Puddlefoot! There you are! I'm sorry, I meant to spell you, but I slept right through until morning," Regina choked, fanning her nose, but she was so hungry, nothing was going to distract her from breakfast. Matthew slowly came to the table, laughing. Puddlefoot appeared with his face flushed in embarrassment. "You must stop that, my eyes are burning," Regina coughed.

"Sorry, I'm lactose intolerant," he snickered.

"Now you tell us!" Matthew sniggered.

"No worries, Regina, Brownies don't require much sleep."

"So what's on the docket for this morning?" Regina asked.

"I've been to the cave. Your traps caught some nice weasels. Henry enjoyed them immensely," Puddlefoot smiled. Regina shivered at the thought of Henry eating something furry. "But he needs to rest. The lightning scorched his side pretty good, and he's not as healed as I would like. I used some more Unicorn Horn on him and he's resting comfortably," Puddlefoot said.

"I want to go see him!" Dyson jumped off his chair and stood beside Puddlefoot.

"You can't… We have to find Pam," Regina frowned.

"NO!" Puddlefoot barked. "It's not safe out there. Besides, I don't know who shot us out of the sky last night, and until I can figure it out, we stay undercover."

"But Marcus and Veronica know where this place is… I'm thinking it won't take them long to find us," Regina snorted.

"Right… Pam showed them where to find us, remember? Remind me again why we are trying to save her," Matthew snorted. Regina backhanded him in the arm. "Well? Why should we help her? She sold us out to Marcus," Matthew said, massaging his arm.

"Because Mrs. H wanted us to," Dyson snapped.

"Do we even know where to look for her?" Matthew shrugged, asking between his bites of cereal.

"I'm hoping she's at the house. At least it's a place to start," Regina suggested.

"We are staying here until Henry is well enough to take us back to Magic House," Puddlefoot growled. Regina cleared her throat, plopping down on the couch. She picked up a magazine that was sitting on the coffee table and began to leaf through it.

She and Dyson watched as Puddlefoot disappeared and began to clean and tidy the fort. He had it all spotless in the blink of an eye. Regina tossed a wadded up piece of paper at Matthew and glared at him under her brow. He shrugged. She sighed and rolled her eyes toward the trap door. Matthew wrinkled up his nose. Regina glanced in the direction of Puddlefoot and then exaggerated her eye roll toward the trap door again. Matthew's eyes brightened with understanding and he nodded.

"I've got to go check on Henry. You three, stay here!" Puddlefoot ordered. Regina looked up from her magazine, glancing at Puddlefoot. Matthew kept his eyes down.

"Let me come with you," Dyson said.

"Not this time, Dyson… Matthew?" Puddlefoot snapped at Dyson and then glared at Matthew until he acknowledged him. Dyson frowned.

"Yeah, I heard," Matthew muttered.

Puddlefoot was gone in a flash. "Let's go!" Regina whispered. Matthew moved the coffee table and threw back the carpet. Regina was the first to descend into the tunnel. Dyson followed and Matthew brought up the rear, making sure the carpet and table moved back into place when he closed the trap door.

"Man, it's dark in here," Dyson grumbled as he crawled through the soft dirt.

They emerged from the tunnel by the large rock. "Where are we going?" Dyson asked.

"Shhh!" Regina scolded, putting a finger to her lips.

"What?" Dyson asked. The three headed into the woods. "We're going back to the house, aren't we?" Dyson said. "We're going after Pam…" he realized.

"Yes, now shhhh!" Regina barked. "Keep your eyes open for Veronica and Marcus."

"I'm more worried about Puddlefoot. What's he going to do when he finds out we're missing?" Matthew whispered.

"Who cares…? I promised Mrs. H," Regina sniffed.

They ran, darting around bushes and jumping over fallen trees. It wasn't long before they were at the back of the farm near the animal pens. Regina stuck her arm out to halt the boys from running into the field. She hid behind the barn and watched the pasture and house for a few moments. They copied her. "Do you see anyone?" Regina asked softly.

"No, but the car is there," Matthew said. "We're going to be in the open when we run across the pasture. They'll see us," he added.

"Yeah, not good! I say we head over to the neighbors' place and follow their tree line. It might at least hide us for half of the distance," Regina suggested.

"Okay, let's go!" Matthew agreed. They dashed between the trees, stopping periodically to see if anyone was coming. The last little bit of pasture lay before them. "I'll go first!" Matthew said, taking off before Regina could protest.

He seemed to make it easily without being noticed. Dyson shot across the open field, following after Matthew. He paused behind an elm tree on the side of the Hillsdales' property. Regina took a few steps out into the open. The kitchen door flew open. Matthew and Dyson dove headlong into a hedge growing in the flowerbed. Regina collapsed to the ground and lay flat on her stomach. She was afraid to breathe.

"That storm was pretty bad, last night. It had to have knocked that dragon out of the sky. We just have to find where they landed. I'll bet they spent the night in that fort of Matthew's," Marcus fumed.

"Why are you mad at me? I'm not the one that saved them," Veronica pouted.

"Someone has to be helping them! How else would they be able to escape the hospital and fly a dragon?" Marcus continued to scream irately. "I bet it's that Magic House!"

"Magic House?" Veronica wrinkled her brow.

"Never mind…"

"How do you know they have a dragon?"

"How else would they have gotten off the roof," he growled. "Stay here and don't let the girl out of your sight," Marcus insisted. "I'm gonna try and find their hideout."

Regina was afraid to look up. "Psst!" she heard Matthew. Regina rolled her eyes forward as far as she could. Matthew was making a crawling motion from his safe place under the bush. Dyson's eyes were unblinking and he was pale. Regina began to squiggle across the damp grass and mud. She hoped she wouldn't have to crawl through a cow patty.

"Gross… Why'd I think of that?" she groaned to herself. The backdoor slammed shut and Marcus marched off straight across the pasture. He was too consumed in his own thoughts, to notice Regina scarcely fifty feet from him.

They waited for Marcus to move out of sight and then made a mad dash for the house. Regina carefully opened the kitchen door. Dyson went in first, followed by Matthew. They crept on tiptoes from the kitchen into the foyer. Matthew peeked around the door jamb and into the family room where they heard the television playing. Veronica was sitting in Mrs. Hillsdale's rocking chair, rocking. She was reading a book, which is what she usually did in her free time.

Matthew put his finger to his lips and pointed to the banister. Regina nodded and took a couple of steps toward the staircase. Matthew and Dyson followed. "Step exactly where I step!" Regina silently climbed the stairs, avoiding the squeaky step. Once they reached the landing Regina pointed for Dyson to check his room, Matthew to go into Mrs. Hillsdale's room, and she would look in her room. If they found Pam, they were to come back out into the hall and let the others know.

Dyson went first. He was back shortly, shaking his head. Matthew went next and it took him a little bit longer, after all Mrs. Hillsdale's room had a bathroom and two walk-in closets, one of which was the baby's room. He returned to the hall, shaking his head. Regina popped the sticky door to her room open. She froze and waited to hear if Veronica had heard the door open. She hadn't. Regina pushed the door open further.

Pam was lying on her bed not moving.

Regina stuck her arm out the door and waved to the boys. The step on the stairs squeaked loudly. Regina gasped! She waved frantically at the boys to stay put, then closed her door quietly and crawled under her bed.

"Pam, you better not be out of that bed! I don't want to have to use this dust stuff on you again," Veronica snarled, heaving. "I'll bet I've lost ten pounds, walking up and down these stairs today." The door crackled when she pushed through it. Regina held her breath. "Oh, are you lucky!" Veronica said, standing over Pam's motionless body. She glanced around the room, in the closet, and under Pam's bed.

"Ronnie, where are you?" Marcus called from down stairs. Veronica sped out of the room and back into the hall, closing the door.

"Checking on our patient. Did you find anything?" she giggled at the top of the stairs.

"No, I couldn't remember where the darn place was," Marcus slammed his hand against the wall.

"That's not surprising. I don't think the witch took us directly to it, the other day," Veronica fumed.

"Get down here... I need a back rub!"

Pam was sleeping soundly on her bed. Regina tried to rally her by poking and shaking her, but it was no use. "She's comatose!" She found an old water bottle that had fallen between the bed and nightstand. She popped the cap and gave it a little squeeze. Water squirted from the spout and hit Pam squarely in the face. She jumped up, gasping.

"What the… Hello!!!" Pam wheezed.

Regina was quick to silence her by placing her open hand across Pam's mouth and whispering, "Shhh!!!" Pam stared at her wide-eyed and startled. Regina moved her hand.

"What are you doing here? They're looking for you!" Pam said, wiping the water from her brow.

"I know. Mrs. Hillsdale asked us to come and save you. Besides, we owed you."

"Owed me? I don't think you know the half of what I've done," Pam wouldn't make eye contact with Regina.

"Can you move?" Regina whispered, just as Dyson charged through the door. Matthew wasn't far behind.

"He's downstairs!" Dyson exhaled.

"Marcus… Yeah, I heard him too," Matthew whispered.

"We'll never get out, going that way," Pam said.

"We'll just go out the window again," Regina grinned. The window had been nailed shut and she could see the ladder lying in the grass. "Great!" she moaned.

"Oh, yeah, Marcus was a little mad when you got away, the last time. He nailed all the windows shut, up here," Pam explained.

"Now what?" Regina said. "We're doomed! I guess I don't have to worry about Puddlefoot being angry."

"No we aren't... I'll bet he forgot about the window in Mrs. Hillsdale's closet. He wouldn't have seen it because of all the clothes blocking it," Matthew said.

"But that window has no ledge," Dyson reminded Matthew.

"What happened to the bed sheets we pulled off the beds earlier? We can finish tying them together, making our rope," Matthew said.

"Veronica wadded them up and threw them over there in the corner," Pam pointed.

Matthew gathered up the sheets. "Let's go to Mrs. H's room," he whispered.

Regina began tying sheets together while the others removed Mrs. Hillsdale's hanging clothes from the racks. Matthew was right; Marcus hadn't nailed the tiny window shut, but it was painted closed.

Pam rummaged through the bed stand drawers until she found a screw driver and brought it back to the window where she began digging at the paint. "I hope I fit through this tiny thing," she commented dryly.

"You will. We just need to hurry," Regina encouraged.

The window finally broke loose and slid open. Regina made a sling out of one end of the sheet and had Dyson sit in it. She tied the other end to the rod that held the clothes. Pam lifted him through the window while the others held the rope tightly. They lowered Dyson to the ground. Matthew was able to climb through the window on his own and he was lowered to the ground. Pam insisted that Regina go next, except she would have to climb down the rope, because Pam wasn't strong enough to lower her.

Regina inched her way out of the window. Pam held the tied sheets up to Regina's hands and helped her transition from the windowsill to the rope. Regina twisted her foot around the sheets and inched her way down a bit at a time until she was close enough to the ground to jump.

Pam had disappeared from the window. Regina heard Marcus and Veronica shouting at each other from inside the house. Pam reappeared. "They're coming!"

"Come on Pam! You can do it," Matthew said loudly. Pam climbed out the window feet first with the sheet in her hand. Marcus appeared behind her. Pam leaped off the sill and flew through the air, clinging to the sheet and swinging in mid-air. She swung back toward the window. Her feet hit the side of the house. She pushed off, swinging out again. Marcus clutched at the sheet and yanked. Pam fell, only to grasp the tether a few feet lower. He shook the sheets with force, trying to knock her off.

Regina gulped, squinted her eyes, holding her hands out in front of her and said, "Don't let Pam fall… Don't let Pam fall… Don't let Pam fall! Harriett!" The wind started to blow. She kept repeating the words. The wind began to swirl. Pam was swinging back and forth, screaming. Marcus couldn't shake her loose so he tried to climb out the small window. He couldn't fit and got stuck.

"Argh!" he swore. "Veronica! Get down there!" he yelled. Freeing himself from the window. He extended his hands through the opening, but without being able to see or having the freedom to move his arms freely, he couldn't aim. Fireballs shot from Marcus's hands and landed all around them. The wind continued to pick up speed. It sucked Pam into its spinning whirlwind. Then it moved over to Dyson and Matthew, spinning them into its web, and finally the tornado swept over Regina. All four were caught up inside the twister. Regina kept her concentration as the wind and siblings spun around her inside the whirlwind. They rode across the pasture and toward the woods.

Screaming and screeching reverberated through the woods, straight to Puddlefoot's ears. He'd been out searching for the children and figured they'd gone to the house to look for Pam, but not knowing the way, he'd wandered, lost for a time. Henry plodded along behind him. "There the urchins are, Henry! Come this way," Puddlefoot urged, turning invisible.

The whirlwind came to an abrupt stop when it made contact with a tree, spitting out Dyson, Matthew, Regina, and Pam onto the ground. "Ouch!" Matthew complained. "I don't know how much more my body can take! I'm tired of crashing," he moaned, rolling his eyes.

"What was that?" Dyson groaned, lying flat on his back.

"Regina, did you see what you did? That was incredible!" Pam yelled, brushing herself off and standing.

"Come on! Let's get out of here! They'll be coming soon," Pam said.

"I can't move," Regina wheezed, lying flat on her back, staring at her hands.

"Give me your hand! Come on!" Pam reached out for her, taking her forearm and yanking her to her feet.

"Here they come!" Matthew screeched. Dyson inhaled sharply and jumped to his feet.

"You got any more of those cyclones in your hands?" Pam coaxed Regina. "'cause now would be the time to cut'er loose!"

"That wasn't me. I don't know how to conjure anything!" Regina protested. Just then, a fireball ricocheted off a tree, just missing Regina.

"Run!"

The four ran through the woods, dodging sparks. A fallen tree tripped up Dyson. He sprawled across the ground, skinning his knees. "Reg! Reg!" he screamed. She turned and saw Marcus almost upon him.

"Dyson, get up!" Regina shouted, realizing it was too late to retrieve him without getting caught herself.

Regina smelled a foul odor. At the same time a blast of fire flew through the air. Regina looked up to see Marcus explode into flames and fall to the ground. "Henry! Is that you?" she cried out, hoping she was right.

"No!!" Pam squealed, taking a few steps back toward Marcus. Veronica had slowed to a crawl. "You have to save him!" Pam cried, collapsing to the ground.

Regina ran back to Dyson and scooped him up away from Marcus and the fire. Henry turned visible right before her, along with Puddlefoot. "Let's go! Climb aboard!" he demanded. Regina lifted Dyson up to Matthew who was already sitting astride Henry.

Regina ran up to Pam, "What did you say? Save him... He just tried to kill us!" she growled.

"He has the antidote..." Pam sniffed.

"Let's Go!" Puddlefoot grumbled. "We can discuss this away from here."

"Come on, Pam! Let's go!" Regina snapped. Pam shrugged, all hope and light left her expression. She climbed aboard Henry. Puddlefoot glared at Regina as he laced his fingers together and offered her a hand up. She accepted.

"Okay, Henry, we're ready," Puddlefoot said, stroking Henry's scales where his tail met his back.

The dust from the pouch was sprinkled over all of them as Henry took to the air. Puddlefoot used Unicorn Horn to repair Dyson's knee. "I'm sorry, Puddlefoot," Regina said humbly, when Dyson had relaxed and was out of pain. "But we promised Mrs. H. We promised to save Pam... Are you mad?" Regina whispered.

Allie Kat Mouser

Chapter Eight

Learning Magic

The day turned into night and they were still flying across the heavens. Puddlefoot hadn't said a word to any of them for hours. Finally, he opened his empty backpack. Dyson watched him carefully. He reached in and offered each of them a peanut butter and jelly sandwich and a bottle of water. They ate silently, afraid to speak.

The joy Regina wanted to feel from saving Pam was tainted by their deception and Puddlefoot's anger. He wasn't making it easy for them to apologize, either. Harriett had warned her not to make him mad, but she never thought he would be this livid. *What have I done?* Pam seemed more concerned about Marcus than she did about Dyson or the rest of them. *Have I put all of us at risk?* She shivered, feeling her stomach tighten with each bite of sandwich. Eventually she tossed most of it away. *How can I fix this?* She sighed aloud.

"Puddlefoot, please… I'm sorry. You're right to be annoyed. I didn't stop to consider the danger. How can I make it up to you?" Regina pleaded. He stared off in the opposite direction. "Oh, Puddlefoot! Don't shut me out!"

A few minutes later…

"Pfft, pfft, pfft, pffft!!!"

"Puddlefoot, not again," Regina moaned, fanning her nose and rolling her eyes. Matthew started to giggle. Dyson joined in. Pam snickered, trying to hide her mirth, but when Regina snorted while holding back a full blown laugh, the whole group cracked up. Even Puddlefoot chuckled. His temper began to soften. Just when everyone had caught their breath and regained their composure, Matthew started the fit all over again.

"Stop it! My sides hurt!" Regina cried.

"Mine too!" Dyson laughed, clutching his ribs.

"So, Pam, it seems like you already know about magic and Magic House. What gives?" Regina hiccupped loudly. "Oops! Excuse me!" she snickered.

"I've known for a while about all of this," Pam continued, laughing, this time at Regina.

"What did you mean back there, when you said Marcus had an antidote?" Regina asked through her giggles. Pam froze. Her merriment subsided and she faced Regina with a long thoughtful look.

"Marcus used some kind of enchanted weapon on Mrs. H. He didn't cut her bad; just enough to get the poison into her system. I was supposed to deliver you to him and he would give me the antidote," she sighed. "I'm sorry, I couldn't do it. But, now… Now he's gone and I'll never get it." She closed her eyes and let the tears trickle down her cheeks.

Regina slouched. She understood and surprisingly, she had no animosity toward Pam.

"What about Veronica? Can't she get the medicine from Marcus?" Matthew queried.

"I don't know. She thinks she's in love. She's under his spell," Pam sniffed.

"I thought it was too late for Mrs. Hillsdale…" Dyson whispered.

"Marcus told me that she had a week. He planned it so she would have a slow and painful death," Pam said.

"That means we have time to make a new potion. We just have to get back to Magic House," Regina said hopefully.

"But we don't know what spell he used and every minute that ticks by, Mrs. Hillsdale gets weaker," Pam muttered.

"Why does he want Regina so bad?" Puddlefoot asked.

Pam shrugged, "I don't know, but he wants her real bad!"

"Look! There's Magic House!" Dyson pointed.

"We're here! You can take all this up with Madam Harriett," Puddlefoot said sternly. "I have to care for Henry."

"I'm sorry, Puddlefoot. I hope Henry is all right," Regina said. He patted her on the shoulder and shrugged.

Henry landed in the forest that they'd flown out of two days ago. The dwarf was waiting and took Henry's reins as soon as they all disembarked. Puddlefoot opened the elevator doors, escorted the four of them into the lift, and pressed a button with the number two on it. He stepped out and the doors closed. A few minutes later, they were in Harriett's office. She was sitting at her desk.

Everyone stepped out of the elevator and stood quietly. "Well, so you are back," Harriett said. "Let me look at you," she walked up and faced each one of them. "Dyson, you tore your pants. How is your knee?" she asked kindly.

Dyson nodded. "Puddlefoot fixed it," he whispered. Harriett hugged him and moved on to Matthew.

"Matthew, I understand you are quite ingenious when it comes to building forts and tunnels." Harriett looked him in the eye and waited. He blushed. She hugged him and moved on to Regina.

"I can certainly tell you are my daughter! Stubborn!" Harriett held her chin between her forefinger and thumb. Regina stared back, dropping her gaze after a moment. She knew she deserved a tongue lashing, but it never came. "I understand you found some of your magic?" Harriett dropped her chin and reached for Regina's hands, she held them up to the light. After twisting them from side to side, she lay them back at Regina's side and hugged her tight. Regina felt the air rush out of her.

"And Pam, dear, it is good to see that you are well!" Harriett pulled her into her arms and held her the longest.

"It's good to see you, too, Aunt Harriett," she smiled.

Regina straightened up and inhaled sharply. "Aunt Harriett? You two are related?"

"Pam is your cousin on my side. She has been a student of the school since her thirteenth birthday, however, she preferred to stay at Mrs. Hillsdale's to be close to you and Dyson," Harriett replied.

"Why didn't you tell me?" Regina said, astonished. "What else don't I know?" She directed her questions to Harriett.

"Plenty! We are a school, after all," she said. "So, tell me about this antidote," Harriett softened her voice and spoke to Pam. Regina clenched her teeth and glared. Pam, Dyson, and Matthew walked over to the fireplace and had a seat on the couch. Harriett sat in one of the chairs, and Regina stood, staring up at the emblem above the fireplace. "Fill me in!" Harriett prodded Pam.

"I'd been in the stables practicing my magic, that morning. I started to come in the kitchen door when I heard Marcus threatening Mrs. H. Then Matthew came downstairs and Veronica forced him to sit at the table. I was about to leave and go call the police when Regina, Dyson, and Sally came down the stairs. I saw Veronica take them back upstairs. That's when I left and went to get the ladder," Pam paused to breathe.

Harriett waited patiently, but when Pam didn't continue timely enough, "Go on," Regina prodded. Everyone turned and looked at her, "Well…" she shrugged.

"Well, I got the little ones out and I sent Reg with them. Then I went to try and slow Marcus down, because he'd seen me free them. He was mad. He threw me in the kitchen. Mrs. H was bleeding all over the place. I tried to help her. She wouldn't let me touch her. She was afraid I'd become infected by the poison." Pam wiped a wayward tear from her cheek.

"Take your time, dear." Harriett said consolingly.

"He told me to cooperate with him and if I helped him get Reg, he'd give Mrs. H an antidote. So I took him to the fort in the woods. I'd hoped they weren't there." She turned to Regina and glared, "I sent you to Holman's place!" Pam paused.

Regina shrugged, "We got confused…"

"Anyway, Matthew tricked him and you all got away," she said with a smile. "Then Marcus made me tell you that Mrs. H would be dead by morning," she cleared her throat.

"By morning? You didn't tell us that!" Regina growled.

"He was hoping you would let Reg come to the hospital, and you did. But then they escaped from him for the second time. He knocked me out with some kind of potion. I woke up with water in my face… And the rest, you know." Pam fell silent.

"Sorry, but you're leaving out something," Regina said, glaring.

"Did he show you the potion to cure Mrs. Hillsdale?" Harriett asked.

"Yeah, he pulled it out of his pocket," Pam said.

"What aren't you telling us? I mean, Pam, you could have come with us and we could have called the police, but you stayed… Why?" Regina wouldn't let it go.

"I… I thought I could talk him out of what he was doing. I mean, I never thought the two of them would actually go through with their plan." Pam wiped the tears off of her face.

"You knew?" Regina gasped. Matthew and Dyson let their mouths drop open.

"I introduced them. Veronica said they were in love and needed money to run away together. I hinted at the cash Mr. H kept in the underground safe in the barn. I didn't know!" Pam sobbed.

"It is alright, dear. We need to focus on now," Harriett said, giving Regina a glance.

Pam turned her back on the group, clenching her fists, and groaned, "But I've really messed up. Marcus is dead and the potion is gone!" Pam could no longer control her tears, she doubled over, sobbing.

"No… Typically, a fire demon cannot be destroyed by fire unless he is injured, or it is his own magic. Either way, between Marcus and Veronica, they put the fire out. We are sure."

"What?" Pam choked.

"Then we have to go and get the antidote and give it to Mrs. H," Regina spat at Harriett.

"You are not going anywhere!" Harriett growled. "We are going to take a different approach," she said calmly. "All this time, we have been playing right into his hands. It is time he played into ours," Harriett thought for a moment. "Pam, does he know about Magic House?"

"Yes!" Pam said, "But I don't think he'll come… He knows that no one has ever broken through Magic House's magic."

Regina felt the flush of anger fill her cheeks, "So, I risked everyone's safety to rescue you! And now you're bringing the enemy here?!" Regina exploded.

"Regina, it is all right… Let us give him a reason to come," Harriett said softly, holding Regina's hand and nodding to Pam. Pam gave a little nod.

"How can you say that?! Isn't this a school full of kids?!" Regina ripped her hand away from Harriett and stormed back to the fireplace.

"Regina, we protect our family. That is what our motto says, and why Pam came back to the foster house after Mr. Hillsdale died. He had protected all of you with enchantments, but when he died, they evaporated. Pam tried to pick up where he left off," Harriett said, then paused, waiting for Regina to calm.

"We captured a goblin a few weeks back. I think he is just the one to take a special message to Marcus," Harriett grinned. Regina stared at the group with a furrowed brow. A dove flew in through the window. "Take my message to the dungeons, please," she said, and then sang a song no one understood.

Regina fumed. When Harriett stepped away from the open window Regina lashed out. "You have known where we were all this time, and you didn't come for us or tell us you were alive... Sort of!" Regina hissed.

Dyson gawked, his eyes filled with tears, "Don't fight!"

"I could not tell you. For one thing, I have no magic of my own, so I cannot leave here, and for another, you were thriving with Mrs. Hillsdale," Harriett tried to explain.

"Why does he want Reg so badly?" Dyson whispered. He couldn't listen to any more arguing.

"Let me just say that all of you come from a particularly important heritage," Harriett said, "but more on that at another time. We have to get you some food and sleep so we can prepare for the oncoming assault. Our first goal is to save Mrs. Hillsdale, so off with you..." Harriett had risen, and she herded them toward the door.

"Wait! I have one more question." Regina turned and stopped, causing the others to run into her.

"Yes?"

"Why wasn't Veronica brought here when she came of age? I mean, I kind of remember Pam leaving for a summer and then returning. I always thought Pam went to camp or something, and came home early because Mr. H was sick and Mrs. H needed her help, but Veronica has been there the whole time."

"She was to be accepted into the mansion four years ago, however she was not stable enough to leave home. That happens… Sometimes a sorcerer cannot be up-rooted, especially if their self-esteem or maturity has not developed. It could be anything. But most of the time, when that happens, their magic stays suppressed. Did any of you notice if Veronica used magic?" Harriett asked, but hesitated when she saw the tears dripping off Regina's chin. "What is it, Reg?"

"I watched you die!" Regina whispered, sniffing, and snorting through the sobs. Harriett cradled her in her arms and held her for a long time, letting her release her anger. She nodded to Pam to take the others back to their room. They tip-toed out into the hall, leaving mother and daughter to patch things up.

"I am sorry! I am sorry you have had such a hard time, and I am sorry I was taken from you when you were so young. I do not know if you remember, but it was Marcus and his brother, Rudy, who came to our house that night. They killed your father and myself, but not before I got Rudy. Others came for you and Dyson that night," she continued.

"Others?" Regina gulped.

"Our protectors."

"I don't understand…" Regina sniffed.

"Okay, I guess you are not going to rest until I explain," Harriett sighed. "When Atlantis was alive and well, we had an order to things; the king and queen, for instance, their court, and their protectors. Then, of course, there were the Valkyries, the teachers, and the wizards. Our land also flourished with brownies, fairies, dwarves, trolls, leprechauns, elves, and others. We also lived among the unicorns, dragons, yetis, gnomes, phoenixes, and many different species too numerous to name. Our ancestors survived because they were smart and escaped Atlantis before it sank to the bottom of the sea, but our descendants struggled for years, not fitting into this new world. They quarreled, splitting into two sects. We have been hunted, ever since. Anyway, magic was slowly dying. We needed a place to live, regroup, and renew our species," Harriett paused to let Regina take it all in.

"So, Magic House was born. It was essential that Magic House exist in harmony with each species contributing to the collective. It secures that all of us survive." Harriett glanced down into Regina's face. She was mesmerized.

"But… Some of the Atlanteans, we call them Cobbleports, meaning 'stone hearted,' opposed our alliance. They are the ones that have turned their backs on a peaceful existence and want nothing but our magic for their own power. They hunt us and steal our powers for their own use."

"The night Marcus and Rudy attacked our house, Rudy killed your father and absorbed his power. I struck Rudy down and that released his power and your father's. All the magic came to me. Now this is where it gets tricky; when I died I had a fraction of a second to send all the power to you, so that you and your brother could escape. Marcus did not know I had that power and he feels cheated. I am sure he has been looking for you for the last four years."

Regina gasped, "That's how I got out of the house with Dyson that night, isn't it?"

"Yes!"

"Okay, go on!" Regina said.

"The year before, Pam's house was attacked. Her parents were killed, but she had been staying with a friend and was not hurt," Harriett paused. Regina looked up for her to continue. "I guess you do not remember her. They lived in another town and we only saw them occasionally." She looked for some spark of recognition from Regina, but none was forthcoming. "Anyway, I digress… Our magical creatures, the ones that protected our houses, notified the rescue party and you were swept quietly into Mrs. Hillsdale's house.

"It was important that our people co-mingle with the human race, but we also needed a way to educate our magical children. So, what better way to have that happen, than to have our offspring grow up in the real world? But when they came of age, they needed a school to learn, channel, and protect their magic and our secret. So, Magic House also became a school." Regina hadn't blinked for the entire story, and even pinched herself to make sure she wasn't dreaming.

Harriett smiled, continuing, "We have many magical creatures here, and our combined magic protects us from our enemies. Marcus and the other Cobbleports believe if they can capture Magic House, then they will control the magical world, and possibly, the whole world." Harriett stopped and let Regina mull that thought over.

"Well, someday we hope to return to Atlantis."

"You told us that all the teachers were ghosts. Does that mean other kids' parents are teachers?" Regina whispered.

"Teachers, researchers, protectors, and whatever else we need, in order to survive," she said, smiling proudly.

"Oh!"

"Now, do you think you can get some sleep?" Harriett asked. Regina nodded and Harriett walked her to her room. The others were just finishing up a feast. Dyson yawned, stood, and headed for the ladder to the loft. He ran back and hugged Harriett around the waist. She escorted him to his bed.

"Feel better?" Pam asked. Regina nodded, breaking off a piece of bread and cramming it into her mouth. She ladled some chicken noodle soup into a bowl and sat at the table. "I'm really sorry for using you as bait. I didn't know what else to do," Pam said.

Regina waved her off and smiled, "I get it. I probably would have done the same thing."

"Well, I'm going to bed," Pam announced. She headed toward the corner where Regina had slept the first night. There was an entirely new section that Pam now occupied. Regina blew it off as no big deal. She'd come to the realization that anything was possible in Magic House, as long as you had an imagination.

Harriett walked past her, kissing her on the top of the head. She ruffled Matthew's hair, "You get some sleep, young man," she ordered, and left the room, invisible.

The morning came all too soon, in Regina's mind. She lay still, trying to pretend she wasn't awake. "Come on, get up!" Pam poked her. "I saw your eyes open. The bathroom is clear. The shower is all yours, and if you feel anything like *I* did, you need a shower," Pam snickered.

Regina yawned, "What time is it?"

"8:00 o'clock," Pam chirped.

"Hey, Pam, what kind of magic do you have?" Regina asked, sitting up and stretching.

"I can commune with the living creatures of the earth, and hopefully learn to move things with my mind," she said. "You're the one that is amazing, though! The way you made that cyclone and controlled it to get us out of there, yesterday, not to mention, you aren't thirteen, yet. I just wonder what else you can do," Pam said.

"I didn't know I could do that. I don't know how I did it," Regina said softly.

"Well, let's go to breakfast and find out what classes we need to take to be able to help Mrs. H," Pam encouraged. Regina bailed out of bed and ran to the shower. She was fully clothed and ready to go in fifteen minutes.

Harriett met them at the breakfast room as they were finishing up. "Come with me." The four children marched behind her into a classroom the size of a ballroom. It was empty of all furnishings and had no pictures on the walls. A transparent woman in a long black skirt and white blouse, with a tweed cape, stood at the far end of the long room. Matthew, Dyson, and Regina shared a wide eyed gasp.

"Ahh, Penelope. Good morning to you," Harriett greeted her. "Children, this is Ms. Calderon."

"Very nice to meet you all," she said, turning corporeal.

Not an unattractive woman, though a little thin, Regina thought. Her brownish-red hair flowed to her waist with smaller braids winding through it. "Where did her lips disappear to?" Regina sniffed.

"Shh!" Pam rolled her eyes.

"Please bow as I introduce you," Harriett instructed the children. "Dyson, eight years old. Matthew, ten years old. Regina, twelve years old and has found some of her magic. And this is Pamela, fifteen years old. I believe you two have met," Harriett waved in each child's direction, who each, in turn, bowed slightly. Matthew and Regina grinned at each other, feeling a little silly.

Harriett then addressed the four standing next to her, "Ms. Calderon is going to assess your magical abilities. Please do as she instructs." Harriett turned and walked across the great room, vanishing midway to the door.

"Stand to!" Ms. Calderon snapped as she stood in front of Dyson. He straightened up and stared, frightened, into her eyes. "Have you ever thought about something real hard and had it appear?" she asked. Dyson shook his head slowly. "Have you ever had your skin crawl as if you were covered in ants, when you were extremely frightened?" she stated. Dyson turned and looked at Regina for comfort. Regina rolled her eyes for him to pay attention. Ms. Calderon cleared her throat, "Have you ever had a dream where you did magic or could read minds, and it seemed natural?" Dyson's eyes widened and a smile began to cross his lips. "Very good! I'm sending you to Dream Lab. There, you will be taught to control your dreams and transfer them to reality. Mr. Cornelius Horn!" she called.

A handsome ghost, approximately twenty-three, with shockingly brilliant blue eyes and pronounced cheekbones appeared. He carried his brawny stature with confidence and grace. Pam gave Regina an approving wink. Regina rolled her eyes. Matthew snickered, watching the exchange. Ms. Calderon ignored them.

"This is Dyson Edwards. His dreams are important! Help him learn from them," Ms. Calderon said. "Dyson you may go with Mr. Horn," and scooted him along.

"Now, Matthew!" He stood at attention at the mention of his name. "You are the technical one, the one that likes to invent things." Matthew nodded. "I'm going to send you with Miss Candy Poppyshirm. She is going to start you in potions and magical defenses," Ms. Calderon explained.

"Magical defenses?" Matthew quizzed.

"And charms and enchantments!"

Matthew smiled and high fived Regina.

"Miss Poppyshirm," Ms. Calderon called. An older woman appeared, with gray hair and half glasses that sat at the end of her nose. She threw some dust on Matthew, they disappeared from the room.

"Regina and Pamela, you will be with me. We are going to begin with conjuring." Regina was pleased that she was going to be with a familiar face. "Are you ready to get started?" The girls each nodded.

"Alright then… Your magic is based on emotion and an inner strength. You have to reach into your soul, bring it up to a place you can see it and use it. Once you achieve the first part, then you must control it," Ms. Calderon explained. Regina sighed.

"For instance, Regina, the first day you happened upon Magic House, you were desperate for sanctuary. You drew from your strength, visualized, and called out to the House."

"I did all those things? All I remember is wishing to be away from Marcus," Regina said, miffed.

"Exactly. Do you remember what you felt when you were calling for Magic House?" Ms. Calderon asked.

"I remember I was terrified… And I called out Harriett's name, like I've always done when I was scared."

"No, this is deeper. This is a truth inside of you. You saw it, you felt it, and you called for it, that day. You must find that magic inside of you again," she repeated.

Regina stared back at her, "You're crazy! How does one do that? I don't even know where to start," she muttered, feeling lost, stupid, and that she was letting Mrs. Hillsdale down.

Pam took Regina by the hand and walked her away from Ms. Calderon. She put her arm around her shoulders, hugging her close. "Okay, Reg. Stop! Don't let negative vibes overwhelm you. I know it's not easy, I've been practicing out in the stables for two years now, and she is asking you to make magic in fifteen minutes." Regina exhaled loudly and slumped.

"Try this… Sit down." Pam directed her to the floor. "Cross your legs…" Regina sat Taylor style. "Yeah, like that! Now, put your hands here and put you middle finger and thumb together. It completes the circle and returns the energy." Pam laid Regina's hands on her knees, palms up. "Breathe in through your nose and out through your mouth." Regina looked across at Pam, who had joined her on the floor. "Close your eyes. Good! Good. Now look inside yourself." Regina opened one eye and peeked out. "Concentrate! Search for the magic! It's there! You'll know it when you see it!" The girls sat motionless for a moment.

"Regina, relax. Search inside yourself for something that bubbles, excites you, and makes you feel special and powerful," Pam coached. Ms. Calderon watched the interaction between the girls. She was pleasantly surprised.

Before long, Regina caught a glimpse, a light, a feeling of excitement. It was more than her mother's name. It was her love! It was her sacrifice! And it was the magic a mother gives a child at birth. She let it rise. It filled her. Her hands came up, and poof! A spark and cloud of smoke were left from the tiny explosion. Regina jumped to her feet and skittered away from where she had been sitting. "What was that?!" she coughed, fanning the air. Pam and Ms. Calderon stared at each other with mouths agape, and then grinned.

"Fire?" Ms. Calderon exclaimed. Pam shrugged. "Alright, Regina, that was a good start... Now let's see if you can tap into the wind," she encouraged, waving for Regina to return to her spot on the floor.

Regina hesitantly stepped forward. Pam reached up, and taking her hand, pulled her back down to the floor. "Again!" she instructed. Regina glanced from face to face as she crossed her legs, placed her hands on her knees, and closed her eyes. "Good. Find the magic... Now, concentrate on the breeze, build it, build it into a wind, and organize the wind into a whirlwind. You're doing it. Focus... Stay focused!" Regina opened one eye and exhaled, startled. "You let it drop! Get it back! Good! Okay... Now send it across the room," Pam coached her. Regina threw her hand toward the back of the room where the whirlwind spun and then broke apart when it hit the wall.

Regina looked up, smiling, jumping to her feet and dancing in circles. "I did it!" she beamed. "I really did it!" Pam joined her in the celebration.

"You certainly did!" Ms. Calderon congratulated her. "Now, we must begin..."

Chapter Nine

It's Magic House

By lunchtime, Regina had to be forced to take a break. "Regina, save the next step for after lunch," Ms. Calderon said. "But… But, I've almost got it!" Regina protested. Mrs. Calderon shooed them out the door.

The girls pranced through the halls animatedly, "Not fair! I was getting so close to picking up the rocks with my whirlwind," Regina grumbled.

They walked through the giant doors into the dining hall, where the lively chatter and excitement from the students was loud and boisterous. Regina hesitated, staring in awe at row after row of round tables, in a room twice the size of the ballroom. The students, of all ages, were dressed in matching school uniforms.

"Hey Pam, I never noticed the crest embroidered on the collar of the girls' capes…And the boys have it on the lapel of their jackets," Regina observed.

Pam giggled, "We don't exactly fit in with our sloppy sweaters and jeans." Regina nodded, dragging her feet. "Get in there," Pam pushed her into the room. Regina tripped over a chair leg, rattling and banging it into the table. The room fell silent.

A flush of embarrassment rose in Regina's cheeks, making her skin itch. She rubbed her arms, staring back into the curious stares of the student body. Pam glanced from Regina to their peers, giving her another gentle nudge, pointing her in the direction of an empty table. Regina exhaled slowly, bowing her head, not making eye contact with anyone, and marched to the chair that Pam now held out for her. "Do you see them?" Regina whispered, peeking over her shoulder quickly to have another look.

"Oh, yeah! The ghosts!" Pam said, pointing to the apparitions floating throughout the room. "Hey, Mrs. B! Nice apron!" Pam complimented the transparent figure floating past with a large tray of assorted sandwiches.

"So very nice of you to notice, Miss Pamela. Not many people recognize my Pilgrim costume.

Regina shook her head, but didn't take her eye off of Mrs. B as she floated by. "No!" Regina muttered. "What are they all staring at?" she glared out into the room. Her eyes locked onto Dickson. He gave her a quick secret smirk.

"Don't worry about them," Pam said, waving her hand through the air. "They always stare at new arrivals." Regina's attention was directed off of her peers and onto empty plates being replaced with full platters of sandwiches, chips, and fruit. Pitchers of juices, milk, and water poured themselves into glasses, and cookies appeared to the students that had finished their meals.

Regina heard the chatter pick up again and now, no one was paying any attention to her. She sighed. Everything she'd seen in the last two days certainly had her miffed. Regina sat down at the table and reached for a ham and cheese sandwich. "Why am I so hungry? I feel like I haven't eaten in a century," she muttered, taking large bites. Her sour cream and onion chips opened with a pop. The apple snapped crisply in her mouth and tasted sweet as candy. The pitcher at her table poured her a glass of water. "How did it know what I wanted?" She leaned in and whispered to Pam.

"It's Magic House!"

Dyson and Matthew bounded in, "Reg! Reg! You'll never believe what we were doing!" Dyson laughed, bumping into Regina and startling her back to reality. The room fell silent again.

"Jeez, I wish they'd stop staring!" Regina mouthed to Pam, but before she finished her thought, everyone went back to their conversations.

"Huh? What? Oh, what have you been doing?" Regina asked, shaking her head, and giving him her full attention.

"They're teaching me how to watch for Marcus while I sleep, and when he's spotted I am to notify Mom!" he shouted. Again, the room went silent for a moment. Regina quickly put her hand across his mouth.

"Shh! I get the feeling we aren't very welcome here, and the less they know about us, the better off we'll be," Regina whispered.

"That's not true, Reg. They're just curious to see Madam Harriett's offspring," Pam said.

"Offspring... How comforting! I thought you didn't know what they were staring at," Regina said peevishly.

"Well, you know what I mean... And Matthew, what have you learned?" Pam redirected the conversation. Regina fumed, watching the room suspiciously.

"I have been studying plants and birds. Did you know that every plant on the grounds of Magic House can be mixed together to make something magical?" He wrinkled his nose. "Nothing as cool as what Dyson's been doing, though."

"I'm sure it is essential to the plan," Pam said.

"Maybe you'll be making an antidote for Mrs. H," Regina said, grinning.

"Do you think? Yeah! You might be right!" Matthew stuffed ham and cheese into his mouth, grinning.

"Well, *he* feels better," Pam giggled. Regina relaxed, laughing with her. Dyson and Matthew joined in, and before they knew it, they were all comparing stories about their morning's adventures.

"Pam, look, lunch is over. We need to get back."

"Right!"

"Bye boys," Regina said as they parted ways. By the time dinner rolled around, the four siblings dragged themselves back to their room on the second floor, where a hearty meal awaited them.

Harriet appeared a few minutes later to oversee bath time and brush out the girl's hair. Regina had been waiting all day to ask her all the questions that had been piling up in her head, but for some reason she couldn't remember a single one. She yawned, thinking she ought to get Dyson into bed before she had to figure out a way to get him into the loft. "Dy? Oh, I'm too late, he's sound asleep," Regina muttered.

"I will take him up," Harriett offered. Regina was so tired, she didn't argue. Harriett floated up the ladder to the loft, tucked Dyson in, and returned to the common room.

"We will be back in Glenville, day after tomorrow," Harriett said.

Regina sighed, stretching her neck and arms. "Oooh! I need a massage…" she groaned.

"What time is it? I can't believe I woke up before the sun…" Regina sighed.

"Oh, good! You're up! It's raining today, which means we'll get to go out and work with all the elements," Pam said.

"Out in the rain? All the elements?" Regina pulled the covers up over her shoulders, snuggling down in her pillow, and wrinkling her nose and brow.

"Oh, sure. When there is a storm, it puts moisture in the air. It's easier to channel the wind, metals, water, and lightning. But it's harder to communicate telepathically with other creatures. It kind of insulates everyone…" Pam trailed off.

"Lightning?" Regina frowned. "Telepathy?"

"Yeah! You'll see!" Pam grinned. "It really helps those of us that can't manipulate all the elements. We use the clouds, fog, and rain as an end run, so to speak."

"What do you mean, 'those of us that can't use all the elements?'"

"Really, Reg? It should be obvious to even you that you can call up all kinds of magic!" Pam said with a grin.

"Yeah, sure… Obvious?" Regina muttered, crossing her eyes. *What is Pam talking about? Yesterday, I gathered the breeze, turned it into wind, and the other day I had one little episode of smoke. How's that 'calling up all kinds of magic?'*

"You're not even of age and you can make magic," Pam said.

"My birthday is in five months, and I'll be of age," Regina sniffed.

"Exactly. Put on your rain gear, and let's go!" Pam slammed her wardrobe door shut and exhaled. Regina threw off her blankets and stepped onto the cold floor. Lying across a chair was a floral print slicker, hat, and a pair of galoshes that matched. She raised her eyebrows and collected them.

"Come on, Reg! How can it take you so long?"

"Holy cow, Pam! Ever heard of patience?" Regina grumbled, walking out the door. She stumbled into a group of girls a year or two older than herself. "Oops! Sorry," Regina apologized for stepping on a tall, pretty brunette's toe. She and the girl came eye to eye. Regina froze. The girl's eyes flashed a silver color.

"Leave it, Cornelia!" her friend whispered.

Pam caught Regina by the shoulders before she slammed up against the wall. "What was *that* all about?" Pam said with a frown.

"You've got me. I've never seen her before. Did you see her eyes flash sparks? It felt like she tried to disintegrate me!"

"Well, she threw you across the hall with that look," Pam said.

"She did? She moved me with just her eyes? Maybe she's jealous because we don't have to wear that smock thing," Regina snickered.

"That's a cape, and it's the school uniform. I'll bet we do, sooner or later," Pam said.

"I'm serious, Pam. Why are they all angry with me? What did I do? I so wanted to ask Harriett last night, but my brain was dead. All I could think about was sleeping," Regina grumbled, spinning in a circle and eyeing everyone.

"Oh, who knows? Ignore them." Regina couldn't help but be both curious and uncomfortable. *I wonder if I can move things with my eyes.*

After breakfast, the girls hurried off to the ballroom where they found Ms. Calderon and Mr. Horn. "Dyson! Is he all right?' Regina hushed in asking.

"He is fine, dear. I asked Mr. Horn to accompany us to the gardens. He is an excellent instructor on teleportation. You see, with dreams, you must transport one object to another place while in your sleep. Most of the time, it is

146

easier to do asleep. It does not get all messy with self-doubt," she waved her hands around. "I have a feeling you might be able to do it while awake," she said, giving Regina a pointed look.

"He's here… I'm so nervous!" Pam said, elbowing Regina in the side gently. Regina pursed her mouth and scowled. *Pam's in love with her teacher!* Regina sang in her head. She wanted to shout it, but thought better of it.

"Oh, good thinking, girls. You brought your rain gear. Shall we go?" Ms. Calderon floated across the room and out the door. Pam and Regina hurried to keep up. They followed her straight through the front doors and onto the lawn.

"The rain sounds just like it does on the roof of the barn, only on my hat," Regina said with a laugh.

Pam smiled, nodding. "But check out the sky!"

Pam was right. The gusts of wind, lightning, and thunder made for a spooky, exhilarating morning. It wasn't like the frightening thunderstorm from Marcus, but like the storms she remembered as a child. She could feel her heart pounding, her breathing seemed nonexistent, and she felt exhilarated. The rain seemed to wash away all her negativity, rejuvenating and cleansing her inside. With that feeling of cleansing, came a feeling of raw power.

"You feel it! Don't you," Pam said, skipping through the wet grass and splattering each puddle with her galoshes.

Regina closed her eyes and turned her face to the heavens, arms outstretched, as she twirled in a circle. She began to sway with the wind and sing with the rain. She blocked out everything except for the earth, the wind, and the rain.

The garden gnomes, little creatures with stumpy legs, big eyes and big noses, peeked out of their caves. Then came the devas, nature's guardians, appearing in bucket hats and in every shape and size imaginable. Fairies fluttered out of the forest with their butterfly wings and their tiny human forms. And finally, the elves appeared. The males looked like old men, while the females were young and beautiful. They watched Regina. She greeted and connected with each one of them, bowing or shaking their hands. They, in turn, welcomed her to Magic House.

Finally, she settled on the unicorns. They'd strolled in from the forest to stand in the grass, a few feet from Regina. The big white male extended his left leg and bowed. His mate knelt down on her front knees. Regina approached him, reaching her hand out to stroke his long, silky mane.

Pam swallowed hard, witnessing the exchange, "He let her touch him! Has anyone ever been allowed to touch him?" Pam gasped.

"She has no idea how important she is," Ms. Calderon whispered to Pam and Mr. Horn. They both shook their heads. No one wanted to interrupt the sight before them.

"How old is she?" Mr. Horn asked softly.

"Twelve!" Pam whispered.

After a moment, the unicorn stood, as did his mate, and they walked slowly back into the forest.

The spell was broken. Regina slowly opened her eyes, feeling her body become her own again. Everyone and everything had been watching. She flushed with the heat of awkwardness and held her breath for the moments that followed.

"Do not be frightened, my dear. That was beautiful! You connected with our world like only you could." Ms. Calderon appeared at Regina's side, taking her by the elbow. She led her deeper into the garden and to the edge of the forest.

"I don't understand what just happened to me." Regina started to cry. Pam rushed to her side, hugging her tight.

"Don't cry, Reg! It was beautiful. I wish I could connect with the earth like you just did," Pam consoled her.

"I don't know what I just did. It felt so natural to breathe in… Everything," she whispered, swiping her arm in a big arc.

"Look! They all felt it too!" Pam pointed out her audience.

"What? I know I just met them all, but who *are* they?" Regina sniffed.

"They are Atlanteans," Pam said, glowing.

"What about the big white bird sitting in the tree over there?" Regina pointed.

"What white bird? I don't see any big white bird." Regina looked at Pam and back at the large bird, perplexed.

"Okay. Enough chit chat," Ms. Calderon broke up their moment. "Pam, it is your turn. I want you to call on that rock and move it into position." She pointed to a boulder sitting in the middle of the forest.

"It's so big!" Pam groaned. "I've never moved anything that big."

"It's only three feet tall! You can do it," Regina said encouragingly.

"It is no different than moving something smaller. Now concentrate! Feel the magic growing inside of you," Mr. Horn coached. Pam closed her eyes and pursed her lips. "Relax. Do not force it." She breathed and let her lips part. "That is it. Let the magic build." Pam inhaled and exhaled soundly through her nose and out her mouth. "Call for the boulder," Mr. Horn whispered.

Pam's hands reached out from her body at waist height, palms up. "Giant rock..." Pam called clearly. The rock rumbled and shook. She closed her eyes tighter and lifted her hands upward. The rock broke apart from its base and moved toward her. Pam exhaled, opening her eyes. She screeched when she saw the boulder floating toward her. It slammed back to earth.

All the creatures that had come out of their homes to watch, ducked for cover, "What about our little friends? We didn't hurt any of them, did we?" Regina gulped, concerned.

"No, dear. None of the little people were close," Ms. Calderon assured Regina. "So sweet, you are!" she mumbled.

"Okay, Regina! Your turn. Blow it up!" Mr. Horn instructed. Regina closed her eyes and let her head fall back. "Gather the energy..." She opened her arms to absorb the thunder. "Bring it up through your being..." Regina felt the energy flood through her. "And, zap!" he shouted.

Regina channeled the lightning through her hands, aiming it at the rock. With a loud report, the boulder exploded into tiny pieces.

"Ahh!" Regina screeched, jumping aside, and staring wide-eyed.

"That was excellent, dear!" Ms. Calderon praised. Mr. Horn clapped.

"Wow!" Pam panted.

"Okay, girls! Let us try something in tandem. Pam, I want you to hurl the stones from the rock Regina just destroyed, at that big tree," Mr. Horn pointed about thirty feet into the woods.

"Regina I want you to blow them up before they hit the tree. Remember, I want controlled blasts," Mr. Horn explained.

"Good idea, Cornelius," Ms. Calderon agreed.

Pam levitated one of the stones from the rubble and commanded, "Little rock: Tree!" The rock flew towards the tree. Regina aimed her lightning zap at the rock and let it fly. "It missed!" she growled.

"It is okay! Keep them coming," Mr. Horn called. "Little rock: Tree!" Pam shouted. Regina plotted the path of the stone in her mind. She exhaled, concentrating the bolt to cross paths in front of the rock. The zigzagged stream of energy met the stone at the same time, exploding into sand particles.

"I did it!" Regina cheered.

"Keep it going!" Mr. Horn shouted.

Pam called for rock after rock, as fast as she could say the words. Regina blew each one to smithereens.

"Well, I would say you have that move down, and then some," Ms. Calderon said, satisfied. Pam and Regina smiled, their eyes bright.

"Um, let us try something else. Since we may not be having a thunderstorm the day Marcus comes, we will need to find our strengths," Mr. Horn said thoughtfully. "I want you two to pretend I am Marcus," he instructed. "Get together and make a plan. Take me out!"

"Won't you get hurt?" Regina gasped.

"No, I am a ghost. The stuff will go right through me. I am going to stay corporal, though. The trick is to catch me before I can turn invisible," he said.

"Oh, yeah!" Regina snickered. "Pam! Come here!" They whispered back and forth, with a few nods and a grin. Pam took up a position opposite of Regina.

"Ready?"

"Fire away!"

Regina grabbed the wind, spun it into a whirlwind, and picked up all the sticks, rocks, and pinecones in its path. Mr. Horn stood between Pam and Regina observing. Pam jumped out from her hiding place and fired a rock out of the cyclone directly at Mr. Horn. He barely turned invisible before it flew through him.

"Good job, but you missed!"

The whirlwind spun around coming at him from different directions. Pam stepped out, "Stick: Mr. Horn!" It missed. "Rock: Mr. Horn!" It bounced off a tree beside him.

"Hahaha! Try again!"

"Pinecone: Mr. Horn! Rock: Mr. Horn! Stick: Mr. Horn!" Pam was turning blue with frustration. She dropped her hands and leaned against the tree, exhaling loudly.

"Rock: Mr. Horn! Rock: Mr. Horn! Mud Puddle: Mr. Horn!" Regina started laughing hysterically. She dropped the wind. All the items inside, fell to the ground. Pam looked around the tree. Mr. Horn was standing before them covered in mud and dirty rainwater. He had mud caked on his nose, his perfectly styled hair dripped in his eyes, and his pristine white shirt was wet with soggy leaves and muddy water.

"Oh! Yay! I got you!" Pam cheered.

"Yes, you did. Nicely done! Okay. I think we have concluded this exercise for the day." Mr. Horn chuckled, shaking the water from his sleeves and wiping it from his face with a white handkerchief. The small group made their way back to Magic House.

"I thought you said you couldn't get hit, and that it would go right through you!" Regina covered her mouth to hide her laughter.

"I did not expect you to deliberately drown me," he chuckled. "Ms. Calderon, I believe my services are no longer needed here. I would hate to go up against these girls in a fight," he said, continuing to brush the remnants of the forest off of his suit.

"Let us hope it does not come to that, but I can see that you are correct. Thank you for your guidance." She curtsied. "Shall we clean up and get you girls some lunch?"

"Yeah, I'm starving," Regina said, hiding her mirth. Pam and Regina secretly high fived each other when the two ghost's backs were turned.

"We will pick this up after lunch in the Ballroom," Ms. Calderon said as she left the girls. They strolled to the Great Hall, chattering, and anticipating their noon meal.

Chapter Ten

Lessons Learned

Standing out front of the Great Hall, was Dickson. He fidgeted with his fingers and paced back and forth. Regina poked Pam and jerked her head in his direction, before he spotted them. "Maybe he's waiting for you," Pam said, smirking. Regina stuck her tongue out in Pam's direction.

"Regina!" Dickson called, rushing up to her. He looked at Pam and waited.

"I'll meet you inside," Pam snickered. Regina raised her eyebrows, making her eyes wide with apprehension, but Pam skirted off into the Great Hall. Regina directed her attention back to Dickson.

"Um, yeah?" Regina coughed, clearing her throat.

"I was wondering…" he stammered, not looking directly at her. Regina stood perfectly still. "I was wondering if you had planned to go to the Tween Dance, next Saturday night?"   "I… um, I don't know. I didn't know anything about it," Regina half whispered, flushing a rosy shade of pink.

"Oh. Yeah, it ought to be fun. It's the first dance they let the twelve- to fourteen-year-olds attend. They'll have cookies, candy, chips, and punch. We can wear street clothes! Oh, I guess you already do, but…" he muttered, pointing to her sweater and jeans. Regina snickered and looked away. "Um, anyway, I thought maybe if you were going, we… I mean… maybe we could have a dance?" he blushed, wiping away a bead of perspiration, then glanced sideways, hoping to catch her gaze.

"Oh, yeah. Sure… I guess… If I'm there," she hesitated and nodded.

"Great! Hope to see you then," he said, eyeing something over her shoulder. He turned abruptly and strolled into the Great Hall.

Regina was startled by his sudden departure. "Look, girls! Our mentor is here!" Regina heard behind her, spinning to face the attacker. Coming up the corridor was Cornelia, flanked by her two admiring friends. "Out of my way, Worthington," she snapped, pushing past Regina with a death stare. Her two friends snickered.

Regina held her ground, returning the same stare, "Actually, it's Edwards!" she corrected Cornelia, who flipped her hair and continued past her. After they had rounded the door into the Great Hall, Regina breathed and shook her head. "What did I ever do to her?" she murmured to herself.

"Sometimes, it does not matter that we have never provoked a certain person. Sometimes that certain person can just have hate in their hearts. So, think about this: 'It is not how they treat *us* that is important. It is how we treat *them* that defines who we are'," Mr. Horn explained, appearing beside Regina. He was all cleaned up and looking younger than she first realized.

"She's really starting to push my buttons," Regina retorted and sighed.

"I can see that, but be mindful of who you want to be," he reminded her. They walked into the Great Hall together.

"Right now, all I want to do is punch her in the nose," Regina mumbled under her breath.

"I see Pam waving over there," he said, pointing.

"Oh, yes. Thank you," Regina said, scampering off to join Pam.

"That was Cornelius! What did he say? How'd you run into him?" Pam's questions came   too fast for Regina to answer. She giggled, instead. Pam sat in awe for a moment then snapped out of her reverie. "What did Dickson want?"

"Something about a dance…"

"Ooh, did he ask you to the Tween Dance?" Pam teased.

"No! That's disgusting! He asked if we could dance or something," Regina muttered.

"What did you say?" Pam giggled.

"Yes, but it's not like I'm still going to be here. After we save Mrs. H, I'm going back to her place. I hate it here!" Regina declared, nibbling on a chip thoughtfully. She washed it down with water. Pam shrugged her shoulders and smiled.

Dyson and Matthew appeared, crowding around their table. "Hey Reg, Pam, what's shakin'?" Matthew chuckled. "This place is great, huh! I never want to leave."

"Yeah! You guys look way too serious. Didn't it go well, this morning?" Dyson teased.

"It went fine," Regina snorted, pushing her chair away from the table. She marched out of the Great Hall with a sandwich in one hand and a cookie in the other.

"What's with her?" she heard Matthew say.

Regina found a private garden with a small waterfall that trickled in the background. She sat on a cement bench and took a bite of her sandwich. Birds were singing and a light breeze tickled the leaves. Regina breathed deep, catching a faint scent of gardenia. She closed her eyes and envisioned the bush with its thick, green, waxy leaves and delicate white petals. Her eyes opened to a carpet of gardenia plants under a group of tall, thin-branched vitex trees. Up in the tree sat that same large, snow-white bird she'd seen out front, yesterday morning.

Regina inhaled deep and let the air out slowly. Her life had taken an unexpected turn into complete and utter chaos. "Mr. Bird! What am I to do? I can't believe four days ago I was complaining about a pimple on my chin. Now, I have a boy asking me to dance, some girl who hates my guts, and a whole magical world looking to me to fight one of our mortal enemies." A tear trickled over her lower lid. "I'm not that strong… I don't want to be that strong! I just want to be a kid," she whispered.

Regina took another bite of sandwich and chewed. The bird looked down upon her, batted his eyes, and spread his wings. "Growing up is not always easy. Being afraid to experience new life challenges will keep you safe, but will stifle your greatness," he said, flapping his wings at their full six-foot length, and then settling back onto his limb. He again looked down at her and stretched his long neck. She nodded her head, stunned, but acknowledged his words.

Regina sat, thoughtful for a time, finishing her lunch. If she understood him, he was telling her, "It was okay to be afraid. It was okay to fail. But it was not okay to quit." She gazed back up at him sitting on his vitex perch, stood, and smiled, before she left the atrium.

Out in the hall, Pam came running up to her, "There you are! I was beginning to worry," she said, out of breath.

"Why?"

"I thought, maybe you... I don't know, left us."

"Why would I do that?" Regina said.

"Oh, Regina and Pam, here you are. I thought I was going to meet you outside the Great Hall after lunch?" Ms. Calderon asked more as a statement than a question.

"We decided to go exploring," Pam said, covering for them.

"Well, you are here, now. Follow me!" Ms. Calderon waved to them to follow her. "I am taking you into the training room, first. Then we will go to the hologram room for a little play acting. Most of the time, the seniors are the only ones allowed to use the holograms, but since we are under the constraints of time, Madam Worthington thought you needed to practice in there.

"Mr. Adam Aikman is going to teach you some defensive moves. You know, how to fall and roll. Stuff that may save you some agony. Then we will go up to the theater and play with the holograms," Ms. Calderon explained.

"No more magic?" Regina squeaked.

"Oh, yes! You will be practicing your magic," she said.

"You know... I've been wondering why we are bringing Marcus inside our House. Isn't that like letting the wolves into the den?" Regina asked. "Or something like that."

"I guess it could be, but the House has its own magic. Since you are underage, your magic is more powerful here. Not out in the world."

"But then, we still have to get Mrs. Hillsdale the medicine. That will take precious time that she doesn't have," Regina argued.

"Regina, you must learn to trust the House!" Regina rolled her eyes and plodded along behind her and Pam. She wasn't convinced.

"I'm just saying..." Regina wouldn't let it go. Pam turned around, walking backwards, pursing her lips together, and glaring. Regina continued, ignoring Pam, "I think we're making this too complicated. We can go to Mrs. H's house, where Veronica and Marcus are. I can bombard Marcus and Veronica with rocks and things, while Pam calls for the antidote. Then we can whirlwind out of there to the hospital," Regina said.

Pam exhaled loudly, slamming her hands against her legs. She turned back around, shaking her head, waiting for Ms. Calderon to fly into a rage.

"Regina, honey, I will take it up with Madam Worthington," she replied. "Here we are." Ms. Calderon opened the door to a room that was stuffy and smelled like sweat. She nudged Regina, forcing her further into the room.

"Hey, the ground is squishy!"

"Yeah, it reminds me of the play yards at the park, but look at the trees and rocks. It kinda looks like the woods," Pam said.

"Mr. Aikman!" Ms. Calderon called. A man in tight pants, slipper-like shoes, and a sleeveless shirt stepped through the trees. Regina gawked at the size of his muscular arms.

"Are these the girls you told me about?" he growled. Regina backed up and hid behind Pam. Ms. Calderon nodded and disappeared, leaving them alone with him.

"Oh, great! Thanks a lot Reg," Pam huffed.

"So, what are you here to show us?" Regina asked, still hiding behind Pam. To her surprise and horror, a fireball flew directly at them. Regina pushed Pam out of the way and dived to the mat.

For the next two hours, Mr. Aikman shot bolts of lightning and balls of fire at Pam and Regina. They rolled, dived for cover, and sprinted out of the path of Mr. Aikman's assault. Their clothes were torn, their hair had come loose from the ties that bound it, and they were dirty from head to toe.

"I can't move another inch," Regina huffed and puffed, out of breath. She had no more finished her sentence when a stream of fireballs flew in her direction. Regina rolled across the mat, dodging each one. She finally made it to an oak tree and crouched behind it.

"Well, Regina, maybe next time you want to shoot your mouth off, you'll remember this little exercise," Pam barked, as another lightning bolt landed at her feet.

"I thought ghosts didn't have any magic!" Regina screamed.

"The ghosts that were assassinated and have had their powers stolen, don't. I was killed in a car crash on my way to a wrestling match, while in high school. Oh, and you've only begun to fight off fireballs," Mr. Aikman bellowed from the middle of the room.

"Did he just use a contraction? He just used a contraction!" Regina squealed.

"I said I wasn't killed by a Cobbleport!" he yelled, letting two fireballs fly. One aimed at Regina just missed her by inches, and the other flew at Pam, who felt the heat, it was so close.

"Pam, you all right?" Regina called.

"Yeah, it didn't burn me," Pam exhaled.

"I'm done with this," Regina said, stepping from behind the tree when the next fireball came at her. "Fireball!" she called, catching it in her hand and heaving it back at Mr. Aikman. He dived to the mat and rolled, averting it.

"Nicely done! But I have to say it took you long enough to get mad!" he laughed long and hard. Pam stood up, dusting herself off, and walked over to Regina. She took hold of her hands and turned them over to examine them.

"You aren't even scorched! That was amazing! How did you do it?" Pam exclaimed. Regina collapsed to the mat and sat there, stunned.

"And that's why you need to stay at Magic House, Regina. You draw your power from it. It's as if you are one with the House." Mr. Aikman winked and smiled. "Okay, let's go visit the holograms."

Pam pulled Regina off the floor and dragged her down the hall behind Mr. Aikman. They entered an empty room. The walls and ceiling were completely green. Mr. Aikman nudged them into the center of the room. Pam exhaled, looking around suspiciously. Regina stood silently with her arms hanging from her shoulders and a blank stare on her face.

"Can I at least have a drink of water, before we start again?" Pam asked, trying to give Regina a few more minutes to regroup, but the room instantly turned black. It was darker than dark. Regina twitched. She couldn't see her hand in front of her face. "I hope you're back among the living," Pam said quietly.

"Now, what?" Regina groaned. The lights came up. Regina twirled with glee. They were transported to the pasture outside Mrs. Hillsdale's house. Pam's eyes opened wide with sheer panic.

"Now, *this* is what I'm talkin' about!" Regina exclaimed. "Come on, Pam! Let's go home!" Regina started running across the field toward the house.

"Reg, stop!" called Pam. Regina ignored her and kept skipping. "Regina! Stop!" Pam screamed.

"Why? What is it?" she stopped and spun around, irritated.

"We aren't in Glenville! It's a hologram. Marcus could be anywhere," Pam whispered. Regina perused the area, wide-eyed. "I think the house is showing you your plan," Pam continued.

Regina considered this. "Okay, we got this," she said confidently, squatting on the ground. Pam knelt beside her. "The goal is to get the antidote, right?" Regina whispered. Pam nodded. "First, we have to find the vial."

"All the time I was with Marcus, he kept it in his right hip pocket," Pam said.

"So, do you think it's still there?" Regina asked softly. Pam shrugged her shoulders, nodding. "Then I will keep him and Veronica busy until you can call for the vial. Easy peasy!" Pam exhaled and rolled her eyes. "Stay behind me!" Regina instructed.

The two girls crept into the house through the kitchen door. The TV was blasting. Regina pointed for Pam to hide in the pantry. Pam pushed the pantry door open and tiptoed inside. Regina continued through the kitchen and through the foyer. She didn't see anyone. She crept toward the family room where the television was blaring.

"Marcus, I want to go to the hospital to see if the old lady is still alive," Veronica called from upstairs. "I've torn this place apart looking for the money, and I can't find it anywhere! Maybe she's cuckoo enough to tell me where it is," Veronica said, coming down the stairs.

Regina opened the coat closet and slipped inside. Marcus was in the house someplace, but Regina didn't know where. She really needed to know where he was. "Marcus!" Veronica spat when he didn't answer. Regina held her breath, listening. She heard footsteps coming down the stairs, hitting the wooden floor at the bottom. Her heart raced, but still no word from Marcus.

Breathe, Regina told herself. *Now… Wait for it…* She threw the closet door open with a bang. Veronica stood a few feet away from her. She had tiny round balls dancing between her open palms and a smirk on her face. Regina hesitated, watching the spheres dance. Veronica raised her hands and the metal balls moved with them. *Do something…*

A decorative plate hung on the wall. Regina flung it at Veronica, striking her in the shoulder. It shattered, leaving a piece of ceramic embedded deep in her arm. A shriek came from Veronica. She collapsed to the floor, letting the balls drop and scatter.

"Where's Marcus?!" Regina spat. Veronica rolled around on the floor, screaming in pain. "I'm sorry, Veronica. I didn't want to hurt you, but you gave me no choice," Regina said, reaching to console her. Veronica rolled over to her stomach and climbed to her knees. "Stay down, Veronica! I will hurt you," Regina warned. Veronica continued to her feet, pulled out the piece of glass, and began to giggle. Her snickers built into outright laughter. Regina felt her skin prickled.

"You gave her no choice, Ronnie! She didn't want to hurt you," Marcus taunted Regina, laughing. Regina spun at the sound of his voice. He was coming up behind her with Pam in his clutches. The same knife he'd used on Mrs. Hillsdale was laid against her throat.

"See, Pam? I knew you wouldn't let us down. You brought her to me," Marcus chuckled. Pam tried to shake her head 'no'. Regina could see big tears streaming down Pam's face. Her eyes were wide with fear.

Regina didn't lower her hands; she knew they were her only defense against him. The problem was how much magic did she have outside of Magic House? Would it be enough to get the antidote, and save herself and Pam? *Stall!* She told herself. "All we want is the antidote, and we'll let you and Veronica have the house," Regina said trying to reason with him.

"And all I want is my brother's and your father's magic," Marcus snarled. "But I'll take the house, too."

"I don't know what you are talking about! I don't have their magic!" She stared into his eyes, watching for the next move. Pam coughed, holding back the sobs. The knife blade pressed harder on her throat. She heard Veronica's squeaky giggles.

"Okay, okay. How do I give it to you? Just don't hurt Pam!" Regina gasped.

"You die," he replied, hurling a fireball directly at her chest. Regina reacted, deflecting it to the side.

Veronica screamed. Regina heard her hit the floor. A quick glance told Regina she was dead, lying at the foot of the staircase with her eyes wide open and lifeless. Regina inhaled sharply, her chest felt heavy, and her feet refused to move. She'd never seen anyone die. She looked into Pam's eyes for consolation, but Pam was busy trying to reach into Marcus's pocket and retrieve the vial.

"You killed my girlfriend!" Marcus pretended to sound aggrieved, but he had no real sympathy and started laughing. "She was getting on my last nerve, anyway," he sighed.

Regina's eyes met Pam's. She rolled them down so that Regina would see that she had her fingers in Marcus's pocket. Marcus also caught on, shoving Pam to the ground. The knife sliced through her delicate skin. She lay before Regina, gasping aloud.

"Noooo!" Regina screamed.

Marcus heaved a fireball directly at Regina as she reached out to Pam. She rolled, averting the assault, coming up on her knees behind the couch in the family room. Regina peeked around it, meeting Pam's eyes. Pam blinked over and over again, fighting off the tears. "I'm sorry," Pam mouthed.

Marcus had taken cover behind the kitchen door. He threw fireball after fireball in Regina's direction. She ducked and crouched, avoiding the onslaught, until the couch disintegrated and a lightning bolt creased her forearm, scorching her skin.

"Ouch," she moaned silently. She closed her eyes, took a deep, bracing breath, then jumped up, completely open to Marcus. He fired. She caught the fireball and threw it straight back in his face. It exploded, and he vanished with just a scorch mark on the wall.

Regina ran to Pam, cradling her in her arms. "Harriett!" she screamed for help. "It's over! You're going to be all right. I'm going to get help!" Regina looked around, confused. "Harriett!" she didn't appear. Why was no one coming to help Pam?

Regina rocked Pam back in forth as she lay in her lap gulping for air. "Matthew will make us a potion for Mrs. H," Regina sobbed. Pam looked up into Regina's face one last time. She opened her hand. In the creases of her fingers lay the antidote vial. She nodded for Regina to take it. Regina carefully held it up to the light, watching the amber liquid reflect swirling patterns on the wall. Pam sucked in her last breath, and gently, like a sigh, the breath left her body and she became still. "No, Pam! No! Come back to me!" Regina sobbed. "Harriett!"

Just then, the lights came on, Pam faded away, the vial disappeared, and the room returned to green walls. Marcus was gone. The house was gone, and Veronica was gone. Pam ran to Regina from an open door in the hallway. "It's over!" Pam said consolingly. Regina wiped the tears from her face, glancing around confused.

"Yes, it's over," Mr. Aikman said, helping her to her feet. "The House knows your plan would work to get the antidote, but the cost would be too great." He spoke softly without any growl in his voice. Regina nodded, understanding that now.

"Pam, are you all right?" Mr. Aikman asked.

She nodded. "They grabbed me in the dark."

"And, Regina, are you going to be all right? That was pretty intense." He sounded more like himself. Regina nodded. "Some things to think about, tonight."

Regina glanced at him and then over to Pam. Her head hung and her shoulders slumped. She had a lot to think about, and most of it had to do with her own attitude. Her mind flashed back to the big white bird today. He'd told her it was okay to fail, but not okay to quit. She wouldn't quit. "I promise to be ready for Mr. Marcus Vermont, next time."

"You girls go get cleaned up! I think dinner is about to be served.

Chapter Eleven

The Magical Ringed Land

Regina shifted the peas from one side of her plate to the other and back again. Trying to sort through her thoughts proved to be harder than she first thought. *How was she going to defeat Marcus?*

"Don't look now, but here comes mommy," Cornelia whispered snidely as she passed by Regina in the Great Hall. Her two sidekicks, close on her heels, giggled. Regina looked up, startled, and saw Harriett heading straight for her table.

"Ohh!" she groaned, pushing her plate away. A transparent ghost whisked it away.

"You really ought to try and eat something, dear," Harriett said in her motherly voice.

"Yeah, I'm not very hungry," Regina muttered, refusing to look up into Harriett's face.

"I told her the same thing," Dyson nagged. Regina glared at him.

"Okay, I did not come here to fight or cause one. If you are all finished, I will escort you to the nursery," Harriett said.

"Nursery? Is Sally all right?" Regina jumped up.

"Oh, yes. She is just fine. She misses all of you. I thought you might like to spend some time with her before tomorrow," Harriett explained, stroking Regina's cheek and patting Dyson on top of the head. "So, shall we go?"

The chatter fell silent as the four foster siblings and the Head Mistress left the Great Hall. Regina hesitated. "Ignore them," Harriett whispered in Regina's ear, and gently nudged her out the doors.

"Can you tell me what the big fascination is?" Regina asked.

"That is a discussion for a later time. I think we have bigger things to deal with, tonight." Harriett winked. Matthew nodded and took the lead.

The door to the nursery opened on its own, as the group approached. "Oh, good. They are still up," Harriett said, smiling. Pam frowned. "The door will not allow visitors if the majority of the children are in bed, but I can see that baths are still underway," Harriett explained. Pam smiled.

Sally had finished her bath and was being dressed in her sleepwear. She heard the commotion and looked up. "Reg!" she cooed, wiggling out of her nanny's hands. Regina caught her as she charged into her arms. Regina hugged and hugged her until Sally pushed herself away, patting Regina on the cheeks.

"Hi Sal! I've missed you!" Regina squeezed her again.

"Mis ou too!" Sally grinned. Pam hung back, waiting to see Sally's reaction to her. She wasn't sure if Sally understood the deceitful part she'd played in the last couple of days. "'ammy," she called, reaching for her. Pam smiled and exhaled, taking Sally into her arms.

"Oh, Sal, I've missed you so much," Pam sang. "You smell really good… Like lavender." She breathed in deep.

"Yeah, Sal! I can smell you from here," Matthew snickered. Pam set her down and she ran to Matthew and Dyson, who each, in turn, patted her on the head. Sally stood before them with her hands on her hips.

"I don't think you're going to get away with just a pat," Regina said, smiling at the boys. Matthew squatted down and gave her an awkward squeeze and Dyson copied him. Satisfied with that, Sally ran to her small section of the room and grabbed a book with a cover of an island surrounded by two mountainous rings, off the small table.

"Ree!" she demanded, looking up into Pam's eyes and handing her the book.

Pam giggled. "Just like at home." She sat down in the big wooden rocking chair and gathered Sally onto her lap. She opened the book, waiting for the others to find a comfy spot on the floor, and began the story.

The Magical Ringed Land… Once upon a time, on an island in the center of the ocean surrounded by two mountainous rings, there lived a magical people. They shared this land with many different magical creatures who helped them prosper. The elves, brownies, fairies, dragons, and many others, did the hard, backbreaking work and the everyday chores. This freed up the people to pursue other, more thoughtful tasks such as writing poetry, creating works of art, and designing buildings, water systems, and indoor plumbing, to name a few. However, as time passed, the people became lazy. They spent their time lying in the sun, celebrating, and creating beautiful gold and silver trinkets that they traded with visitors that came to the Ringed Land.

The lazy people failed to appreciate their magical friends and good fortune. After many years, the magical community began to resent the people of the kingdom, calling them selfish and idle, and so magic sent them a warning.

It was a beautiful spring day, when a mystic appeared on the bow of a ship that sailed into the kingdom. He carried a crate under his arm. The people watched this funny little man with his long beard, pointed hat, and long flowing robe, walk to the middle of town. He stood upon his box and began his warning of an awful fate that would happen to them.

"You will be given a test!" he said. "This test is the only way to make sure you have a future of happiness, and to prove you are worthy of magic." The people murmured amongst themselves, but turned their backs on the mystic and began to walk away. The mystic shouted, "Get your affairs in order! Be mindful of all creatures and of all magic. When your people have respected magic for ten-thousand-years, you will have your paradise returned."

Well, the king and queen that ruled the Ringed Land didn't believe the mystic. To prove to their kingdom that he spoke false words, they decided a child would bring happiness and calm their fears. The queen gave birth to a beautiful daughter. She was loved by all. Things went back to normal, and for a time, all the mystic's warnings had been forgotten.

Several years later, on a bright, sunny day, the Ringed Land began to tremble and shake. Houses cracked, falling off their foundations, smoke billowed through the Earth's crust, and the fresh water ran off into the ocean. The people gathered at the gates of the palace, waiting for their king to save them. The king instructed everyone to collect all their valuables and meet at the docks.

The king and queen had finally realized the mystic had spoken the truth. It was time to heed his advice, but it was too late for the Ringed Land. To protect all life, every living being was to be brought to the docks. "Guard! Do not leave a single creature, no matter how large or small, behind," the king ordered, for they would not sail without everyone.

The queen made sure each boat carried magical creatures, as well as citizens of the Ringed Land. When all were loaded, they sailed away from their beloved home. Each ship headed in a different direction. They would travel across the sea in search of a new land to call home.

See, the king and queen were not sure how far or wide the shaking and destruction traveled, so they thought that if the boats traveled in several directions, one of them would find a safe place and send for the rest of the kingdom. Once they found a new land, they would rebuild a bigger and better kingdom for everyone. They would prove their value and be returned to the Ringed Island.

But before this could happen, several volcanoes erupted and sank their island to the bottom of the sea. This caused the ocean to grow, creating huge waves and giant whirlpools. Some of the boats were swallowed up by the sea and some were pushed so far from the others that they lost touch and were left to sail alone.

The king, queen, and daughter's boats sailed for many, many months, until they found a land bigger and more promising than any they had ever seen, but this land was harsh and wild. The inhabitants of the new land didn't understand the strange magical beings or their magic, so the king built a house, a giant house that reached the clouds, and he protected it with magic. The more magical friends that were found over time, the bigger the house grew.

In time, they learned to love the new land, but they also learned to protect each other, and to this day, they prosper, working hard, and waiting for the ten-thousand-year test to end.

Sally was fast asleep by the time the story ended. Her nanny picked her up, letting everyone gently kiss her on the forehead, and put her in her bed. They all tiptoed out of the room and into the hallway.

"That was quite the story! Any truth to it?" Regina asked. Harriett ignored her. "Hmm!" Regina said with a sideways look, but continued on to her room.

Regina's mind had been racing since early afternoon. Even though the fairytale Pam had read gave her a small reprieve, it seemed to give her more to think about. She couldn't help but wonder if this was the magical house the king had created. *It had to be! Where else would this place have come from?* But if that were true, what happened to the king and queen? Or for that matter, the daughter? It can't be the same, because the story had no enemies, like Marcus. *Oh, all of this is making my head hurt...*

"I want to talk to all of you," Harriett said, and herded them all into the common area on the couch. Regina plopped down, throwing her head back against the sofa, and crossing her arms over her chest. She knew she wasn't going to like what Harriett had to say, whatever it was.

"I want you all to hear me. Regina, especially you! Tomorrow, when the battle commences, you are to stay in this room and not confront Marcus!"

"Not leave! What have I been doing for the last three days, if not learning to fight Marcus?!" Regina was livid, standing, and pacing the room.

"Yeah! What *she* said! I… We thought we were going to be helping Mrs. H!" Pam wailed, slumping down in her chair.

Harriett held up her hands to calm the room. "The only reason you have been training, is to protect yourselves in the unfortunate event that the House fails, or Marcus breaks through our defenses," Harriett explained.

"I don't believe this…" Regina turned her back to march off.

"Regina, this is exactly why you are being restricted to this room."

Regina sighed loudly. She hesitated and returned to the sofa.

"You mean; I won't even be able to help with my dreams?" Dyson groaned.

"No, sweetheart, you are not ready for a battle." Harriett smiled and rubbed his shoulder. Dyson frowned.

"What about the antidote I've been working on?" Matthew asked.

"Well, it is not ready. After all, it has not been tested, and furthermore, we do not know what poison Mrs.

Hillsdale has been given. Giving her the wrong potion could be just as deadly."

All the children sat solemnly on the couch with Regina staring out the window next to her bed. "Now, promise me you will not leave this room to fight Marcus until I come to get you," Harriett said. She waited for an answer. No one said anything.

"Dyson?" Harriett cleared her throat. He looked up and nodded reluctantly.

"Matthew?"

"Yes," he snorted sharply.

"Pam?"

"Yes!" she said as snotty as she could, hugging a throw pillow.

"Regina?" She wouldn't answer, getting up and walking to the window. "Regina? I am extremely serious! You need to stay out of the action and let the House handle it. Now, promise?" Harriett barked, knowing Regina was angry and didn't understand.

"Yeah, sure. Why not?!" she said heatedly, throwing up her hands.

"You all know that a promise cannot be broken in Magic House. So, as hard as it is going to be on you four, stay here and protect each other," Harriett said and turned to leave, disappearing at the door.

"You can't break a promise in Magic House?" Regina coughed. Pam shook her head. "Why? What will happen?"

"Nothing. the House won't let you do anything that involves breaking the promise," Pam tried to explain with a sigh. "We are stuck here until it's over."

"I can't believe this…" Regina moaned.

"If you think about it, they couldn't really sic a bunch of kids on a great sorcerer like Marcus. And *you* are the one he wants. What if he got you? Then all would be lost," Pam said.

"All of *what* would be lost? There's more of that cryptic talk!" Regina was at the end of her patience.

"I don't mean anything. I mean, you're the Head Mistress's daughter, aren't you? How would that look for her to serve you up to the enemy?"

"I'm going to bed," Regina spat, shaking her head.

Regina tossed and turned well into the night, having vivid nightmares of Marcus shooting fireballs at her. She saw Veronica juggling metal balls and flinging them at her like bullets. She screamed in pain as they penetrated her skin and caused her to bleed. She woke up in a panic, unable to quiet her pounding heart, and sweating so much that her sheets were soaked.

Regina threw the covers off and sat up. "I need some air," she mouthed, slipping into a pair of yoga pants and a sloppy sweatshirt. She crammed her feet into a pair of athletic shoes and stuffed Mr. Wuzzles under her pillow. The door to the hall opened, allowing Regina to exit the room. "Hmm… So much for 'being stuck,'" she whispered.

Regina walked down the hall and stood in front of Harriett's office. She knocked softly. No one answered. She tried the knob. It turned. Regina stuck her head inside and saw no one sitting at the desk. She slipped inside. The fire flickered in the fireplace, creating an eerie glow on the crest above it. The snake, an Ouroboros; A never ending circle, meaning protection and life eternal. Regina stared at it, thinking.

"Where does Mrs. Hillsdale fit into this eternal life cycle? She's a descendent of Atlantis. Doesn't she count for being protected or saved?" Regina questioned the snake. Just then, she heard someone coming down the hall. She looked in vain for a place to hide. She remembered the elevator that led to the redwood forest. Regina stood in front of the blank wall, sweeping her hands in a circular arc in front of her and said, "Revealalecto!" The elevator door appeared before her. She heard the doorknob twist behind her.

Regina held her breath, entering the elevator. She pressed the *Cloud* button and said, "Accendelecto!" The doors closed and the lift started to move, just as the office door opened. Regina heard nothing more until the lift came to a stop. The doors opened. She recognized the fog, so thick it dripped like rain. *I wonder if Puddlefoot will talk to me.* She thought, hurrying down the hall, blinded by the mist. She smelled the pine of the forest and knew to turn.

"Puddlefoot? Are you here?" Regina called softly and waited. The sky overhead was as clear and beautiful as the first night she saw it. After a moment, Regina caught sight of a figure coming toward her.

"Regina, what are you doing up here? Students aren't allowed on the top floors," Puddlefoot growled in his deep, heavy voice.

"I know! I couldn't sleep. I've been benched!"

Puddlefoot tilted his head and wrinkled his brow. "Benched?"

"Yeah, I'm not allowed to fight Marcus or save Mrs. Hillsdale." Regina fought back tears.

"You're not allowed to save Mrs. Hillsdale?" Puddlefoot half asked a question and half made a statement. Regina hesitated, considering his comment.

"Yeah, Harriett made me, us, promise we wouldn't leave the room to fight Marcus," she groaned.

"Oh, well you *are* pretty young to be engaging a full-blown sorcerer." He thought for a minute. "I thought you said you weren't allowed to help Mrs. Hillsdale?"

"Well, yeah. If I can't fight Marcus and Veronica, how can I save Mrs. H?"

"Oh, there are many ways to help Mrs. Hillsdale," Puddlefoot said.

"But…" Regina considered. "Wait; I don't have to fight Marcus to help Mrs. H, do I?" she whispered.

"I don't know what you mean," Puddlefoot muttered.

"Thanks, Puddlefoot! Thanks!" Regina beamed and ran back down the hall. The elevator was still in the same place she'd left it. Regina jumped in, pushed the *two*, the doors closed, and she said, "Descendalecto!" It rumbled into action, stopping, and opening into Harriett's office. Regina bound out of the lift and headed for the door. "Oh!" she exclaimed, turning around and saying, "Concealalecto!" The elevator vanished. Regina ran out the door. A ghostly figure materialized as the office door shut.

Regina ran back into her room, jumped into bed, and lay there cuddling with Mr. Wuzzles. "I need a plan! And this time, I need a plan that will not get everyone killed," Regina pondered.

"Where have you been?" Pam asked, propping herself up on her elbow.

"I have an idea. I just need to work through the particulars," Regina said. Pam snickered, laying her head down on her pillow.

"Make sure you include me," Pam whispered.

"And me," she heard from Matthew above her.

"And me too," Dyson chimed in.

"Only if you all can keep a secret. Now get some sleep and let me think."

Chapter Twelve

The Promise

Regina tossed and turned, trying to figure out how she was going to rescue Mrs. Hillsdale from the hospital. *The hard part is getting to the hospital and getting Mrs. H back to Magic House, not to mention, in time to give her the antidote, assuming Marcus and Veronica even show up to Magic House, or that it can be retrieved. Oh, my; this is impossible! I have no idea where to start. 'Oh, Regina, you have to have faith that Harriett knows what she is doing.'* Her mind raced, twisting and fretting over the possibilities. Then she heard Ms. Calderon's voice. *How am I supposed to have confidence in this place when my mother chose Magic House over me, leaving me in foster care? Ugh! Those are thoughts for another time...*

By the time the sun crested the easternmost mountain, Regina had half a plan, and that hinged on her sibling family. She needed them. She needed Pam's magical ability to call on things, Dyson's cleverness at observation, and Matthew's technical skills. All would help the success of her mission. The hard part would depend on Puddlefoot. He would have to agree to help them. *I hope he's gotten over being mad at me.*

She hit the shower before the others woke up. When she finished, Dyson and Matthew were sitting anxiously on the couch. Pam strolled passed Regina on her way to the bathroom, smirking, and winked. Regina noticed her clothes were draped neatly over her arm. Regina raised her eyebrows and grabbed the sleeve of Pam's shirt, yanking it to the ground.

"Reg!" Pam groaned. Regina snickered.

"Well?" Dyson almost screamed.

"Shh!" Regina laid her index finger over her lips.

She had no intention of explaining what was on her mind, in case the house was listening. Dyson groaned, plopping onto the couch. "They might be listening," she mouthed at Matthew and Dyson. Both boys straightened up and scanned the room suspiciously.

Pam hadn't been in the shower for more than five minutes when she emerged. She headed for her side of the room and put away her clothes. Regina was busy making beds and picking up dirty clothes.

"You don't have to do the chores of home, here," Dyson teased.

"I know," she said, shrugging. "I miss home, and I liked my chores."

"I don't miss the stables," Pam giggled. Just then, Harriett appeared in the room.

"Kids, I am here to escort you to the Great Hall for breakfast," she said, smiling.

"We're not feeling very social. May we eat in our room?" Pam asked. She wasn't about to let Harriett think they were just cheerfully going along with the promise she'd coerced them into making. And besides, if Harriett thought they were resigned to things, then maybe she wouldn't expect them to cause trouble.

"I'm with Pam. I don't feel much like seeing the student body or their insulting stares," Regina said, having caught on to Pam's genius.

"I suppose. Yes, that might be a better plan," Harriett agreed.

"So, has Marcus shown up yet?" Matthew asked.

"No, dear. He has not." Harriett watched him, trying to read his expression. For his part, Matthew keep his expression of genuine curiosity.

"Will the house get the antidote? He carries it in his right hip pocket," Pam queried.

"We know! Yes, the House's first goal is to retrieve the antidote and deliver it to the hospital for Mrs. Hillsdale. It is also going to protect the students and the four of you. This is not the first time the House has been called upon to protect our society. I do not want any of you to worry," Harriett assured them. "Oh, and I will be the first to let you know when it is all over."

"How do you know this is all going to happen today?" Dyson asked.

"The Oracle has foreseen the battle. Do not worry. Everything is going to be all right," Harriett said again. "I will have breakfast sent up." With that, she turned and left.

"Why don't I trust her?" Regina muttered.

"Because she doesn't sound convincing!" Matthew answered. The rest nodded.

Five minutes later, breakfast was sitting on the table where Sally's room had been. They had eggs, bacon, ham, cinnamon rolls, and various juices. "Eat up!" Regina snickered.

After breakfast, the children returned to the couch. Pam and Regina picked up a deck of cards and began a game of Speed, but neither of them were committed to the fast pace. Matthew flicked through station after station on the flat screen.

"Pick one, already," Dyson said, irritated. Matthew settled on a game show, tossing the remote control to Dyson, who rolled his eyes.

"Hey, Pam! Look outside!" Regina exclaimed.

"Rain!" Pam's brow wrinkled in concern. "Does a storm effect Marcus the same way it does us?"

"I think so! But the House can use it too!"

"Not good! He has the power of fire. This could be a long battle and Mrs. Hillsdale doesn't have a lot of time. All he has to do is stretch out the fight for twenty-four hours and she's a goner," Regina said. "It's already late in the morning. We're wasting precious time. We have to go!"

"But the promise…" Matthew said, jumping to his feet.

"We aren't going to fight Marcus! Get your rain gear and let's go," Regina ordered.

Five minutes later, the four of them opened the door to their room and stepped into the hall. It was empty. Not a ghost or person to be seen. "Wow, it's creepy out here," Pam whispered.

"I think Magic House is preparing for Marcus." They all startled when they heard a loud pop. "Or, he's already here!" Matthew grumbled.

"I think you're right! I bet the house hides everyone. We'd better hurry," Regina whispered.

"The students had to have been here when we showed up, the other day. We couldn't see anything or anybody, right?" Matthew said.

"But, we know what's going on and where everything is, so let's go!" Dyson picked up his pace. "Where are we going?"

They tiptoed down the hall, until they stood in front of Harriett's office. Regina knocked. No one answered. Regina pushed the door open and walked inside. The silence gave her the chills. "Come on! Come on! Hurry!" she motioned them inside.

"What are we doing?" Dyson asked, puzzled. "Going? Where are we going?" He shuddered.

"Up!" Regina stood in front of the wall where the elevator had been. "Revealelecto!" she called.

Slowly, the wall disappeared and the lift door opened to reveal the inside of the elevator. Just as they started to step in, the office door creaked. Everyone froze, their eyes fixated on the opening. A head full of semi-dark hair appeared. Regina inhaled.

"Dickson?" she exhaled, exasperated. He froze, staring wide-eyed at the four siblings. He turned a bright shade of red and swallowed hard.

"Regina! What are you doing in here?" he blurted, flabbergasted.

"Shh," she hissed. "You first. Why are you here?"

"I was… Umm, I was wanting my pouch back. You know the one Mrs. Worthington took from me the other day, in the hall," he stammered miserably. "Okay, I told. What gives with you guys?"

"Reg, come on!" Dyson said, following Matthew into the lift.

"Yeah, Reg! Let's go, before Harriett shows up!" Matthew said.

"Where's your pouch?" Regina rolled her eyes. "Get it and leave here!"

Dickson stepped up to the file cabinet, waving his hands. The middle drawer popped open. He waved his hand, again, over the open drawer and his pouch floated out.

"What's in there?" Regina asked, watching him closely.

Dickson stared back, intensely. "Nope! I'm not telling you anything else until you tell me what you're up to."

"Never mind. You're coming with us!" Pam pulled him into the elevator. Regina followed.

"Accendelecto!" Regina commanded.

"What are you doing? Let go of me!" Dickson demanded, but the elevator had already started its accent. "Where are we going?"

"Up!" Regina said, glaring.

"Up? Up where? To the top floors? We aren't allowed on the top floors!" Dickson tried to find a button to stop the elevator.

"I'm pretty sure you weren't allowed to steal your pouch back, either," Pam fired back. Dickson glared at her.

"Why did you pick now to come for your pouch?" Matthew asked.

"Well, everyone knows when the House goes into wacko mode, all the ghosts go somewhere to oversee it," Dickson said with a shrug. "I knew my pouch would be alone, so to speak." He patted his breast pocket.

"Wacko?" asked Dyson.

"Into protective mode. Someone has entered the grounds that wasn't invited."

"Aren't you scared?" Pam asked.

"Na! It happens more than you'd think." He smiled. "So, where are we going?"

"*You* aren't going anywhere! I just needed time to get away before you told on us," Pam said.

"I'm no tattletale! And since you brought me this far, if you don't take me with you, then I'll scream my head off and they'll come running," Dickson said, smirking.

The elevator opened to the foggy corridor. Dickson was poised to start hollering. "Oh, all right! But you better not cause me any trouble," Regina said. Pam pursed her lips. Regina crossed her eyes.

They followed Regina down the long hall to the redwood forest. The trees were beautifully stretching for the sky. Regina hadn't seen them in the daylight, but today's weather left them looking spooky and cold. She noticed snowflakes floating through the rain.

"Dickson, you aren't dressed for this adventure. Sure you wouldn't rather stay behind?" Pam asked.

"Oh, no. I'll be fine," he assured her.

"Puddlefoot! Puddlefoot, please! I need a favor!" Regina called. He stood at her feet in a flash, startling Regina and the others.

"Whoa! What *is* he?" Dickson gasped, stepping away.

"Dickson, meet Puddlefoot. He's a Brownie. Puddlefoot, meet Dickson. He's an unfortunate accident!" She introduced them. Puddlefoot shook Dickson's hand. Dickson stared apprehensively, but allowed the exchange. "Good! Everyone acquainted?"

"Let's get on with this," Matthew said, rolling his eyes.

"Yeah. Puddlefoot, we need a ride to the hospital!" Regina came right out with the request. Pam slapped her on the shoulder. "What? I'm running out of time! Besides, Puddlefoot prefers directness." She winked at him.

"Do you have permission for this run into town?" Puddlefoot asked.

"Yes!" Pam lied, before Regina could speak.

"Now's no time to fib, Pam. Umm, no. Not exactly!" Regina said.

"Well, then I can't allow it," Puddlefoot said, and turned to walk away. Pam grimaced and rolled her eyes.

"Puddlefoot, you told me that you respected honesty and you know of our struggle to save Mrs. Hillsdale. By the time the House gets the antidote from Marcus, she could be dead! You, of all people, know what she means to all of us. Please, help me! Please, help us!"

"Henry is still too weak to carry six people," Puddlefoot said, and started to walk away again.

"Can't we use another dragon?"

"Oh, it's easy for *you* to say! Just use another magical creature to get what you want!" Puddlefoot said sarcastically.

"Mr. Puddlefoot, umm, I thought our motto was to save all creatures great and small. Doesn't this Mrs. Hills… Hillsdale count as 'all creatures?' I mean, what about that song they teach us in school?" Dickson said. "'Welcome to Magic House! We welcome you all! Welcome to Magic House great and small…'" Dickson began to sing.

"Okay, I give! Regina, you win, but there'd better be no surprises. We slip into the hospital and back out. No other stops, right?" Puddlefoot glared. Everyone shook their heads in agreement.

Henry strolled up to Puddlefoot and stood by. "Dyson, do you think you can be the lead rider on Henry?" Puddlefoot asked.

"Yes, sir!" Dyson said with a sparkle in his eyes and a grin. Henry bent his head down to the ground and Dyson climbed aboard, making his way to the saddle. He stopped to stroke Henry between the shoulders and Henry blasted his customary fire out of his mouth and nose. Another dragon ambled up with the assistance of an elf. He looked similar to Henry, except he had blue wings and a blue blaze on his chest. Puddlefoot took his reins.

"Thank you, Melwin!" Puddlefoot said.

Dickson hadn't closed his mouth the entire time they'd been in the forest, except when he sang the little ditty. Regina took one look at him and giggled, punching Pam in the arm. "You better ride with him. He looks terrified," Pam snickered.

"This is Charlie!" Puddlefoot introduced the second dragon. "Pfffft"

Dickson, startled out of his stupor, chuckled, fanning his nose. "Yeah, he does that… A lot," Regina groaned, which got Matthew and Dyson laughing too. Before she could stop, everyone was in hysterics.

"I think I'll ride with Matt and Dy," Pam choked, stepping toward Henry. That left Regina and Dickson to ride Charlie with Puddlefoot.

"Henry, you know where we're going, so up and away with you," Puddlefoot called out.

As they climbed over the trees and into the cloud-filled sky a ghostly figure slid out from behind a tree.

"For the souls who left our house cold with fright

Give them strength to win the fight

Give them courage to help those they hold near

Give them shelter, and rid from them their fears.

Let them see the light for which they still hold within

And bring to life all they imagine."

"Much success, my darlings," Harriett said, completing the spell, and blew them a kiss as she watched them fly out of sight.

"Don't forget the invisibility dust!" Dyson screamed, as they swooped through the clouds toward the hospital.

"Pffffft… Already taken care of!"

"Oh, Puddlefoot," Regina muttered, shaking her head. Dickson was too overwhelmed to laugh or fan his nose.

Chapter Thirteen

The Rescue

The hospital roof was within sight, and a few minutes later, they were landing. Dyson guided Henry to the widest section of the rooftop with the fewest obstacles, and Charlie followed. They landed softly. Puddlefoot corralled the dragons in a corner overlooking the north parking lot. "Henry, shields!" he commanded. Henry and Charlie kept their invisibility cloaking activated.

"Okay; now remember, we collect Mrs. Hillsdale and get out of here. No messing around," Puddlefoot said, glaring at Regina.

"I'm with you Puddlefoot! I promise, we'll stick to the plan!" Regina assured him. Puddlefoot nodded, his eyes narrowed skeptically.

Dickson slid off of Charlie's side, landed with a loud thud, and crumpled to his knees. Regina was there to give him a hand up. "I'm sorry! My feet are a little cold and they hurt when I hit the ground," he said, blushing at the concern in her eyes.

"Puddlefoot, I think he's freezing! It's pouring rain and he's soaked. Tell me there is a raincoat in your pouch."

"Not in my pouch, but let's see what's in the backpack." Puddlefoot reached in the main pocket, rummaging around. Dickson stood shivering and waiting patiently.

"Puddlefoot, stop the torture! He didn't mean to insult you back at Magic House," Regina said. Dickson nodded. Puddlefoot smirked, pulling out a plastic navy rain cap. Regina handed it to Dickson. He examined it, looked at everyone else wearing theirs, and eventually placed the fashion blunder on his head. Puddlefoot snickered, but then pulled out the raincoat to match. Dickson accepted it gladly.

"Wait, wait, wait!" Puddlefoot waved his hand across and in front of Dickson. The rain that had soaked through his clothes and hair vanished and appeared in a puddle beside him. Dickson was abruptly dry; not even a little damp.

"Thank you!" Dickson bowed, smiling, and donned the rain gear.

"That was pretty cool, Puddlefoot. What else do you have in that bag?" Regina reached for it. Puddlefoot evaded her grasp and slipped the straps over his shoulders.

"Let's go! Dyson, I need you to stay here and make sure Henry and Charlie are taken care of. If we run into trouble, get them out of here!" Regina instructed.

"But…" Dyson started to protest.

"Please, Dy. It's important that our escape be secure," Regina pleaded. Dyson shrugged and clambered onto

Henry's back. Regina exhaled, relieved it wasn't a bigger argument. "Okay, good! Puddlefoot, will you go first? Remember! Everyone stick together."

"So, Dickson, just in case we need help with your magic, what can I look forward to?" Regina whispered.

"Umm, I can manipulate the metals of the earth. My pouch has gold and silver dust, some iron, and a tiny bit of lead."

"Good to know! But why did Harriett take it away from you?"

"When it's sprinkled onto a ghost they can't turn invisible for a couple of hours. Doesn't hurt them, but it makes them mad to be mortal," he said and shrugged, grinning. Regina thought for a moment.

"I was hoping it might help us move Mrs. Hillsdale," Regina sighed.

"Hey, Reg, if we had some Unicorn Horn and with his gold we could, maybe, heal Mrs. Hillsdale for a short time. I learned it in the lab, yesterday," Matthew said.

"Puddlefoot, don't you have Unicorn Horn in that pouch of yours?" Regina perked up. He nodded. "Dickson, can you separate out the gold?" He nodded. "Then we have our answer" Regina said.

"But, if we don't get her to Magic House within an hour and give her the antidote…" Matthew said.

"What?" Regina barked.

"She'll die, no matter what we do for her."

"Great! No more pressure *here*!" Pam grumbled, flailing her arms around.

"All right, it's a plan. Maybe we can find another way, once we get inside. It depends on how sick she is. Can we get out of the rain, already?" Puddlefoot moaned.

"Right! Let's go. Puddlefoot, take the lead, and Pam go next. I'll bring up the rear."

"Is she always this bossy?" Dickson whispered to Pam.

"She is the princess, after all," Pam muttered sarcastically.

"I am not a princess!" Regina yelled. "I just thought about this all last night and came up with this plan!" She began waving everyone out into the open and across the roof, toward the door.

"Well, what was your plan to get Mrs. H out? If I hadn't dragged Dickson along, then what?" Pam said, sounding put out.

Regina shrugged and said, "I never said my plan didn't have a few holes."

"Shh, you two!" Puddlefoot reached for the door.

A dark figure stepped from behind a giant dual pack, catching Regina's eye. "Look out!" she screamed, feeling a sting in her right shoulder, at the base of her neck. She flinched. "Duck!" she shrieked. Small metal balls bounced off of the door and everything around them.

"Ouch!" Pam screeched.

Dickson threw up his hands, freezing the small projectiles that were continuing to fly at them. He fought back with the person throwing the balls. Dickson's magical ability was far greater than his opponent's. Regina grinned in approval, reaching inside her raincoat and rubbing her shoulder. Her hand came back bright red. She carefully pulled her coat back over the wound, wiping her hand on her pants.

Puddlefoot raced toward the unknown person, Dyson aimed Henry in Puddlefoot's direction. "Stroke his scales!" Puddlefoot shouted. Dyson massaged him between the shoulders and Henry breathed out a flame that reached the dark figure, catching the perpetrator's sleeves on fire. Puddlefoot then doused her arms with rain water.

"No!" Veronica wailed, collapsing to the ground.

"Give it up, Veronica! We're too strong for you!"

Puddlefoot reached into his pack and pulled out a rope. He tied her hands behind her back. He then walked Veronica over to Henry, where they both vanished behind the invisibility shield. "Henry, if she moves light her up!" Puddlefoot commanded. Henry roared that he understood. A moment later, Puddlefoot walked back into the open. "Henry will keep her put," he explained.

"What should I do with these balls?" Dickson asked, still holding them. "I'll take the gold," he added, separating out the gold orbs. Puddlefoot held open his backpack and Dickson dropped the other spheres into the pack. He then dropped the gold into his own pouch.

Pam had her arm cradled up against her chest. "She's bleeding! A lot!" Matthew yelled, rushing to her side. Pam's face looked pained and had taken on a greenish tinge. Puddlefoot appeared beside her and reached into his pouch. He sprinkled a tiny bit of Unicorn Horn on her wound. Out popped a round sphere made of silver. It dropped to the ground. Her wound healed immediately and the color began to come back into Pam's cheeks. Puddlefoot picked up the single ball and dropped it into his backpack.

"Wow! That was close!" Matthew breathed a sigh of relief.

"Okay! Let's go!" Regina said, opening the door and stuffing her rain hat in her pocket. "Keep your eyes open!" The group started down the metal stairs, made the turn, and tiptoed down the next flight. It wasn't long before they reached the fifth floor. Puddlefoot opened the door and peeked in. "The coast is clear!" He disappeared and crept into the white corridor, followed by the others. "Puddlefoot, where are you?" Regina panicked.

"Pffft!"

"Oh, I had to ask," she sighed. Dickson and Matthew couldn't stop sniggering. "Guys, don't encourage him." The boys laughed harder. Regina and Pam rolled their eyes.

"Where are you children going? What is that smell?" a nurse said, waving her hand in front of her face and wrinkling her nose. "Visiting hours aren't until later this afternoon. You might want to check the bottoms of your shoes before you come back," she added. They all straightened up and stood still. Matthew snickered. Pam punched him.

"Oh, I'm sorry! My brothers, sister, and I just wanted to see our mother. We won't stay long. I promise," Pam answered her.

"I'm sorry. That isn't possible. Come back after lunch."

"But that's only fifteen minutes from now," Pam said. "The doctor called us this morning and said he didn't think she would last till this evening. Can't we please see her," Pam whimpered, waving her hand from behind her back for Regina to sneak everyone away.

"I'm so sorry, dear. I didn't realize you were here to see Mrs. Hillsdale. She can only have two visitors at a time." The nurse softened her voice. She looked up and was a little taken aback by the fact that Pam was standing all alone.

"Thank you! I'll have the others wait in the waiting room. We'll be quiet. You'll never know we're here." Pam shuffled to the door of the room. The nurse smiled and returned to her station.

The door swung shut as Pam stepped inside room 524. Mrs. Hillsdale was lying very still in her hospital bed. She had more tubes and wires coming out of her than she had the last time they were there. Her knife wound oozed green goo and was twice as large. Regina covered her mouth to keep from retching. Matthew took Regina's hand and squeezed it. Regina swallowed hard, forcing her stomach contents back where they belonged.

"How are we going to get her out of here without the alarms going off on the monitors?" Pam whispered.

"You guys get her ready to travel. I'll meet you on the roof," Regina said softly, watching from the door. They all shrugged. Pam nodded.

"Matthew, you know more about this cure thing than we do. Get to curing her," Pam said, waving him to step closer to Mrs. Hillsdale.

"I need two parts Unicorn Horn, and one-part gold," Matthew instructed. Pam grabbed a small drinking glass off of Mrs. Hillsdale's tray table and passed it to Dickson. He held open his pouch and twitched his fingers. Flakes of gold that amounted to a pinch flew out and into the glass. "Puddlefoot, some Unicorn Horn, if you please."

Puddlefoot once again reached into his pouch and took two pinches of the substance that looked a lot like raw sugar, and put it into the glass. Matthew stirred with his index finger. "I need enough water to make a paste." Pam dribbled a few drops of water from Mrs. Hillsdale's pitcher into the glass. Again, Matthew stirred. "I guess this looks right. Cross your fingers that it works," Matthew sighed, daubing the mixture onto her open wound.

Mrs. Hillsdale's eyes fluttered open, "What's going on?" she whispered, confused.

"Don't talk! We're getting you out of here and taking you to Magic House," Matthew explained.

"Regina, go!" Pam commanded.

Regina slipped out the door and up the hall. She heard the commotion in the room she'd just left. *Don't worry about them and focus on what you have to do.*

"Hi!" she said to the nurse behind the counter.

"Yes, dear. Can I help you?" the nurse said.

"Oh, I can't stand seeing my mother that sick, so I stepped out to get some air. I was wondering if you could explain those machines beeping behind you. I was thinking about becoming a nurse, someday."

"Those are the heart monitors. They tell us all about the patient's oxygen levels, pulse rate, blood pressures; stuff like that."

"Well, which one is my mom's?"

"The third from the left."

Regina squinted her eyes and felt the magic rise in her. She sent the dials spinning, causing the alarm to go off. The nurse looked up startled. She inhaled sharply and started to run for room 524, but Regina made the monitor beside it, do the same thing. The nurse turned back staring at the two monitors. She held her breath, returned to the panel of machines, pushed buttons, and twisted the knobs. She tried to get them back to center, but they continued to spin. Regina smiled thinly and set off the next one in the row. By this time, the nurse was flummoxed to the point of ringing for help.

Regina glanced over her shoulder to see Mrs. Hillsdale wrapped in a blanket, with her rain cap on her head. Pam, Matthew, and Dickson tiptoed down the corridor to the stairwell door. They all disappeared from the hall.

"Pfffft!"

Regina exhaled, "Umm, I guess I'll get out of your hair. It looks like you have a real mess, here." She backed up a few steps before she turned and ran for the door leading to the roof. As she ducked into the stairwell, she set all the monitors back to normal, except Mrs. Hillsdale's. It was now ringing because she wasn't hooked up to it any longer. The nurse groaned loudly, but didn't go straight to Mrs. Hillsdale's bedside. She continued to fiddle with the dials.

"Puddlefoot, you didn't have to get my attention by expelling gas! You could have tapped me on the shoulder," Regina complained. "What is that nurse going to think of me?"

"I would have, but look at your shoulder," he said, glaring. Regina's raincoat had moved enough for her shoulder to be exposed. She grabbed the corner of the plastic coat and pulled it back in place.

"Oh, imagine that! It's fine! Just a little blood..."

"Your whole shoulder is bright red," Puddlefoot said, pulling the coat back and examining her blood-stained shirt. "Did you get hit by one of Veronica's pellets?"

"Yeah, I guess. But it doesn't hurt... I'll be fine."

"I hope so, because I used all the Unicorn Horn on Mrs. Hillsdale and won't be able to heal you."

"It's fine. Don't worry," Regina assured Puddlefoot, not telling him she was starting to feel a little woozy.

Puddlefoot watched her for a moment and said, "Let me have a look at it."

"No, really! I'm fine! We need to get Mrs. Hillsdale back to Magic House," Regina said. Puddlefoot pulled out a plastic poncho and covered Mrs. Hillsdale with it.

"Great! What are we going to do with Veronica?" Pam snorted.

"I say we leave her here," Matthew said with a chuckle.

"I agree! Untie her and I'll keep her trapped in a cyclone until we get out of her range!"

"That will work," Puddlefoot nodded.

Pam and Dickson took Mrs. Hillsdale and joined Dyson, on Henry, while Regina created a whirlwind and trapped Veronica inside. Matthew, Puddlefoot, Regina, and Charlie waited on the roof for a few minutes, letting Henry get farther away.

"What do you think happened to Marcus?" Matthew muttered.

"Good question!" Regina replied. "Okay, Charlie! Let's go!" Puddlefoot nudged him. Charlie leaped into the air and headed straight for the clouds. Regina dropped the whirlwind when she couldn't see the rooftop any longer. A few minutes later, Charlie was above the clouds.

"Whoop! Whoop! We did it!" Matthew cheered. His voice echoed throughout the clouds. Regina smiled, patting Matthew on the back. She was feeling weaker and weaker by the minute.

Charlie caught up with Henry and the two dragons flew side by side, high above the clouds, in order to keep everyone dry. "How much time does Mrs. H have left?" Pam shouted.

"Forty-five minutes," Puddlefoot answered. "Take her down, Henry." They dropped below the cloud cover.

"There's Magic House," Dyson pointed excitedly.

"I hope they have the antidote ready!" Regina said, sighed, and slumped over.

"Regina! Regina! Wake up!" Matthew screamed. "What's wrong with her?"

"She was hit with one of Veronica's metal balls," Puddlefoot answered.

"So, heal her!"

"I can't! I don't have any Unicorn Horn, but I have a feeling it wouldn't work anyhow," Puddlefoot muttered.

The forest was within sight. The two dragons swooped through the wind-ruffled trees, landing in the snow. The energy of the storm had begun to increase, with lightning and thunder hammering the school. Puddlefoot lifted Regina down to Dickson. He and Matthew carried her through the door, into the hall, and laid her on the floor. Dickson stretched his sweater sleeve out and wiped the snowflakes from her face.

"She is so still and her breathing is so shallow. Is she going to be all right?" Dickson asked.

Puddlefoot whistled for Melwin. He strolled out of the forest. Dyson handed Henry's reins over to Melwin and charged to Regina's side. Puddlefoot handed Charlie's reins over to Melwin and whispered something. Melwin took the dragons and hurried back into the forest.

"Pam, Matt, take Mrs. Hillsdale to the infirmary. I'll take care of Regina." He led them into the corridor and down the hall. Mrs. Hillsdale appeared to be perfectly healthy, but her time was running short.

Puddlefoot brought up the elevator and reached in, punching the button to the basement. "What's wrong with Reg?" Pam asked.

"She was hit with one of Veronica's balls and she's lost a lot of blood," Puddlefoot explained.

"Well, fix her!"

"I don't have any more Unicorn Horn! I sent Melwin to get me some. He's probably administering it as we speak. Now, get downstairs! Remember, you aren't hidden by the cloak of the house because we left, so when you get to the hospital, Pam, say this spell:

'All that was and now is obscured

Draw on our magic, which is more matured.

Return to brilliance and keep us secure.'

It should blend you back into the hospital," he explained, letting the elevator doors close.

Puddlefoot ran back to the forest entrance. Dickson and Dyson fidgeted, watching Melwin dab Unicorn Horn on her wound. "Nothing is happening," Melwin groaned.

"I was afraid of that," Puddlefoot muttered, pacing, and thinking. He didn't know what to do for her. *Only one person could help!*

Chapter Fourteen

Pffffft!

"Madam Harriett!" Puddlefoot called out. She appeared almost instantly.

"Oh, my! What happened?"

"She was hit by one of Veronica's metal spheres, but…" Puddlefoot looked around, wondering if he should say what he was thinking.

"Yes?" Madam Harriett said, her eyes wide.

"I just wondered if, maybe, the ball that hit Regina was marked with the same poison as Mrs. Hillsdale," he whispered the last. "You know, I could be wrong, because Pam was also hit and she healed up just fine."

"We need to get her to the garden," Harriett said with a frown.

"What about the antidote?" Dyson asked.

"We do not have it yet," Harriett said softly.

"We just sent Mrs. H. down to the hospital to get it. She has forty minutes left," Dickson said, wiping the melted snow off of his brow.

"The House has been fighting Marcus since early this morning. He brought reinforcements, and it is almost like he is stalling. You children were correct in thinking he might take this course," she sighed. "Time is running short for Mrs. Hillsdale, but we have days before Regina succumbs to the poison; plenty of time to figure out the potion."

"The garden? Why the garden?" Dyson snapped. His heart was beginning to pound in his chest. They were talking about Regina and not including him in the discussion. Dyson felt the tears sting his eyes. Harriett wrapped her arms around his shoulders, consoling him.

"We need to take her to the unicorns. If the male unicorn will offer his horn, it might be enough. I think it is worth a try."

"Will it help if I call for the ball that's in her shoulder?" Dickson asked.

"Good idea!" Harriett motioned for him to continue. "Be careful not to touch it! We do not need *you* infected," she warned.

"Puddlefoot, will you go and ask Grigor to help us?"

"Yes, Madam Harriett."

"Okay, Dickson; carefully pull out the metal ball." Dyson pulled back Regina's raincoat and stretched the neck on her shirt. The tiny hole from the ball was already starting to swell and fester. Dyson hid his eyes.

Dickson raised his hands over the hole and squinting his eyes, he called for the ball. It took a few seconds and

Regina winced in pain, but the sphere finally appeared. Dickson held it suspended in mid-air.

"Where do you want it?" Dickson asked, glancing at Mrs. Worthington. She produced a small yellow envelope. Dickson dropped the ball inside of it.

"Thank you, Dickson! I would like the spheres you collected from Veronica, on the roof tonight, as well."

"The only ones I have are the gold... Puddlefoot has the others. Since that ball is lead and the one we took out of Pam was silver, wouldn't it be logical that the poison ones are lead?" Dickson asked.

"I do not think we can take the chance, and since you mixed them with your magic dust, it could be contaminated." Harriett held her hand out for the pouch.

"But it can't be contaminated in my pouch! We used my dust on Mrs. Hillsdale!"

"I see. But I still need your pouch." She snapped her fingers and waited for Dickson to place the pouch in her hand.

"Ohhh! How did you know, anyway?" he groaned, handing it over reluctantly.

"Thank you!" She glared, regarding him with knitted brows.

Puddlefoot was returning, and walked toward them with a seven-foot man covered in shaggy, matted hair. "What is *that*?" Dyson whispered to Dickson.

"He is not comfortable with humans, so please be respectful," Harriett shushed them.

"No problem!" Dickson smiled, punching Dyson.

"Grigor, we need your help," Harriett said. "Will you please carry Regina down to the garden?" Grigor picked Regina up under the arms and knees, securing her tightly in his arms.

"What is he?" Dickson whispered to Puddlefoot.

"A Yeti," Puddlefoot said.

"Cool!" Dyson and Dickson said together.

The elevator opened onto the first floor hallway. "This place looks just like it did last week; full of junk and rat infested," Dyson choked.

"Now, be mindful of our uninvited guests. They are lost within the walls of Magic House. We do not want to be spotted, if at all possible." Harriett grabbed Dyson by the collar and pulled him back into the lift. She scanned the hall. "Coast is clear!" She walked out first and Dyson followed reluctantly.

"I don't understand why we aren't hidden like everyone else." Dyson said.

"Because you left Magic House this morning, losing the cloak. The House is seeing you as it does any foreigner."

Puddlefoot rolled his eyes and disappeared. He didn't like being out in the open, especially on the bottom floors. Humans didn't understand him or his kind, and he would rather skip encounters with them all together. But he liked

Regina, even though she had tricked him a couple of days earlier. He knew she had a good heart and he was worried about her now.

"Pfft!" All this stress made his stomach upset. He hoped no one heard or smelled it.

"Puddlefoot!" Dickson held his nose. "I'd disappear after that silent *air freshener*, too!" Dickson snorted. Dyson snickered.

"Mrs. Worthington, where did you go?" Dickson asked. "I'd say you two were chickens! Leaving two kids and a Yeti to do all the fighting! If I remember my studies, Yetis have no magic! How'd I get myself into this fight, anyway?" he mumbled. Grigor whined a long growl.

"Trust me, this is better. If you are spotted, they will not know we are here and we can protect you better," Harriett sniffed.

"Pffffft!"

"Oh, Puddlefoot!" everyone said at the same time.

"That ought to give us away for sure! My eyes are burning!" Dickson sniggered. Dyson snorted loudly, trying to suppress his laughter. Grigor moaned softly.

"Quick! Turn to the right and head for the foyer. Go that way, where the light is shining through the windows." Harriett pointed in the direction of the front doors. The house healed about six feet ahead of them as they made their way down the hall and into the entryway. Dickson was in awe, watching the rubble float into place and turn the hall and foyer into flawless, perfect rooms. Behind them the paint, plaster, and carpet crumbled back into the ramshackle mess it had been.

"Dyson, is this what the house did when you guys showed up for the first time?" Dickson whispered. The silence proved to be unnerving for him.

"No! We got lost for hours at first, climbing through holes and tripping over bricks. But the worst part, was the giant, glowing orb that followed us," Dyson shivered.

"At the time, we were really scared, but now that I think back on it, I think it was a teacher making sure we didn't get hurt," Dyson said thoughtfully.

"Was Regina with you?"

"No. I was with Matt, and she was with Sally, our little sister. Why all the questions?"

"I'm just trying to fill the time and figure her out. She seems a lot older than twelve," Dickson said.

"Nah. She's just Reg! She likes to make everyone think she's this tuff chick, but she cries a lot when no one is looking. I've heard her," Dyson said with a shrug. Dickson smiled.

They'd reached the front door, stepping out onto the porch, and looking down at the many steps. "We are out in the open. Marcus and his lot can see us. We must hurry into the trees," Harriett urged.

"Isn't the forest going to look deathly and icky?" Dyson asked.

"I have a spell that will allow you to see it's greatness. The problem is… Magic House will lose it's cloak and the Cobbleports will see also. When that happens, Grigor will become visible too. I just hope we can find the unicorns and get back inside before Marcus discovers us," Harriett explained. Grigor growled.

"You mean he's been invisible all this time, too?" Dickson blushed. "I bet we looked pretty silly, walking beside a floating girl."

"Watch your step! It is wet," Harriett said, ignoring Dickson's rambling.

Sheets of rain fell from the sky. The wind whipped from all directions, making it difficult to navigate. Dyson missed the bottom step and stumbled into a puddle on the driveway. "Dyson, are you okay?" Dickson choked, scooping him up. Dyson's pants dripped with water.

"Yeah, but now I'm all wet! Never mind me, though. Let's get Regina to the garden!" Puddlefoot appeared and waved his hands. The water flew out of Dyson's pants and returned to the puddle on the drive. "Thanks!" Dyson said, amazed.

"There they are!" Everyone turned to see Marcus hanging out of an upstairs window. "Regina, I'm coming for your magic!"

"Ohh, what do we do?!" Dyson exclaimed.

"Get to the garden!" Harriett said. Dyson looked back at the window. Marcus was waving his hands in a circular motion and mumbling something.

"We need to hurry!" Just as Dyson said that, the House filled in the window with bricks. Marcus was blocked.

Puddlefoot picked up Dyson and threw him over his shoulder. Dickson chuckled at the sight of Dyson flying through the air.

"Quick! This way," Harriett shouted. They followed her voice to the south end of the garden. "Just keep running in this direction!" Dyson's stomach hurt from the bouncing up and down on Puddlefoot's shoulder.

"Pffft! Pffft! Pffft!" Puddlefoot exploded with every step he took, but no one was laughing, now.

"Through here! Hurry! Hurry!" Harriett yelled. "We are almost there! Just through these trees!"

"Where are we going?" Dickson grunted. "You know if I had my pouch, I could hurl bullets at him!" he glared at Mrs. Worthington. She didn't answer or look in his direction.

"Here we are! Get inside there!" Harriett pointed.

"It's dark!" Dyson complained.

"Don't worry," Puddlefoot puffed. He turned visible, and reaching into the backpack, he pulled out a flashlight. Dickson breathed a sigh of relief.

"Dyson, lead the way!" Harriett ordered. They cautiously followed the light deeper and deeper into the cavern.

"I hope there are no female dragons in here," Dyson mumbled.

"Female dragons? I hadn't -- considered that," Dickson whispered, staring blindly into the darkness.

"I think we should stop here," Harriett whispered.

Puddlefoot reached into his pack and pulled out a lantern and some matches. Grigor lay Regina down. Puddlefoot lit the lantern and set it on the ground next to Regina. Dyson knelt beside Regina, using her rain hat to make a pillow, and wiped the moisture from her face with his sleeve.

The light reflected off the walls, catching Dickson's eye. "Look how the light makes the metal ore sparkle," Dickson said, drawing everyone's attention to the cave walls. He walked closer to get a better look.

"Where are the unicorns?" Dyson groaned.

Dickson looked over his shoulder, brushed the cave wall with his hands, and rubbed them together. He then dropped a dozen metal balls into his pants pocket. He repeated the process several times.

"Puddlefoot, can you find the unicorns?" Harriett requested.

"You know, Madam Harriett, they only come when they want," Puddlefoot shrugged. "I'll go wait at the entrance." Grigor followed him.

"How about you give me my pouch, and when your unicorn comes, we mix his horn with gold and bring her back to life," Dickson interrupted.

"Good try Dickson, but no. What are you doing?" Harriett asked. Dickson turned around and walked back to the group.

"Just looking!" he said, with his hands behind his back.

"That would put Regina in the same predicament as Mrs. Hillsdale," Harriett finished her thought. "We are never going to defeat Marcus without Regina's magic," Dyson complained.

"They are here! I can't believe they are here!" Puddlefoot exclaimed excitedly. Grigor picked up Regina and carried her to the entrance of the cave. He lay her at the foot of the male unicorn and stepped away. Wide eyes and gaping mouths showed on the faces of the small group as they watched from the shadows of the cavern.

The female lowered herself to her knees and the male straddled Regina. He sniffed her shoulder, raised up, and drove his horn through the wound in her shoulder. Regina screeched in pain, writhing. The male unicorn pulled the horn from her shoulder, stepped away, and bowed to the small group. He snorted and began to leave.

"Thank you very much," Harriett said, running to Regina's side to console her. She was coming to. The unicorns nodded and left.

Harriett pulled Regina's shirt back and saw that the injury was healing. In fact, it was almost closed. "Is she going to be all right now?" Dyson fell to his knees at Regina's side.

"The wound is healed, but it will only buy us some time. She still carries the poison," Harriett whispered.

"Let's move her back inside," Puddlefoot suggested, and Grigor carried her where she would be dry. The rain continued to fall outside the cave, giving them cover and washing away their footprints so that Marcus wouldn't be able to track them.

Regina started to rally, and rubbing her brow, she murmured, "Where am I?"

Dyson latched himself to her neck, "A male unicorn jabbed you with his horn! We're hiding in a cave, and we don't know if a female dragon lives in here," Dyson spluttered, overwhelmed.

"Huh?"

"Marcus is out there, hunting us," Dickson groaned.

"Where's Mrs. H?"

"In the infirmary, with Matthew and Pam," Harriett said.

"Help me sit up." Puddlefoot put his arm around her shoulders and lifted her gently.

"Man, my shoulder doesn't hurt as much!" Regina felt around the injury. Her eyes widened, "Do you guys see the big hairy man, over there?"

"Oh, yeah. That's Grigor. He's a Yeti," Dyson said calmly.

"Okay! Good to know! Hey, Grigor." Regina waved and smiled.

"I got the ball out."

"Thanks!"

"Let me have a look," Puddlefoot said. Regina let him stretch the neck of her shirt and examine the wound. "It looks a lot better!"

"How do you feel?" Dickson whispered to Regina.

"Sore… It feels like someone stuck their hand inside my shoulder and mixed things up," she said, wiggling it around in a circle. "But not bad. So… What's up, gang? Are we going to sit here in the dirt and wait for Marcus to find us?" Regina asked. She was tired of talking about herself.

"No! As soon as you can move, we are going back in the mansion and wait for it to get the vial from Marcus," Harriett insisted.

"Regina, I know that look… What do you have in mind?" Puddlefoot exhaled with a loud groan.

"Seems to me, Pam and I practiced this part, the other day," Regina winked, totally ignoring Harriett.

"No! I will not allow it!"

"Not that you care, but Pam's not here!" Dickson's sarcasm continued to grow.

"So, Dickson, do you think you can take Pam's place?" Regina stared, waiting for a reaction.

"If it gets me out of this cave and there's a sandwich waiting for me, I can!"

"Is anyone listening to me? I absolutely forbid you to engage Marcus!" Harriett stomped her foot. "Besides the promise!"

"The promise doesn't apply here. You brought us out in the open... technically." Regina said. Harriett glared.

"Madam Harriett, he has already seen us. It's unlikely that we would get past him anyway, and Mrs. Hillsdale is running out of time. We have to get that vial," Puddlefoot said, patting her back. She stared between the three of them and gritted her teeth, but calmed and sighed.

"Good! Here's what I think we should do..." Regina huddled Puddlefoot and Dickson together and whispered her thoughts.

"Pffft!"

"Good! Smells like he agrees! How about you Dickson? You in?" He shrugged with a nod. "Harriett... Mom, take care of Dyson. Don't let that dragon over there, get him," she giggled and pointed into the darkness of the cave. To their surprise, two big red eyes were watching them closely. Dyson jumped and clung to Harriett. Regina giggled some more. "She's fine, as long as you stay out of her nest," Regina explained.

"How do you know that?!" Dyson stuttered.

"She told me, of course. When I was asleep! Never mind. Just stay put!"

"Here, Dickson," Harriett handed him back his pouch.

"Thanks!" Dickson leaned in and whispered something to Puddlefoot, while patting his hip pocket.

"Good idea, but you'll have to be careful!"

"Let's go boys!" Regina said, watching them. "You going to let me in on the secret?"

Puddlefoot studied her for a moment, "No, I don't think so."

The three walked out of the cave into the pouring rain. Grigor joined them. Regina pulled her hat down over her ears and buttoned up her coat. She snickered as they stood outside the cave getting their bearings.

"What's so funny?" Dickson said, squinting at her.

"I think our soaked Yeti smells worse than Puddlefoot!"

He chuckled, "I'd have to agree with you!"

"Let's go. I want to get as far from Dyson as I can. It wouldn't do for Marcus to know where he is." She led them through the woods, away from the cave, and to the opposite edge of the garden. She could see Magic House, its crumbling facade silhouetted against the blackness of the sky. "This looks like a good place to confront Marcus. We have protection, ammunition, and the element of surprise."

Regina had to stand in the open for this part, but it couldn't be helped. She closed her eyes, drawing her breath in, deep and cleansing. She felt the connection with the house and the garden building inside of her, removing the pain from her shoulder, and giving her confidence.

Dickson watched in awe, just as Pam had done. He saw the other magical creatures come out of their homes to stand with her. After a while, her eyes fluttered open and she blew a kiss to her audience. They returned to their hiding places. A fairy fluttered close to Regina's ear and said something in a high squeaky voice. Regina looked across the lawn. Marcus had clambered out the front door and was stepping through the rubble of the steps and porch. "Here he comes, and he's not alone," she said, pointing to the house.

"Did you practice fighting against five, no, make that *six* Cobbleports?" Puddlefoot said sarcastically.

"Not exactly…" Regina chewed on the inside of her lip and cracked her knuckles. "This would be better if Pam were here." The Yeti emitted a long, deep growl.

"Well she's not, so think of something else. I'm only useful with spells, charms, and enchantments, and I can manipulate water, streams, and ponds. I have to say water is my forte," Puddlefoot bragged.

"Get down, now!" Dickson shouted, heading toward the grass. Regina followed his movement.

"There she is!" Marcus yelled.

Chapter Fifteen

Cobbleport's Attack

"Puddlefoot!" screamed Regina. "Get out of here!" He disappeared and scampered up a pine tree. Regina began gathering the wind, spinning it into a whirlwind. Thunder sounded. Lightning flashed.

"Ohhh!" Puddlefoot groaned, perched on a branch high in the tree. "Marcus is grabbing the energy. A lightning bolt will be…" Puddlefoot screamed as a bolt of lightning streaked toward them. Regina wasn't about to be swayed. She absorbed the bolt of energy within her whirlwind. A fireball followed. She missed it! The ball of fire blasted a hollow log. Tiny screams echoed in Regina's ears. She gasped, letting the whirlwind collapse. The energy dispersed all around them, causing their skin to prickle.

"What are you doing?" Puddlefoot hissed.

"I can't… That was an elf," she bent down and stroked his forehead. The tears began to trickle down her cheeks. "He killed an elf and it's my fault. I called them out for their magic!" Regina shuddered as she watched the elf vanish forever from her sight.

"Still the little girl, Regina?" Marcus mocked her. Regina's body stiffened. The tears dried up. She forced a breath, holding it, and glared at Marcus, but she couldn't move. She snorted loudly. How could she risk injuring another innocent being? This was real. This was not a game she was playing in the forest, at home with the boys. Lives were being lost. Someone else could die. *I could die!* Her bravado gave way to fear, and it gripped her.

"Complete the circle!" Marcus called out, motioning to his team. They inched their way around Regina and company. "I'll bet I can find some more of your little friends… Shall I blast away that hollow tree stump?" Marcus taunted.

Regina's eyes grew wider and her fingers began to tingle from the lack of oxygen.

"Regina, get it together! You have to move! Pick up your feet and breathe!" a little voice in her head screamed. Movement seemed impossible, no matter what she told herself.

"Dickson, the backpack!" Puddlefoot shouted, dropping it out of the tree at Dickson's feet. "Regina! Regina, snap out of it!" Dickson positioned the pack and opened the pocket containing the metal balls. He magically extracted the metal spheres from his hip pocket, adding them to the ones in the pack.

"We can't do this without you, Regina!" Puddlefoot growled in the deepest, angriest voice anyone had ever heard from him.

Dickson closed his eyes and lifted the projectiles out of the backpack. "Regina, help me!" Dickson swore as a lightning bolt crashed between him and Regina. She jumped, startled from her paralysis. Seeing Dickson's projectiles strung out reminded her of what was at stake.

"Focus!" she mouthed aloud. Raising her hands, she started building the whirlwind again.

"That's it! She's back! Phew!" called Puddlefoot to Dickson.

Lightning bolts and fireballs crashed around her. Marcus noticed she'd joined the fight again. He fired fireballs in her direction between lightning bolts. The storm's energy had slowed, irritating him. He swore.

"Pfffffft!"

"Dad-gum, Puddlefoot! Shoot those at the Cobbleports!" Dickson chuckled. Regina ignored them and concentrated on her whirlwind, building it into a roaring cyclone, collecting everything Marcus heaved their way. Marcus and the Cobbleports ducked for cover when she directed it in their direction.

"Get around behind them!" Marcus screamed, ducking for cover behind a giant boulder. "Complete the circle!"

"Grigor, keep them at bay!" hollered Puddlefoot.

Grigor stepped out of the thicket of trees in the forest. He yanked some of the smaller trees out of the ground, roots and all, and heaved them at the Cobbleports.

"Now!" Regina whispered to Dickson. He threw a couple dozen small balls into the cyclone.

Regina flung the cyclone at several Cobbleports as they left the protection of their hiding places to get behind her. The cyclone gobbled them up, spinning them inside the fierce wind with the lightning, forests debris, and lead balls.

"Stop! Stay out of her line of fire," Marcus cautioned the others. "The House must be enhancing her magic."

"Ramon, take her down, but remember she's mine!" Marcus shouted.

Ramon, also with the power of wind, started a cyclone of his own, bigger and faster than Regina's. It consumed hers and then began to track toward Dickson. Dickson hunkered down behind between two boulders. Grigor picked up a three-foot-tall rock and along with Regina's power to move objects with her mind, they heaved it at Ramon. He used his whirlwind to block it. The two massive forces collided into an explosion. Pieces of rock splintered in all directions with the two main halves falling to the ground. Three Cobbleports, two men and a woman, were spit out on the front lawn. They lay face down, beaten and battered.

"Thanks, Grigor!" Regina shouted, catching her breath as she darted behind a large pine tree.

"Metal balls, back in the pack," Dickson called for all the small balls. They flew back to him at lightning speed and dropped back into the pack.

"That was pretty impressive, but if Grigor hadn't been here, we would be toast. Do you have any other brilliant moves?" Dickson whispered in a snarky voice. Regina rolled her upper lip up and glared in his direction.

"We took out three with that move! Jeez! And as a matter of fact, I do! Stay here and wait for my signal! Then fling those balls straight at them. Remember use the storm!" She exhaled and charged out from behind the tree.

"The storm?" he said confused.

"Yeah! Absorb its energy," she shouted, diving for a downed tree and rolling up against it. A fireball was headed for the rock that Dickson was hiding behind. Regina focused on the bright yellow and red light, and jerked her head and eyes back in the direction of Marcus. The ball of fire changed directions, striking Marcus in the hands from where it was conjured, blowing up in his face. He screeched in pain, collapsing to his knees.

"Cool!" Regina cheered, ducking behind the log again.

"Yeah, your own magic can hurt you more when used against you," Puddlefoot said. Regina raised her eyebrows and smirked. "Just trying to help," Puddlefoot shrugged.

"I'm coming!" a female Cobbleport hollered. Marcus held his hands out. They were consumed with flames. She directed the rain into a waterfall and drenched his hands to stop the burning. She repositioned herself behind a split dead tree stump.

Dickson closed his eyes and concentrated on the storm. "Feel the power," Regina coached. "Feel the energy grow inside you!" Dickson inhaled. He took another deep breath and held it, pulling the projectiles from the pocket of the backpack.

Regina focused on the tree stump where the water Cobbleport was hiding. "Tree stump," she called. It rattled and broke loose. Regina threw it straight at Marcus. He ducked, protecting his hands and rolling up to his knees. His hands dripped melted flesh and his hair sizzled around his face.

"More water, Sheila!" Marcus screamed, not caring that she was out in the open. Sheila crouched, unprotected, trembling with fear. She conjured the rain into another stream. Dickson shot several metal spheres, at lightning speed in her direction. They found their mark, pummeling her and knocking her to the ground. The waterfall disappeared. A giant black hole opened up, swallowing her.

Marcus moaned. Ramon appeared from his hiding place. He raced to the female Cobbleport lying on the front lawn. He lifted her into his arms and followed Sheila through the hole before it closed.

"Nicely done!" Puddlefoot said. "Send them running!" Dickson looked up into the tree and grinned. He retrieved half of the balls, dropping them back in the pack.

Grigor whined a long steady growl of warning. Dickson dove into the mud as a fireball zinged over his head. Fireballs continued to come at them from both sides. Dirt flew, along with pinecones and other forest debris. Regina crouched behind her fallen tree.

"Who'd we miss?"

"Look! There's only one Cobbleport on the grass." Dickson pointed out.

"The other one must have come to. He's hiding behind that rock to your left!" Puddlefoot shouted.

"Ready?" Regina called to Dickson. He nodded. "Big Rock!" Regina called to the huge boulder shielding the Cobbleport. It was twice the size of the one she and Pam had relocated earlier that week. It shook and rumbled, breaking apart from its base. No one moved as they stared in amazement, watching it float through the air. She gathered more strength from the storm and heaved the giant boulder at Marcus, leaving the fireball throwing Cobbleport flummoxed and out in the open. Marcus pulled a lightning bolt from the storm, but with his damaged hands he wasn't able to direct it fast enough and it shattered it into smaller pieces, burying him in the rubble.

Dickson stepped out from behind his boulder and shot the projectiles toward the exposed Cobbleport. The demon avoided the spheres and still managed to get off a couple of fireballs. They all missed their targets. The ground opened up. The Cobbleport jumped through the black hole, sending a fireball soaring in Regina's direction at the last second. Puddlefoot intercepted it, drowning it with his own waterfall.

Marcus roared, working his way out from under the debris of rocks. "Regina Worthington!" he screamed with all his might.

Actually it's Edwards. She clinched her teeth as the wind picked up, gusting. Lightning bounced all around them and thunder deafened their efforts to communicate. Dickson was struggling to return his projectiles into the backpack, when the wind sent them out of control.

"Ouch!" Dickson moaned.

Puddlefoot had his hands full, swaying and swinging in the tree. "This can't be good," Regina mumbled to herself as she held tight to the tree branches of her downed pine tree. Puddlefoot flew over her head and landed with a thud. "Dickson! Dickson what happened?" she screamed through the blowing wind.

"I was hit by one of my metal spheres," he shouted.

"Was it a poison one?"

"I don't know! It's still in my leg!

"Well, get it out!" Regina screamed, fighting against the wind and debris in the air to get to Puddlefoot.

"Ahhh!" Dickson screamed. "Nope! It's a silver one!" He sounded relieved.

"Put pressure on the wound to stop the bleeding!" Puddlefoot's shouts were barely heard.

"Puddlefoot, are you all right?" Regina called, relieved to hear his voice.

"Kind of… Got the wind knocked out of me, but I don't think anything is broken," he said hoarsely.

"If you can move, I could use a little help over here," Regina called.

"I'll do my best," he grumbled, inching across the ground. "Where are you?" he called softly, when he reached the fallen tree she'd been hiding behind. Just then, Grigor scooped Puddlefoot up and delivered him to Regina.

"Thanks Grigor!" Puddlefoot patted him on the leg. "Regina, how'd you get *here*?"

"I was coming to you when the wind grabbed me and blew me into these pine trees! I have so much dirt and junk in my eyes, I'm blind."

"Dickson, where's Marcus?"

"He and the guy on the grass are still in the same places."

"Who's stirring the wind?"

"Pffff!"

"Puddlefoot, really?! Never mind! My eyes are killing me!"

"I think it's just the storm gaining intensity. Marcus can't manipulate the wind!"

Grigor cradled her head in his big hairy arm, blocking the wind with his oversized hairy body, and Puddlefoot gathered the rain from the storm. He lifted her eyelids and directed a steady stream, rinsing her eyes over and over, until they were cleaned out. "Wow! That's better! Thanks!" She hugged his neck.

"Pffft!"

"Puddlefoot!"

"We have company," Dickson screamed.

"What? Who?" Regina covered her eyes and yelled to Dickson. A ball of fire flew in her direction. She quickly ducked back into the cluster of trees. Grigor had a solid hold on Puddlefoot so he didn't blow away, and they were shielded by a large boulder. The fireball slammed into a pile of brush that burst into flames. Puddlefoot doused it with water.

"Look! Across the grass!" Dickson shouted. Regina recognized the same raincoat and hat she'd been wearing.

"Oh no! Pam!" A gust blew into them, causing Regina to tumble backwards. She slammed against an oak tree before Grigor caught her.

"Pam, get down!" Regina screeched, realizing Pam was walking into Marcus's line of fire. Thunder clapped, drowning out her voice. Regina sent a shot of lightning at Marcus to distract him from Pam. It exploded at his feet. He danced away, unharmed. Pam was still coming straight for him, "Pam! Get down!" Regina shouted. *What is she doing?*

Marcus screamed in pain, trying to heave a fireball at Dickson. Regina watched a gust take it in another direction. "Pam is calling the wind and throwing it at Marcus," Regina hollered. He raised his hand with another fireball, but a gust took it just as it left his hand and landed it on his injured comrade, lying on the ground.

"Argh!" Marcus growled, watching the Cobbleport vanish.

"Pam! Get back!" Regina stood and screamed at her, but it was too late. Marcus collected the static from the thunder, crying in agony, he guided the bolt of lightning straight into Pam. She crumpled to the ground.

Regina screamed, bolting from cover, into the open.

"Regina! No!" Dickson shouted. Grigor snatched her around the waist, holding her tight. The tears burst from her eyes. She couldn't move. She couldn't think. Her energy and will evaporated. Grigor deposited her next to Puddlefoot, behind the boulder.

"Pam! We have to get to Pam!" Regina tried to wiggle free. Puddlefoot held her firmly and wouldn't let her move.

"Listen to me!" he shouted, shaking Regina by the shoulders. "Pam is gone! You can't help her, but we'll *all* be dead if you don't snap out of it!" His voice calmed and became more soothing. He hugged her tightly.

"What was she thinking?! Why didn't she protect herself?!" Regina cried.

"I don't know," Puddlefoot whispered, shaking his head. "Maybe she was confused."

Regina thought for a moment, wiping the tears off her cheeks. "Okay, let's end thi…" Regina snarled. "Dickson, what's happening?" She heard no answer. "Dickson!"

"Yeah, I'm still here," he groaned.

"How's the leg?"

"Leaking…"

"How bad?"

"I'll make it."

"Where's Marcus?"

"I assume, in the same place. He's made a barricade out of the tree stump and the pieces of rock you threw at him."

"What should we do, Puddlefoot? I don't know what to do!" Regina cried. "He's ten times stronger than me, even with his hands melted away!"

"Regina, you work best when flying by the seat of your pants, so to speak." Puddlefoot raised his eyebrows. Regina groaned. "Okay. Sorry. What I meant to say, is you work better when your emotion is running high. You think, you act, and you succeed. Look, you've taken out five Cobbleports, so far."

"I've run them off!" Puddlefoot looked down his nose at her and pursed his lips together.

"Find your anger. Find your passion, and let's *get* this guy!" Puddlefoot made for a strange cheerleader, but it was working. Regina felt the magic start to build in her again. She also felt her injury from the lead ball taking its toll on her. She felt weaker and more vulnerable. She chose to ignore it.

"I think we need to bring him out of his hiding place and into our strength. Maybe the other magical creatures can help us," Puddlefoot suggested. "Call them. I'm sure they will be happy to help you!"

"No. I can't be responsible for anyone else getting hurt or killed," Regina said adamantly.

"Okay. Use the House. Call on the House to add to your magic. Have you noticed it has stopped raining and the wind has died down?" Puddlefoot grinned.

"Hey! And the storm is breaking up! Blue sky! Is that good or bad for us?" Regina chewed on the inside of her lip and cracked her knuckles.

Puddlefoot took ahold of her hand to stop the anxious behavior, "Good for us," he whispered.

"How do I get in touch with the House?"

"The House has been with you since the beginning. Open your mind. Don't think you've gotten this far on your own," Puddlefoot said sternly.

Marcus sent fireball after fireball at Regina. Puddlefoot poured water from standing puddles, dousing each, making them sizzle and evaporate. Dickson had been shooting his spheres, a few at a time, at Marcus, causing him to take cover behind his barrier, while Regina recovered.

"I'm here!" A tiny fairy with a shrill little voice appeared to Regina. "So are we," several more fairies added.

"Us too!" said a couple of elves.

"We want to help," said a garden gnome, representing other garden gnomes and some devas. "After what they did to poor Seamus, we owe Marcus a thrashing!" the group nodded and chattered amongst themselves.

"No!" Regina insisted.

"Let them help!" Puddlefoot snapped. Grigor growled.

Regina thought for a moment, "All I want you to do, is keep him busy and drive him deeper into the forest. Please stay out of his line of fire, and above all, don't risk your lives," Regina implored. They all nodded in agreement. "Now, go drive him out of the garden and into the woods!" she punched her fist into the air and then sighed, giving Puddlefoot a sidelong glance.

The fairies buzzed around Marcus like pesky flies. The garden gnomes shot shovels full of dirt into his face, and the devas blew thistle stickers into his arms, cheeks, neck, and hands. The elves appeared with their canes, zapping anything they were pointed at. Marcus howled in irritation, swiping at the magical creatures, and yanking out stickers. Grigor heaved rocks, logs, and trees at Marcus, driving him from his pile of rocks. As Marcus charged through the garden he attempted to shoot fireballs in their direction, but missed everyone. They were too quick for his big magic.

In the meantime, Puddlefoot ran to Dickson, grabbing the backpack, and helping him limp deeper into the forest. Puddlefoot found a cluster of small oak trees with two huge, granite rocks. "You should be able to see everything from here. Whatever you do, don't leave this spot!" Puddlefoot ordered. Dickson nodded.

"Regina Come! We have to find a safe place to execute our trap," Puddlefoot ordered.

"You mean spring our trap," Regina snickered.

"Pffffft!"

Regina rolled her eyes and smirked. "I guess I deserved that..." Regina pinched her nose between her thumb and forefinger and ran. She found a spot behind a copse of trees and a tower of rocks. Puddlefoot moved back to the small hill and disappeared. With their new positions, they had formed a triangle. The plan was to drive Marcus in between them.

Grigor and the others had succeeded in chasing Marcus out of the garden and into the woods. "For a big guy, Grigor is unusually quick," Regina commented.

"Don't lose focus," Puddlefoot barked.

"Yeah, yeah!" Regina smiled, watching Marcus dive behind a large granite rock on the edge of the woods, but the magical creatures didn't let up. He sustained direct hits from thistle points, flying garden fertilizer, and burn marks from the canes' electrical zaps. Grigor collected several rocks the size of baseballs, and threw them directly at Marcus.

Marcus bolted from the cover of the rock and into the forest before him. "Hey, Worthington!"

"Actually it's Edwards," she whispered.

"Did you chicken out? You really shouldn't have left these little pests in your place. You know eventually I'll hit one of them. Did you run home to your dead foster mother?! I'm not leaving! Where did you go?!" he screeched, enraged.

Regina poked her head out of her hiding place. She waited patiently for Marcus to step into the circle. He stopped short of her target and hid in a small grove of pine trees, flinging fireballs in all directions. He'd lost tract of Regina and her crew while dodging the little people.

"Come on! You're almost there!" she muttered.

The magical creatures had done all they could. Grigor threw one last stone, shattering and severing a small tree trunk enclosing Marcus's hiding spot. He sprinted forward into another tight grove of trees. Marcus was now between Regina, Dickson, and Puddlefoot.

"Regina, how does it make you feel that you got Pam killed? Your own cousin," Marcus taunted, trying to find where she was hiding. "It felt good to absorb her magic! I bet she didn't know she could heal! My hands are all better!" Regina squeezed her eyes shut, letting a wayward tear trickle off her lashes. She couldn't think about that right now, or more would die at his hand. She said nothing.

"I noticed you were being carried out here by a Yeti! Did Veronica hit you with one of my poison lead balls, at the hospital? So how's that working out for you?! You know, no magical creature can save you!" Regina stayed down, deciding that silence was her best defense. Fireballs danced around her.

"Are you even conscious or has your five days of extreme pain begun?!" Marcus snickered. "Is Mrs. H, is still around! Her death is on your head, too!"

Regina found it harder and harder to sit still.

"Don't let him get to you!" Dickson whispered.

"It's okay, Reg! I've waited four years! I can wait a little longer for your magic," Marcus shouted.

Regina gritted her teeth, "As long as Mrs. Hillsdale is here, being tended to and healed, it was worth the risk!" Regina called back to him, putting up a brave front.

"Oh, so you got her out of that hospital! I figured once Veronica shot you, you'd given up. Wow, I didn't think you had it in you! Good job! But don't pat yourself on the back, yet! I'd be careful who I killed next. It would be a shame if you blew me up with the antidote. See? I have it here in my pocket!" Marcus patted his right jean pocket. "Your precious Mrs. Hillsdale isn't out of the woods yet, and for that matter, neither are you," Marcus chuckled. "You have quite the conundrum! Shall you keep the antidote for yourself, or give it to Mrs. H?" Marcus gloated and held his hand up, showing her the vial.

Regina inhaled sharply. *The house hadn't retrieved the potion, yet.* She trembled. "Great!" She felt her heart pound in her throat. She also knew her body was beginning to falter from the poison. "Don't pass out. Just a little bit longer… You can hang on to save Mrs. H," she encouraged to herself.

Regina shifted her weight. She peeked around the rock. "How much time did Mrs. H have left?" she whispered so that only she heard. "I have to end this, now!" Regina stood slowly, walking out into the open. Dickson watched her from his hiding place, ready for her next move. Puddlefoot stayed invisible.

"Ready to die?" Marcus laughed and heaved fireball after fireball in Regina's direction. She stood her ground, dodging them this way and that, while the others waited to spring into action.

Regina smirked. Marcus heaved a larger than usual ball of fire in her direction "Vial!" she whispered. "Fireball!" she called loudly. Just then, Puddlefoot appeared with Dyson sitting on the back of a dragon. Marcus turned, startled, shock oozing from his expression, not knowing whom to attack first.

Regina felt the vial appear in the palm of her hand as she caught the fireball in the other. She threw it straight back at Marcus. At the same time, Dickson fired his lead projectiles. They flew inches behind the fireball. Marcus waved his hand, casting the fireball away, easily.

"Is that all you got?" he chided.

"Pfffffffffft!"

The Dragon shot a stream of fire from her nose and mouth, directly through Puddlefoot's natural gas. It exploded into a giant fireball. The spheres flew through the fireball, hitting their mark, right in the middle of Marcus's chest. He flew backwards, stumbling. He reached into his pocket for the vial, knowing he'd been poisoned by his own magic. Regina held her hand up, showing Marcus that she had the vial.

Marcus stared, gaping at Regina, "Nicely played!" he coughed.

Marcus opened the earth and disappeared.

The magical creatures cheered, whistled, and jumped for joy. Dickson came out of the cluster of trees, grinning, and hobbled toward Regina. "We've done it!" he grimaced, smiling.

Harriett appeared at Regina's side, catching her as she collapsed to the ground. "Here! Get this to Mrs. H! She can't have much time left," Regina murmured, fighting to keep from losing consciousness. Harriett accepted the vial and disappeared. Puddlefoot charged to Regina's side as she lay in the mud.

"Thanks, Puddlefoot! That was one great fart!" she tried to giggle, but a smile was all she could muster.

Chapter Sixteen

Team Work

Dickson limped closer. Dyson slid off of his dragon perch and ran to Dickson's side, becoming the crutch that he needed. "How can we help her?" Dickson's smile had turned into a frown.

Regina's eyes fluttered. Standing amongst the trees was the male unicorn and his mate. They ambled toward her. Dyson closed his eyes and looked to have gone into a trance. "He says that his magic horn can't help you Regina, but he can heal Dickson," Dyson explained. Regina nodded. Her only hope now, was that they would be able to duplicate the antidote in time to save her.

Puddlefoot joined the male unicorn, who had knelt beside Dickson and offered up his horn. Puddlefoot took a sharp knife from his pocket and scraped the horn a couple of times, letting the dust trickle into his pouch. He then sprinkled a small amount on the hole, seeping blood, in Dickson's leg. "That ball must have nicked the artery," Puddlefoot observed. "It's been bleeding a lot!" The hole healed completely in a matter of seconds. Dickson breathed a sigh of relief.

TD Cooper   Magic House

"Thank you," Dickson said, and bowed to the unicorns. They walked slowly back into the forest.

"What are we going to do about Regina?" Dyson said, fighting back tears.

"Yeah, we can't just let her go through all that pain that Marcus was talking about," Dickson said.

"I think we are going to have to get her to the infirmary. They can make her comfortable. Maybe they can test the antidote and make her some, right away," Puddlefoot replied with a heavy sigh.

"Are we sure that was the antidote?" Dickson cleared his throat.

"Yeah. Marcus was going to take it when he realized you'd poisoned him. Remember, he reached into his pocket," Puddlefoot said.

"I *did* poison him. I shot nothing but lead balls at him."

"What happened to them?"

"I have them right here, in the pack," Dickson grinned, feeling impressed with himself.

"Good thinking!" Puddlefoot said, patting Dickson on the back.

Regina groaned. She was beginning to have pain in her arms and legs. Her stomach was cramping and she was having a hard time staying awake.

"Dyson. Dyson, come closer," she mumbled softly. Dyson bent his ear to her mouth. "How did you get that dragon to shoot fire, and how did you know what the unicorn was saying?" Regina asked, and then coughed, spluttering.

"I discovered in the cave, that I could talk to the female dragon. When I explained what we were doing, she wanted to help. She said it wasn't that female dragons were so hard to deal with and that they couldn't be trained, it was that they didn't like to be treated like pack mules." Everyone chuckled. "I guess I can talk to magical animals," he said, shrugging.

"Yes, he seems to have a special connection with our magical friends," Harriett said, appearing suddenly, lifting Regina's head and placing it in her lap. "Regina, how are you feeling?"

"I've been better… How's Mrs. H? Is she going to be all right?"

"She was already starting to rally. We got to her with a couple of minutes to spare."

"And, Matthew? Did you tell him about Pam?" Regina coughed. Dyson dropped to his knees beside Regina and laid his head on her chest. She ran her fingers through his tangled curls.

"I did. He took it as well as you would expect. Mrs. Hillsdale -- not as good. She is really worried about you as was Pam."

"So why didn't Matthew come out here with you?"

"He took the vial back to the lab. He was anxious to begin testing it to replicate the antidote." Harriett smiled, stroking Regina's long, wavy hair, and rubbing Dyson's back.

Regina's eyes rolled up and fluttered. She forced them open, focusing on the tops of the trees and the sunlight that had peeked from behind the clouds. She noticed the same white bird she'd seen on the first day of training, and again, in the atrium, yesterday. "There's that beautiful bird again. Do you see him? He's snow white, huge, and I feel like he watches out for me." Everyone looked in the same direction that Regina was staring.

"Regina, honey, there is not anything up in the tree," Harriett whispered.

"Yes, he's directly above me."

"You know, there's a mythological, magic bird called a Caladrius. It has the ability, if it desires, to cure any sickness by sucking it out of the person and spitting it into the sky. If the person is unworthy of being saved, the Caladrius refuses to look at them," Dickson said. Everyone looked at him, curious.

"What? I like to read," he admitted.

"Do you think that is..." Regina didn't have the strength to finish her sentence and passed out.

"Oh, Regina! Don't leave me!" Dyson burst into tears. "Mr. Caladrius, please save my sister!" he pleaded.

Dyson had no more than finished his plea, when the giant, snow white bird swooped down to the ground beside

Regina. Puddlefoot, Dyson, and Dickson scampered out of its way. Harriett continued to support Regina's head, keeping it out of the mud. The bird hopped onto Regina's chest and stared at her. Everyone watched carefully, not daring to interrupt.

"Do you see what I see," Dickson whispered to Puddlefoot. He nodded.

The Caladrius spread its wings, hiding its next act from their eyes. After a few minutes, the bird launched itself toward the sky. Dickson, Dyson, and Puddlefoot watched as the bird flew above the trees, making a hacking, cawing sound, and spit tiny black balls into the sky. The black dots vaporized into oblivion.

"Come quick!" Harriett shouted. Regina's eyes twitched and flickered open. She stared into each person's startled face.

"What? Do I have three noses, or something?" Regina jested, staring up into the agonized faces of her family and friends.

"How do you feel?" Harriett smiled.

"I feel pretty good, actually. My neck doesn't even hurt." She smiled, rubbing the place where the projectile had entered her shoulder, at the base of her neck.

"Would you like to try and sit up?"

"Sure! I feel as good as new!"

"Regina! Regina! Where are you? Regina!" A voice she hadn't heard, for what seemed like a lifetime, echoed through the garden and into the forest.

"Mrs. H! Dyson! It's Mrs. H!" Regina jumped to her feet and ran straight to the sound of her voice. Dyson sprinted behind her, fast on her heels. "Mrs. H! You're all better! We did it!" Regina sobbed, clinging to Mrs. Hillsdale's neck, while Dyson hugged her around the waist. Both children and Mrs. Hillsdale cried and laughed at the same time.

Grigor, curious to see Regina's progress, stepped from behind a giant pine tree. He looked like a soggy shag carpet. Regina snickered when she caught sight of him. "Puddlefoot, can you get rid of some of the water in his fur?" she whispered.

"Sure!" Puddlefoot took several swipes with his hand across Grigor and the water flew off of his coat and into an existing puddle. He looked like he'd been shampooed and blown dry when Puddlefoot was finished. Grigor groaned a long vibrating moan. He rubbed his fur, smelled it, and sneezed.

"I don't think he likes being clean and shiny," Regina giggled, dashing to Grigor's side. She hugged him tightly around the waist. He purred and patted Regina on the head. Everyone laughed softly. She took his hand and they walked together for a short while.

The female dragon walked with Dyson to the edge of the forest. She paused before returning to her cave. "Henrietta just offered Grigor a ride to the top floor, if he'd like," Dyson translated. Grigor hummed his acceptance. Regina hugged him around the waist before he climbed aboard, "Thank you," she said, looking into his big brown eyes. Everyone waved goodbye as the female dragon flew into the brilliant blue sky.

"Well, that was fun! What shall we do for an encore?" Everyone glared at Regina. "I'm just kidding! Jeez!" she snickered, as everyone laughed with her.

"I'm hungry!" Dyson groaned.

"You're *always* hungry. It seems to me, that you were hungry the morning I found you in the closet, crying," Regina chuckled. *Wow! That seemed a lifetime ago!* She thought to herself.

"Reg! Really! I wasn't crying!" Dyson shouted, flushing a deep crimson. They all laughed.

"I say we head to your room and have a ten course celebratory meal," Harriett suggested.

"That sounds nice, but our fight wasn't without losses," Regina said, frowning. They shared a quiet moment, each remembering Pam, feeling the pain of her sacrifice. "You know, I think she was trying so hard to make up for her part in Mrs. H's illness, that she forgot to protect herself. She charged into a situation without thinking it through, kind of like I did, in the hologram room," Regina said, her eyes brimming over with tears.

"That is a good lesson for everyone. 'Think before you act!'" Harriett said. The whole group bowed their heads and stood silently, not willing to move.

"It's beginning to get dark. Shall we go inside?" Mrs. Hillsdale was the first to speak. Regina reached for her hand and walked out of the forest, into the garden.

The garden gnomes had been busy creating every type and color of flower. They lined the edges of the garden, and along every path. Regina couldn't believe her eyes. She held her breath and covered her mouth with her open hand. She spun in a slow circle, taking in the natural beauty, in awe of her new magical friends.

The devas and fairies raced up to Regina, each handing her a flower as she passed by them. The elves had strands of precious stones and gold, fashioned into necklaces that they offered her. Regina accepted gratefully, bowing to each, and touching her lips in a salute. The rest walked a few steps behind, watching the interaction.

"She really *is* special," Dickson whispered to Mrs. Hillsdale. She nodded. Harriett smiled and mussed his hair. He grinned.

"Pfffft!"

"Oh, Puddlefoot!" everyone said with a groan. He blushed a rosy color of red and they all laughed.

"Hey! Look at Magic House!" Dickson pointed, beaming. Magic House had returned to a pristine, magnificent mansion, in all its glory.

"It truly is over, isn't it?" Regina said softly.

"It is, dear," Harriett said, hugging her. Regina sighed, feeling the tension leave her body and mind. She tingled all over, finally feeling that she'd found a place where she actually belonged. Regina shook off the goosebumps climbing up her back and neck, inhaling the fresh fragrance of each flower she'd been handed, and walked toward Magic House.

Regina hesitated as she passed the spot where she'd seen Pam fall, noticing there was no trace that she'd ever lay in the grass. "She has been taken upstairs where she has some personal decisions to make," Harriett said cryptically.

"What does that mean?" Dickson snorted. "Is she going to become a ghost?"

"We do not know. Like I said, she has decisions." Regina glanced back and forth at each of her companions. They made the long climb up the front steps in silence, and entered through the mahogany front door.

"BOO!" Matthew shouted from behind the door. Regina gasped, startled, nearly jumping out of her skin.

"Matthew, it is not wise to scare Mother of Magic!" Harriett scolded. Regina nodded with a cross look.

"Hey, guys! It's good to see you again!" He charged at Regina, ignoring the warning, and hugged her so tightly, she coughed when the air was forced out of her lungs. "Oh, sorry!" he snickered, loosening his grip. Dyson dog-piled the both of them, causing them to stumble to the floor. The three laughed, rolling onto their backs.

Dickson extended his hand to Regina, offering her a hand up. Instead, she gave him a solid yank, and he fell among them on the tiles. Dyson scrambled to his feet and raced up the curved staircase.

"We almost have the antidote copied, so if anyone ever uses that poison again, we'll have the cure," Matthew said, pulling Regina off the floor.

"Like Veronica?" Regina looked down her nose, glaring and shaking her head, as she offered Dickson her hand.

"She'd better hope I never run into her again," Regina snorted.

"I smell a roast with potatoes and gravy," Dyson exclaimed from the top of the stairs, making a point of interrupting the unpleasant conversation.

"Save some for the rest of us!" Mrs. Hillsdale snickered. Regina rolled her eyes.

"We'd better hurry. He'll eat it all, if we don't get in there and stop him," Regina laughed.

"I'll see you someday, I'm sure," Puddlefoot interjected quietly from the bottom of the staircase.

"What?" Regina came to a stop, midway up.

"Umm, yeah. I didn't want to intrude. Magical creatures don't typically socialize with humans," Puddlefoot stuttered, shifting his weight from foot to foot. Regina recognized that he was clearly disappointed, but uncomfortable, at the same time.

"Well, I don't care what protocol is! Today, you're joining us, Mister," Regina said, racing back down the stairs. Taking him by the hand, she forced him onto the first step.

"Pfff…"

"But no more air freshener!" Regina raised an eyebrow, leveled a finger at him, and stared him in the eye. He smiled bashfully, cutting the explosion off. Everyone snickered.

Dyson burst through the apartment door, "Look, you guys! There is some of everything! Just think of your favorites and they appear on the table!" Dyson couldn't contain his excitement and sat down, filling his plate.

"See, Puddlefoot? You have your own chair and a whole loaf of sourdough bread, with a large glass of cream." She escorted him to the table and helped him up into the chair.

"I don't know what to say… Our kind has never been included, or invited to sit at the table with humans," Puddlefoot stared dumbfounded at each of them.

"Don't be silly, Mr. Puddlefoot. We welcome you to our table today and whenever," Mrs. Hillsdale said with a smile. Puddlefoot sat in the chair, but he wasn't tall enough to see over his plate. Regina noticed his struggle and called for three books out of the bookcase. She guided them over to his seat, giving him the boost he needed. Puddlefoot settled in, joining them in the laughter, reminiscing about Pam, and recounting the fight they'd waged.

The evening turned into night. Dyson had fallen asleep on the couch and Matthew squirmed, listening to all the stories of the day. He felt he was behind on the day's events, but the hour had grown late.

"I'm going to bed," Matthew yawned. Puddlefoot had left hours earlier, and Mrs. Hillsdale had retired to her own section of the room. Pam's stuff still sat next to Regina's, and Harriett was sure that was why she kept talking. Dickson was trying to be a good sport and keep up with her, but he too, was exhausted.

"Come, Dickson. I will see you to your room in the dorms after I put Dyson to bed. Say your good-nights," Harriett said, understanding that he was too kind to leave Regina.

"Um, okay." Dickson stood, and he and Regina's gaze locked. Harriett carried Dyson to bed, and Matthew followed them up to the loft.

"I'm sleeping in tomorrow. How about you?" Dickson stretched and yawned. Regina nodded.

"Dickson? Are you ready?" Harriett called

"Oh, yeah!" he stuttered, the moment broken. "Goodnight!" he said softly to Regina. She blushed.

Chapter Seventeen

Choices, Obligations, and Family

Regina's eyes blinked open to a bright sunny day. She stretched and yawned, and glanced to her right. All of Pam's belongings, including her bed, closet, and nightstand, had disappeared. The room had morphed back to its original size.

"Oh, you are finally awake. Come to my office when you are ready. We have details to go over," Harriett said, smiling.

"Details? Can't I have a day to do nothing and not have to make any decisions?" Regina complained.

"You've been asleep for three days, Reg! How much more *nothing* can a person do?" Matthew said snidely.

"What? Three days?" She wrinkled her nose. Harriett nodded. "Who sleeps for three days?"

"You needed the rest, from the stress and sickness. How do you feel?"

"I feel fabulous!"

"Good! See you in an hour. Take a bath," Harriett said, then turned and disappeared. Regina stuck her nose in her armpit. Her face scrunched. She lifted her hair and pieces of dried, dead leaves fluttered to the pillow.

After a long soak in the tub and a hearty breakfast, Regina knocked on the door to Harriett's office. "Come in, dear!" Regina carefully opened the door and walked through. Mrs. Hillsdale, Matthew, and Dyson all sat before the fireplace.

"What is this? Am I in trouble?" Regina asked, glancing back at Harriett.

"No! Heavens, no! You all have choices to make, and it is just easier to have you all here, so everyone understands each other."

"Sounds so final!" Regina groaned.

"Shall we get started?" Harriett asked, ignoring Regina's sarcasm. They all agreed.

"Mrs. Hillsdale, let us start with you. It is our belief that if you return to the farm, Veronica could, at some point, retaliate against you. You have no magic to fight against her, and she knows you are a willing participant in our world, so you are fair game."

"What about Marcus?" Regina interrupted.

"He has not been seen since the altercation. Those spheres had to have caused damage, and have possibly made him very sick. We are assuming he had more antidote, but we do not know for sure. Our feeling is he has been banished from the Underworld for failing, and is in hiding," Harriett explained.

"Hmm… 'Underworld?'" Regina pondered.

"Just what it sounds like; underground."

"How do we know he's still alive?"

"Well, we do not. Assuming it was the poison balls that terminated him, Dickson would have acquired his magic. So far he shows no traits." Harriett watched Regina raise her eyebrows and nod.

"Mrs. Hillsdale, we would like to offer you a place among the students. We need nurturing people such as yourself, to see to our many children in the dorms. They need hugs and kisses from time to time, as well as stories read, knees bandaged, and everything else a mother does. What do you say?"

"No!" Regina barked, fidgeting in front of the coffee table. "I was hoping that we could go home and, and, I don't know… Be the family we once were! Well, minus one. I have magic to protect us!"

Mrs. Hillsdale pulled Regina onto the love seat, and said, "Reg, Harriett is right! It isn't safe for any of us to go back to the farm. Especially you. They'd know where to find you, Dyson, and Matthew. We can be a family here." She comforted Regina with a squeeze.

"Yeah, Reg! I want to stay. I've met some really cool people in the lab. They like my innovative ideas, and they help me develop them," Matthew said.

"And I've been out in the garden, helping my new dragon friend. You know, her egg hatched, and she has been letting me take the little fellow out for short walks during the day," Dyson said, slumping back in his chair, he continued. "This *is* home, Reg! Mom is here, and Mrs. Hillsdale, too! Maybe we'll get to meet dad, someday!" Dyson exhaled and scooted back in his seat.

Regina almost fell off the couch. "Dad?" she mouthed.

"Well, wasn't Mr. H magical? Doesn't that mean he should be here, somewhere?" Dyson said thoughtfully. Matthew perked up and stared at Harriett.

"Not all magical humans decide to live at Magic House after they die," Harriett explained. Regina sighed. She would have liked to have seen Mr. H healthy, one more time.

"But what happens to our house and the animals?" Regina asked.

"We will take care of it any way Mrs. Hillsdale requests, whether that means rental, sale, or any other idea she has. It is her property. Not ours."

"I would love the position of Head Floor Mom," Mrs. Hillsdale said, quickly changing the subject.

"Fabulous, Carla. A room is being prepared for you as we speak."

"You mean; we don't get to stay here?" Regina was really having second thoughts.

"You may stay in this room until the new term begins, but I am confident, by then, you will be ready to join the rest of the student body in the dorms. There are friends to be made. Most families dine together and take vacations when school is out of session, just like real families. In fact, you will become part of the Atlantis family. We are large and loving," Harriett said, smiling.

"Yeah, come on, Reg! Think of all the magic we are going to learn!" Dyson hugged her neck and whispered in her ear. "Besides, we can't do magic out in the world."

"Not to mention, English, math, and history," Regina giggled. "Okay. I'm convinced." She hugged Dyson and mussed Matthew's hair.

He grabbed her hand and threw it off his head, guffawing, "And don't touch my hair!"

"Great! Now, I understand there is a dance tonight, in the ballroom." Harriett looked directly at Regina.

"Oh, no! I don't dance," she said adamantly.

"How do you know, until you try? You didn't believe in magic a week ago, either," Mrs. Hillsdale teased. "Come. We will go pick out an outfit, comb out that rat's nest you call hair, and see about some lipstick," she said, taking Regina by the hand and marching her out the door.

Regina glanced over her shoulder. Dyson and Matthew were laughing so hard, they rolled onto the floor, and Harriett sighed with a loving, motherly smile. Regina stuck her finger in her mouth and mimed a gagging motion.

Four hours later, Regina stood at the doors of the ballroom in a short, fitted, maroon skirt with gold buttons down the front, a black tank top, and a black leather jacket. Black ankle boots and a maroon handbag finished the ensemble. "What do I need *this* for?" she'd asked Harriett, waving the purse in her face.

"Well, put this lip gloss in there, a handkerchief, and a brush," Harriett instructed.

Regina shrugged, rolling her eyes, "Lame!"

Regina had insisted on wearing the choker necklaces that she was given by the elves. Her hair hung long and soft, with a natural swirl. Harriett and Mrs. Hillsdale had spent hours arguing about make-up and settled on a swish of blush and a soft, pale pink gloss on her lips. Regina felt like a painted up doll out of the toy store.

She fidgeted at the door leading to the ballroom, pacing back and forth. She had huge reservations about stepping across the threshold. "Oh, Pam! Where are you? You were supposed to go with me tonight," she whispered.

"I was not! I am fifteen, and not allowed," the familiar voice said behind her. Regina spun around.

"Pam?!"

"Nice outfit! I never thought I would see you in a skirt," Pam teased.

"Is it really you?" Regina stared at the transparent figure, highlighted by a golden aura that encircled her.

"Jeez, do I look *that* bad?" Pam giggled.

"I don't understand! How…"

"Magic House can do almost anything although they cannot make me alive again, but they let me come talk to you!" Pam continued to giggle. "It is kind of cool, though. I do not sleep or eat. I *do* miss ice cream, though," she said, wrinkling her nose.

"So, what are you? I mean, what have you decided?"

"I have not chosen anything, yet. Aunt Harriett said there would be some kind of ceremony that the high-up muckity-mucks would have to bless."

"So, where have you been, all this time? I mean, I've been worried."

"Mostly upstairs…"

"I thought only the magical creatures lived up there, in the giant redwoods."

Pam raised her eyebrows and shrugged. "They do, but so does the guard, the court, and of course, uncle…" Realizing her error, Pam covered her mouth. Regina raised her brows in surprise. "Oops! I should not have said that! Just forget that came out of my mouth. Well, I have to be going!" At that, Pam disappeared.

"Pam! You get back here and explain! Pam!" Regina spun in a circle, but she was gone. "Oh, Pamela Ann Smith, if I ever catch up with you, I'm going to…"

"Regina! Is that you?" Dickson called from behind her. Regina sighed loudly. She spun on her heel and faced Dickson with a smile. "Are you coming in?" he asked shyly.

"Um, sure. I guess…" He offered his elbow in a courtly gesture. She accepted, and he escorted her into the ballroom.

"Wow! Will you look at this place! I take it, the theme is the Zodiac? The black lights make everything glow! And the stars... Look at the constellations in the sky. I see the Big Dipper, and the one with the belt…" Regina's eyes glowed with wonder.

"Orion."

"Yeah, that's the one! My dad and I used to star gaze on the warm summer nights. He used to point out the patterns… Well, the ones he could see, and the stories that went with them. I wish I could remember them now," Regina ruminated.

"Let's dance, before you change your mind and leave." Dickson smiled, taking Regina's hand, leading her out to the middle of the dance floor.

She felt awkward and waited for him to make the first move. Everyone on the dance floor stopped what they were doing and stared in their direction. "What are they looking at?" she whispered in Dickson's ear, but before he could answer, they all began to clap. It got louder and louder, as more and more students realized that Regina was the one in Dickson's arms.

"Why are they clapping?"

"You saved Magic House!" he said with a smile.

"Not by myself! It was a joint effort," Regina said. The clapping subsided and everyone returned to the dance floor. Regina realized, much to her surprise, that she had been dancing the entire time she was being honored.

"You're quite good at this… Dancing. How long have you been doing it?" she asked.

"Tonight is my first dance," he said, grinning. Regina felt a warmth flush her cheeks. The music picked up. She watched the kids jump, move, and gyrate to the music. "Come on! Let yourself go," Dickson encouraged. Regina imitated the girls around her, and before she knew it, she was enjoying the music.

"Let's check out the punch," Dickson said. Regina grinned and nodded.

Dickson picked up a paper plate and a couple of cups. He chose two frosted cookies, and dipped the ladle into the red punch, pouring it into the paper cups. He handed one to Regina and let her choose a cookie. He led her out to the atrium. They sat on a bench and sipped their punch. Regina told him the family's plans. Dickson smiled.

"Oh, that's a great song!" Regina said, smiling.

"Shall we?" he asked. Regina nodded with a grin. Dickson took the empty cups and paper plate and tossed them in a wastebasket on their way back to the dance floor. A slender brunette approached, and Dickson introduced them. "Regina, this is Candy. She's a first year, and she can call on the water."

"Nice to meet you. First Year?" Regina asked.

"Yeah. I'm thirteen, and just found my magic. Is it true, you can call on all the elements?" Candy asked.

"I guess," Regina said, grinning and shrugged. "I'm sure there has to be lots of people that can do that."

"No. You're the first, since the king of Atlantis," Candy declared.

Dickson made another introduction. "This is Tom. He's a second year, and he can call on the earth. We call him Dirt Man, because he can dig a hole faster than a backhoe," Dickson laughed. Tom blushed. "No, really. He's good with all elements that make up the physical parts of the Earth."

"Hi!" Regina said, nodding.

"Oh, and this is Mary. She's like me, and can call on the metals. She's a second year." Regina stuck her hand out and shook Mary's. "She's dancing with Garrett. He's a second year and can call on fire." Garrett reached for Regina's hand as if to shake it, but instead, he snapped his fingers. A spark flashed. Regina jumped, pulling her hand back. They all laughed "He's also a show off," Dickson said, rolling his eyes. Garrett bowed.

"No one can play with the wind?" Regina asked.

"Oh, sure! Sam, over there." he said and pointed. When she looked, he waved. "And Charlie was one of the guys with me, when Mrs. Worthington took my pouch, in the hall."

"Did you ever give it back?" Regina asked, grinning.

"Nope! She either forgot, or decided I could keep it." Dickson pulled it out of his pocket. "Ha!"

"I miss Puddlefoot," Regina sighed. "Oh, sorry; that was a little random."

"I don't miss his air freshener," Dickson said, grinning. Regina nodded, laughing.

"Hey, are you up for an adventure?" Regina whispered.

Dickson stared at her for a long moment. "Sure! Why not! What do you have in mind?"

"The top floor!"

Dickson hesitated. "You're going to get me into trouble…."

She grabbed his little finger and dragged him out the door. They scampered down the corridor with the music blaring behind them, and turned into the hallway.

"Where did we get off the elevator? Right about here, I guess…" Regina pointed. Dickson shrugged. He didn't think she would really find a way to the top floor. She wiggled her brows at Dickson, looking around to see if anyone was watching them or following. She breathed a sigh of relief and whispered, "Revealalecto" swooping her arms in a circular motion.

Dickson's face tightened and his eyes narrowed when the door to the elevator opened. "Come on, Dickson," Regina giggled, yanking and pulling him by the arm into the lift. Dickson dragged his feet, searching for the words to object.

"You're going to get me into trouble, aren't you?" he repeated.

"Don't be such a chicken. My mom is the Head Mistress. Haven't you heard?" She winked. Dickson rolled his eyes.

"Somehow, I don't think that is going to be an advantage to us."

"Ascendalecto!" Regina said. They rode the elevator all the way to the top floor. The doors opened, and Regina stuck her head out to see if anyone was in the corridor. "Coast is clear!" she whispered.

"What are we looking for?" Dickson said, still standing inside the elevator.

"I just wanted to have a look around. Maybe say hello to Puddlefoot."

"Or find Pam?" Dickson whispered. Regina glanced up at him, wrinkling her brow. She tiptoed through the fog for a few steps. Dickson wasn't behind her.

"Aren't you the least bit curious why they don't want us up here?" She turned and put her hands on her hips. "What do you think the reason is for all this misty stuff?" Regina asked, waving her hand through the fog.

"To make it spooky in here? How would *I* know? To hide stuff, maybe." Dickson said. He crept out of the elevator and stayed close behind Regina. "What am I doing here?" he whispered, berating himself for agreeing to come.

"I think you're right. It's hiding other doors."

"Doors to where? Can we go?"

"Well, who knows? Maybe to a treasure room!" Regina raised her brows and grinned. "Can you feel any gold or silver calling you?" She winked. Dickson groaned.

"How about a throne room? Have you ever wondered if that children's book is actually the history of Atlantis?" she said dreamily.

"No. It's a kids' story."

"Oh look! A door! You open it!" Regina said with a smirk.

"No. I'm good! I really think we ought to forget this, whatever it is we're doing, and go back to the dance," Dickson said, taking a couple of steps backwards.

"Okay. I'll make you a deal: You investigate this room with me, and if we don't find anything, I'll go back downstairs," Regina whispered, twisting the door knob.

The door squeaked, and a strange smell issued forth. "Do you smell that?" She looked back at Dickson. His face wore an expression of wide eyed awe.

"I smell the ocean! The beach! Is that a seagull I hear?" Let me see," Dickson said, nearly pushing Regina out of the way, and opening the door wide enough to walk through. He sank deep into the soft white sand. "Regina! Get in here!" Waves crashed and rolled on the beach, about fifty yards in front of him. Seagulls and pelicans squawked and circled high above them. "Are you seeing what I'm seeing?!"

She gave him a gentle nudge, coming up behind him. "I'm going to have to remember this place when I have time to come body surfing. Those are some serious waves," she giggled.

"Okay. That was a room! Now, let's get out of here," Dickson said, suddenly apprehensive, backing out of the open door.

"Aw... But we didn't learn any secrets!" Regina followed him into the hall, letting the door close behind her.

"The House has an ocean! That seems pretty secret, to me," Dickson huffed, shaking the sand out of the toe of his shoe. "Besides, you didn't say anything about learning something secret with your deal," he said. Regina stopped dead in her tracks, while Dickson continued to the elevator, his voice fading to a murmur.

This is the only time I'm going to get the chance to find out... Regina thought, sprinting in the opposite direction. She disappeared into the fog.

"Regina, come on! I don't know how to get the elevator to work," he groaned. "Where'd you go?"

Regina found another closed door and barged through. She froze. The light was dim, it smelled like candle wax, and a single voice sang in a chant. When her eyes adjusted, she could see some kind of ceremony taking place. Several people, with golden rings on their heads, wearing long white robes trimmed in gold, and each carried a lit candle. They formed an aisle. Above floor level, at an altar, was a young girl kneeling on a cushion. Two people wearing similar robes, stood on either side of a blonde girl. One held a satin pillow with a golden band on it, and the other was chanting softly. A man dressed similarly, was presiding over the ceremony.

Behind the altar were two massive, tall-backed chairs. They were padded with red velvet cushions and trimmed in gold. A tall, muscular man, with raven hair down to his shoulders, sat on the left. His robe was open to the waist and tied with a gold sash. Regina gazed upon his honey-tanned skin, lifting her stare to his amber eyes. She barely noticed his golden crown with emeralds, rubies, and sapphires around it. He looked up, startled. Regina inhaled sharply, holding his gaze. A feeling of familiarity crept over her.

"Regina! Regina, where did you go?! Come on! You're going to get us into troub…" Dickson yelled, rushing into the room, bumping into her. The woman holding the pillow, startled at the commotion, dropping the crown. It bounced and then rolled to Regina's feet. She bent down and picked it up, recognizing the snake. Her gaze jumped back to the blonde kneeling on the pillow, then back to the familiar man, and then back to the girl. Regina started to slowly back out of the room.

"Hey, Pam! Look Regina! It's Pam!" Dickson exclaimed. Pam's blue eyes sparkled and she snickered, "Leave it to Reg, to bust up my coronation ceremony!"

The woman next to Pam stopped chanting. Regina quickly glanced at her, then back to the chairs. The woman sitting in the chair on the right, caught her attention. Regina gasped, "Mom!?"

The tall man rose from his chair, taking a couple of steps forward. He glanced back at Harriett and back to Regina. Harriett nodded with a half-smile. "Regina," he said softly. Regina shifted her gaze to him.

"Daddy!" she whispered. He nodded and smiled, still looking concerned.

Regina held her breath. The man she'd called father for the first eight years of her life was standing before her. He looked exactly like he had, the night she watched him die, except he looked more *official*, somehow. Her mind raced. She'd had a special bond with her father. They'd spent hours together, studying the heavens and reading mystical stories. *How could he abandon me?* Her instincts were to wait for an explanation, but she wasn't sure she was ready to hear it. Regina tripped over Dickson's feet. She shoved the crown into his hands before turning and bolting from the room.

Dickson stared at the scene before him, and had no logical explanation for what he was watching. "Regina! Wait up!" he yelled, as she crashed into the elevator's back wall.

Tears rolled down her cheeks. "Descendelecto!" she shouted. The doors on the lift began to close. Dickson shimmied through the closing doors of the elevator. They bounced open.

Regina sighed. "Descendelecto!" she repeated. Nothing happened. Regina forcibly, pounded the button with a two on it. Nothing happened. She jabbed at it again, crying, "Descendelecto!"

Her father appeared in the corridor outside the elevator. The fog had lifted. The walls appeared black, and the sky glowed with a full moon and bright stars overhead. He spoke to Dickson, "I am sorry, son. I need to have a word with Regina. Will you be kind enough to return to the dance alone?" her father said in an authoritative voice. Dickson searched Regina's eyes, and when he saw that she was resigned to stay, he nodded.

"I'll talk to you tomorrow?" he said, more as a question than a statement.

Regina hugged his neck. "Thank you for a nice evening," she said, stepping out of the lift. The doors closed and she heard the elevator depart.

"Come with me!" her father commanded. Regina followed behind. They entered a cozy room. The first thing she noticed, was the Atlantis crest above the fireplace. The rest of the room reminded her of her father, with all the things he loved; big leather furniture, a pool table, and a wall lined with books. She remembered how much her father had loved to read. He had a painted portrait of the entire family on one wall. Regina recalled the time they'd posed while a woman painted it. She'd hated it at the time, but she was pleased he looked at it daily, now.

"Have a seat," he offered, tossing his robe over a chair and setting his crown on the table. He had silky pajama pants on, underneath. A folded t-shirt was within reach. He put it on and joined Regina on the couch.

"I owe you an explanation," he stated, not looking her in the eye. She pursed her lips and stared. "I thought it would be better if you did not know I was here. You have been having enough trouble with the other kids, as it is."

"How is not knowing you were up here, *helpful*?" she said, suddenly angry.

"If you have not figured it out yet, I am the king of Atlantis and your mother is my queen, so that makes you a princess, and your brother, a prince. Your peers do not know this for sure, but they suspect. We thought it would be too much pressure on you."

"Great!" she groaned. "So, what does all this mean for me?"

"Well, you are extremely powerful. Your mother and I were hoping, if you stayed hidden from our world, you would be older before you had to deal with everything that goes with our family obligations, but that did not happen… Obviously." He paused. "Along with the teasing and taunting, you will have to attend extra classes to teach you your duties for the day that you become the leader of our people."

"Leader? Why do I have to be the leader? You're a ghost! You can't die!"

"I died already. I'm here only until you come of age to take over."

"And when is that?" she cried.

"Let us not get into that right now. There is a lot of time. He paused to watch her exhale, but she didn't relax. "Hey, nice job against Marcus. You handled all of that like a true leader of Atlantis," he said, grinning.

She glared at him. "And just how did I manage to handle all of that like a pro? I have to say, I surprised myself with my leadership and calm, but…"

He chuckled. "Remember when your mother told you the story of Marcus and Rudy?" she nodded. "I had the power of a king, even then; the most coveted of powers. Your mother made sure she transferred them to you," he said, and smiled calmly.

"I don't understand…"

"If I had died naturally, I would have transferred all my power to you when I died and you assumed the throne, but since that did not happen, well… You know the rest."

"But I'm not supposed to be able to do magic until I'm thirteen."

"Royalty can call on their magic when under stress, like protecting our people, for instance. Your brother is using his, and he is only eight. Once you find your magic, it does not go away. So use it wisely, and learn as much as your teachers can teach you. Be careful. You can also hurt someone if you lose your temper."

"Oh, Daddy! I've missed you so much!" She jumped into his arms and hugged his neck.

He returned the embrace. "I have missed you too, Reggie. Do not tell your mother, but I *am* glad you found me." He chuckled louder.

"Can I come up to see you anytime I want? Oh, and can I tell Dyson?" She giggled.

"Yes! Any time!" He hugged her tighter.

"What's going to happen to Pam? I don't want to do this without her."

"I am going to be right by your side, every step of the way," Pam said cheerfully, walking through the door, wearing her crown and robes. Harriett wasn't far behind. Regina jumped up and wrapped her arms around Pam's neck, almost knocking both of them to the floor.

"You scared me! I didn't think I was ever going to see you again!"

"You cannot get rid of me that easy. You should know better," Pam said, laughing. "Let us not talk about depressing things, today. I want to celebrate. We are still together, and our family is stronger than ever!" Pam, the eternal optimist, beamed with joy. Regina joined her, happier than she'd been in a long time.

The End

If you enjoyed this book and would like to keep up to date on my work, you can find me on Facebook @ https://www.facebook.com/tdcoooper or on the web @ http://tdcooperbooks.com. There you can find links to my Twitter and blog feeds as well as G+. I have also posted a few short stories that you may enjoy.

Thank you for reading!

TD Cooper

Made in the USA
Charleston, SC
06 February 2017